AT THE
END
OF THE
WORLD

KEVIN J. FELLOWS

AT THE END OF THE WORLD

A NOVEL

KEVIN J. FELLOWS

Modern Folklore Press

At the End of the World
A Novel

Structural editorial by Kat Howard
Copyedited by Rachel Oestreich
Cover design by Ana Grigoriu-Voicu
Author photo by Seanna Fellows

For information, contact Modern Folklore Press
PO Box 230681 Las Vegas, NV 89105.

First Edition

ISBN: 978-1-7351300-1-9

INFECTIOUS MAGIC

For regular news and updates, sign up for the Infectious Magic Digest. Readers of the Digest also receive cover reveals, occasional free poems and stories, and opportunities to become ARC readers.

You can also receive stories and poems every month, as well as behind-the-scene updates and more by supporting Kevin's Patreon.

Find Kevin at his blog and these networks.

CONTENTS

All roads indeed lead to Rome, but theirs also is a more mystical destination, some bourne of which no traveller knows the name, some city, they all seem to hint, even more eternal . . . If we could follow that vanishing road to its far mysterious end! Should we find that meaning there? Should we know why it stops at no mere market-town, nor comes to an end at any seaport? Should we come at last to the radiant door, and know at last the purpose of all our travel? Meanwhile the road beckons us on and on, and we walk we know not why or whither.

Richard Le Gallienne - Vanishing Roads

To those missing from my life.

PROEM

WHAT WENT BEFORE

Anne allowed Noble to lead her across the rusted, time-stained trestle. The trains were long vanished and had rambled into the silent annals of engineering history as faded remnants of progress, the tracks long buried under the guise of walking paths. The dog tugged, eager against her leash. She was an Alaskan Noble and looked like most people's image of a wolf. The rail bed unwound a space for fresh air and exercise, a respite for the engineers and researchers who spent their days cramped in the shared workspaces of trendy, repurposed tech company offices. Anne never exercised and couldn't recall the last time she'd sought fresh air.

She ignored the joggers and bikers, though in her signature form-fitting Urbletics she appeared to be one of them. She hadn't realized until now it was late fall. The Bay in November, like so many times of the year, was foggy and as cold as market fish. Her limo had delivered her to the office before dawn, when the world was hidden behind a curtain of mist and darkness. It was only Noble's destruction of her client's attaché that had led them outside while Maggie stayed in the office to soothe the client.

"Noble, you've done it now."

The wolfhound ignored her and pulled against the leash, drawing them deeper into the dim woods. There were more trees than she'd expected of the dense suburban area. The trees closest to the trestle still sported fall colors, but these, inside the wood, were in summer green.

Shit—time to get back to the office. Maggie should have things under control by now. They needed to wrap up this final deal to ensure Project E266 had the funding to succeed. Just because they had a working prototype didn't mean it was successful. It would be a success only when E266 was common at pharmacies and medical offices. She and Maggie estimated they needed nearly a billion dollars, and they were still a few hundred million short. Anne pulled hard on Noble's leash, but the hound refused to turn and she was no match for its size and strength. *Shit.*

The trees loomed as monstrous silhouettes. Leaves camouflaged sharp, clawed branches that scraped the colorless sky. Old—no, ancient—trees clung thickly together as if entwined in some perverse, centuries-long lovemaking. The trail wasn't visible. When had they left it? Her watch showed nearly two-thirty. *Shit, shit.*

"Noble, no! We have to go back."

Noble pulled harder, dragging her deeper into the woods. *Damn it.*

Then Noble stopped and growled.

A cracking and crunching sound snapped in her ears, and a furious cloud of sticks and leaves exploded from the right. Something charged toward them. Noble whined and bolted, ripping the leash from her hands as a gigantic creature rumbled out of the trees. Anne couldn't move, she couldn't breathe. *Shit.* Her Urbletics lacked pockets and her phone sat on the conference table beside the E266 kiosk design. Her breath spasmed. The creature slowed, then stopped and stared at her. It was the size of an elephant, tusked, and hairy—a mammoth.

Her mind flashed to her childhood, to the night she had tried to escape music camp. Her father had left her and her sister to develop into the prodigies he knew them to be. In the darkness, she had slipped away from the dorm full of dunder-headed seven-year-old girls, girls who spoke of andante, largo, dolls, and pink backpacks in the same sentence. She'd fled into the woods behind the school, running blindly in the darkness and straight into the path of a bear—black and nearly invisible in the night. A mass of muscle, claws, and teeth. She hadn't been able to breathe then either. She had stood frozen until the bear slipped back into the darkness. As much as she worked to live up to her father's expectations, and as much as he had accepted her gifts belonged to science, she never forgave him for the camp—or the bear.

This was no bear. This was definitely a mammoth. Impossible, unless some Cal DNA research experiment had gone wrong—or right?

The mammoth moved sideways and circled with a shuffling, heavy walk. It smelled of ancient forests and musky, matted fur. It stopped, bellowed a mournful call, then resumed staring at her. *Shit, shit, shit, fuck.*

Her breath refused to return to normal and her thoughts were disjointed and scattered. Mammoths and elephants are related; they don't eat meat, they graze. If she didn't anger or frighten it, it would leave her alone. Right?

Damn it, Maggie, why aren't you here? You left me to take care of the wolf again and now look.

The mammoth shambled into the clutching trees, apparently deciding she wasn't a threat. After several moments, Anne's breath returned to normal. She didn't dare call for Noble, but she darted in the direction the wolf had fled.

She emerged through the trees into a field of recently tilled earth smelling of ripe farmland—dung, hay, and dirt. A small wooden farmhouse stood beyond the field in the sagging manner of old buildings. Forever falling, but never fallen. Noble ran up to her and sniffed the skin of her calves and ankles.

"You left me, Noble. Left me alone with the beast." She picked up Noble's leash and walked through the tilled field. She needed to get back to Project E266. "We'll use the farmer's phone to call the limo and get back to the office."

Noble wagged her tail and sniffed at the rich soil.

PART I

NICO WALKS TO THE END OF THE WORLD

Many will advise against this place.
A few will say seek it.
- Notes of a Traveller
(Written in small, elegant characters on the back of a crisp map.)

*N*ico tried to be alert to other travelers along the muddy road—a basic rule of the road—but he was tired. Ten years ago, at forty, he could have covered a few more leagues. This route had been his father's—a meandering run through towns needing pots mended or new spoons. Maybe a different path would have found better results for the odd bits he peddled. He was no tinker, but the route was what he knew, and he walked it by long memory.

The three men walking ahead were close enough for him to hear their conversation, if they were having one. They were not. Nico's soft, woven creel full of wrapped glass trinkets thudded against his back, and the straps cut against the skin under his arms. He was hungry. Budens was just a few more leagues. His muddied boots trundled against the road and he was glad that it had at least stopped raining. The Atlantic's criminal winds and relentless waves battered this coast on two sides. Rain was a possibility on any day, though it rarely lasted more than an hour or two.

He was looking at his boots and noticed another pair of boots facing his. He stopped and looked up into the stubby face of one of the men who had been walking ahead.

"Purse, mendigo," the man said. He was the smallest of the three and wore a long, mud-stained brown coat. He held a dagger in his right hand. The other two wore the same and also held daggers. There was no one on the road behind him; no one ahead. No houses for another league.

Nico lifted the leather pouch from his belt and handed it to the thief.

"Pretty light, mendigo. Where's the rest?"

"My creel's full, so my purse is empty."

"What's in it?"

"Glass figurines and a book."

"Glass?"

Something hard struck his head, and everything fell black and muddy.

LIGHT AND SENSE RETURNED SLOWLY. It was nearly dark, and he was not alone. Nico leaned against a stone wall. Had he crawled there? His hair was wet against his head. He rubbed through it and his hand came away stained with rain-diluted blood. Where was his creel? A man dressed in odd black clothes —a short coat with thin stripes of gold thread and matching trousers—bent over something. The man's shoes were once a shiny black, but were now stained with mud. He collected something, placing whatever he found into a basket—Nico's creel.

"Hey, what—"

"Ah, finally awake, my friend." the stranger said, turning to Nico. The stranger wore shiny, mirrored spectacles that hooked behind his ears. "Most of these are fine. Only a few busted. Now, what you need, is a new map."

The man placed the last of the scattered figurines into the creel. "Thank you," Nico said. He felt the lump on his head and feared this man might be working with the others.

"Not at all. I must have found you just after the damned thieves clocked you."

"Clocked?"

"Here you go." He handed the covered creel to Nico. A few broken pieces of glass remained embedded in the muddy road. "How far do you have left to go?"

Nico saw himself reflected in the small oval mirrors of the man's spectacles. "Not far."

"I'm a bit of a peddler too. At least, until I sell this last map." He pulled a folded parchment from inside his coat and held it out to Nico.

"A map of what?"

"A wealthy port city less than half a day's journey from here."

"I've been there. I know my way without a map."

The man shook the map at him. "I doubt you've been to the End of the World. And you have to get there soon, no later than tomorrow night, or the map will be worthless. Sooner would be even better."

Nico took and unfolded the map. It lacked detail outside a circle, but inside lay a depiction of a small city and harbor. The familiar trading towns of Almedina, Burgau, Figueira, and Vila da Luz were sketched at the edges, but just beyond Rocha Negra, east of Vila da Luz, was the start of a road he'd never heard of—the Goresetch. The Goresetch led into the circle and city. The mapmaker had marked the city's name in strange characters he couldn't read. The End of the World, the stranger called it. Who named a city Fim do Mundo? Similar characters filled the back of the map—from the orient? Elegant-looking thin lines, but written at different times and with different quills. The writer had used every available space, as if it were their only paper. He handed the map back.

The man put his right hand in a pocket at the side of his pants. He continued offering the map with his left. "Two coins and you put me out of business. A city like that would flock to art such as your glass. They'd love it. There's a kind of magic at the End of the World."

Nico looked at his creel. He'd sold nothing in five days. Maybe a new route, a new city, was what he needed. "But I was just robbed."

"Dude, you haven't reached your age peddling without knowing how to preserve a few coins."

There was no question he wanted the map, and the stranger had guessed right. Nico pulled off his left boot and shook out two dull and worn dinheiro. He replaced his boot. The man handed him the map for the coins.

"Pleasure doing business, and safe travels. Don't let anyone else jump you." The man turned toward Almedina. "Don't forget, be at the End of the World before tomorrow ends," he said, waving a finger over his head.

Nico tucked the map into his coat and headed home, wondering if he had been robbed twice.

BEFORE DAWN, Nico swallowed the last chunk of stale bread with a swill of flat, watery ale. Lura stood with her arms crossed in her worn gray house smock and stained gray wimple. The cottage smelled stale. Even the fresh bread tasted stale, but he hadn't married Lura for her cooking. Her basketweaving was little better than her food, and while they sold, it was never enough. Their thirty years together had faded in his mind. What had drawn them together? Why had they stayed together? Had she been beautiful, wealthy? Certainly not wealthy, and he had never been handsome. However they found each other, they had become comfortable. She drew him home, always. The cure for his wanderlust, however temporary.

That's what a lifelong love turned into—comfort. There was something more, too, something he couldn't quite remember. It happened more often lately. Last week, he had forgotten for several panicked moments which fork in the road to take outside Burgau. He wasn't old enough to lose so much memory. He felt no different at fifty than he had at thirty.

He rose from the table and lifted the creel over his back.

"Where will you find people longing for glass baubles today?" Lura asked, smiling.

"At the End of the World."

"Well, if you find the end of the world be careful not to fall off and leave me widowed. Whatever would I do without your vast income?"

Let her joke. He had determined upon waking that he had not been robbed a second time but given an opportunity. The map sat in his pocket like a promise.

She leaned toward him, and he remembered. She had been and still was beautiful. Her lush brown hair was giving in to silver, and her sparkling eyes were set with fine smile wrinkles. She had chosen him—plucked him away from his father like a child adopting a puppy. He gave her a peck on the lips, and she smiled. "Return to me."

∾

HE LEFT their tiny home made of wood and thatch and surrounded by carob trees and wheat fields. The eastern sky was still dark, but ribbons of purple rippled above the horizon. Hearth smoke filled the air and his breath was visible. The muddy road out of Budens was rutted with cart tracks and footprints. He had to pass through Burgau and Almedina, then Vila da Luz, then down the league-long stretch of the Goresetch Finger, and finally to the End of the World.

"I should be there by evening," he told the sky. "Well before the end of the day."

The padded glass ornaments in his creel thudded against each other as he walked. The creel was heavy. He carried every glass bauble in his inventory, making more room by leaving behind his new book, *Don Quixote*. If he sold the lot for anything near the price he expected, he could live for a year without making another trip. A year spent with Lura, reading and watching her weave baskets if the wanderlust didn't grab him.

BURGAU CAME into view just as the sun emerged through the trees. A small fishing community with a large beach, Burgau was full of practical people but afflicted with sea salt. It hung in the air and stung the nose, a fine, pale crust that clung to anything that didn't move. Just a few hours' walk lay between Budens and Burgau, but less than a handful of people from either town ever visited the other. They were born, lived, and died without ever leaving their village. Budens was home and Lura, but he couldn't stay for more than a week at a time. The pull of the road drew him away on adventures of commerce. When he was young, even if he sold his wares at cost, it felt like a success, especially if there was a book among the things he carried in return. The journey was its own payment.

Yet that form of payment no longer satisfied. There had to

be some small profit. The glass baubles were a brilliant idea, but they had not sold quickly—nor at all. Farmers and fishers were not interested. Decoration was for those who appreciated art and beauty for its own sake. A more cosmopolitan place, like an actual port city, would appreciate art and have the money for it.

He stopped at a tavern for a drink and some bread with a little crottin of cheese, neither of which was stale. He left one of his two remaining dinheiros on the counter.

The tavern keep snatched the coin. "Still selling glass statuetta?"

Nico nodded. "Has someone asked for me?"

"No, just wondering if you gave them up."

"I have to sell them. I can't eat them."

"True enough. Where to this time?"

"The End of the World."

The tavern keep stopped wiping the counter. "Now, there's a town strange as sunless mornings."

"You've heard of it? Strange how?"

"Man dressed all in black with mirrored glass over his eyes stopped in here last night; said he was from the End of the World. I thought he was being secretive, but he started talking. Told me he just couldn't take the life there. Said he came from the future, but fell into the End of the World. He gave up trying to leave and tried to fit in. Never had enough chips or something, so he gave up living there. Said this wasn't the road home, but it was better than the End of the World."

"Odd."

"Imagine you're correct."

Nico finished his ale and left. If the man was so eager to leave, was it a place he wanted to visit?

Yes. It was a place he'd never been.

~

ENERGY AND PURPOSE drove Nico away from Burgau and over tree-lined hills and vineyards toward Vila da Luz, fueled by the feeling he was running out of time. He stopped in the empty road under a warming, early season sun to study the map. The writing on the back had been done at different times and with different inks, like notes. Why had he never heard of the End of the World, or even of the Goresetch road? He knew many distant towns and cities, had traveled to several, but heard nothing about a place called the End of the World. He would have remembered a name like that. Wouldn't he? A kind of magic, the man had said. Also, if he didn't reach the town today, the map would be useless. Why would that be? Must have been a sales trick, pressuring him into acting before it was too late by creating a false limitation. He was familiar with those tactics, though he didn't use them himself. The map was probably a copy among hundreds. And probably already worthless. The city, despite its name, would be no different from any other.

He didn't believe in magic, but he had experienced wonder. It's what drove his wanderlust. He'd seen a man with six fingers and mountains so tall they blocked the sun half the day. He once visited the grand city of Lisboa, guarded by men in glimmering steel who were mounted on the finest horses; the city was dense, with people stuffed into every street like fish in a basket. And there was the stoic cathedral Santa Maria Maior de Lisboa, which had remained proudly upright and whole through earthquakes that had crumbled its neighbors. Miracle to some, but a wonder to him. He believed in wonders, and they beckoned him to the road. He collected wonders. So many he knew he'd forgotten some. Books, too, were collections. Collections of memories recalled by the reader, but they were someone else's memories, or no one's if fiction. The failures of his memory crawled at the back of his mind, stalking with the stealth of time lurking in the shadows. What happened when you lost the connection to your memories? Smells could reconnect them, sometimes a touch. But were the rest just gone forever, like a breath?

He folded the map and returned it to his pocket. He needed to hurry. It would be late when he arrived at the End of the World, and the limitation felt true.

THE GORESETCH WAS hardpacked and dusty. In the twilight, Nico couldn't see the dust, but it tasted stale and clogged his nose. A current-driven breeze blew from the south across the Goresetch, warm and humid. Beneath the wind, there was a hint of smoke. That familiar scent of hearth and civilization mingled with the dust. He was close now, but he took another rest and pulled a glass figure from the top of his creel: a mule, like the one his father had used to carry tin pots and tools. He never cared to learn the tinker trade, but he loved that dutiful mule. He had fed and watered it as if it were his pet. He'd named him Viajante—wanderer. Loading creel baskets over Viajante's back early in the morning, before sunrise, was a promise of a trip out of Budens. With few days at home for friends, Viajante, or Via as he grew to call him, was his closest friend. Viajante never complained about the distance or the weight on his back. It was through their travels he had met Lura. His father tinkered for her mother. That year was a warm, lavender memory. It returned, seeped into his mind like heat returning to frostbitten fingers. He put the glass mule in his pocket.

Nico walked another hour in full darkness, stopping several times to listen and search for lights. Nothing. Only the flapping of bat wings at twilight had made a sound. The seabirds were quiet in their roosts. His legs ached and his back was stiff, the weight of the glass in the creel bending him forward. The night was moonless, but that wasn't right. It should have been a quarter moon. There must have been clouds he couldn't quite see, though there were stars. He drifted to one side of the road, then the other, unable to see the way forward. Only the softer edge of grass on the edges outlined where the road passed. The sound of the road behind changed. It was quieter and felt more isolated. The air smelled different. Gone was the scent of sandy pines replaced by the smell of the open sea. Was it too late? Was the limitation real? Was the map?

A warm, yellow light poked a finger toward the road. Drawing closer, he saw more lights and the shadowed outlines of buildings. Voices drifted from behind dimly lit windows. There was laughter, some harsh words, and a few delighted squeals. He exhaled long, unaware he had been holding his breath.

A half dozen masted ships swayed as black silhouettes against the blacker sky. A harbor city in the truest sense. Hope lightened his step. A few people walked along the docks under the light of the ships' lanterns, and at the far end of a quay a red light glowed at the top of a stone structure. A warning light.

A friendlier light, and some hearty laughter, spilled from a particular inn and tavern. The Scale and Tentacle called to him with its welcoming glow and cheerful sound, like a familiar haunt. There was a crowd inside, the room brightly lit. His arrival drew no attention. His stomach rumbled. There was a seat and a small table in the back, and he set his creel down and sat. A wooden menu, handwritten in charcoal, was extensive and looked delicious: roast lamb, pork tenderloin, buttered sole. Expensive items. Could one dinheiro buy a meal and shelter for the night?

The prices were all marked as 2cv, 3cv, or 5cv. How many dinheiro made a cv? What was cv?

A woman bumped the table with the side of her thigh. She was no older than twenty, wearing a stained gray smock and apron, her blonde strands escaping a gray wimple. Her hands were full of dirty plates and mugs. "Looking for sup? Kitchen's mostly closed, but there's fish stew."

He placed his coin on the table. "What can I get for this?"

She shook her head. "Nothing. New in town? You need to see the changers."

"Changers? Money changers?" He pulled open his creel. "Would you take something in trade?"

"Only chips here. The changers will be open in the morning. You can find several down at the docks. But you're in luck. Padrok, the owner here, will give you your first meal at the End of the World for free."

"How generous. Thank him, please, and stew is just what I need."

"You also need to visit the Mayor. All croppers are to report to the Mayor's Palace within a day of arrival."

"Croppers? I'm required to meet with the Mayor?"

"Yes. The sooner the better."

She returned with a bowl of warm fish stew and a chunk of bread. "We sometimes give a cot to newcomers, but we're full tonight."

The stew warmed him while he thought about the serving girl's instructions. It wasn't unusual for a city to charge a license fee to peddlers; it was the cost of doing business. He hadn't thought of that. He also needed to see a money changer first. Chips—perhaps cv was chip-value? Had he traveled so far beyond the king's realm that his dinheiro was no good for trade? But where would that be? Even if he'd crossed to Spain, which he certainly hadn't, the dinheiro was honored.

Nico was grateful for the stew. Outside, the night had grown cool and foggy, and the streets were nearly empty and quiet. He drew out the map and sought for a landmark that might indicate a safe place to sleep. Sleeping outside was nothing new for an itinerant peddler. In the warmth of summer he could enjoy it, but March was a different story. There was something on the map that looked like an open field in the center of the city. A commons?

A well-dressed couple walked past him arm in arm, lost in a lovers' conversation that was more giggle than words. They stopped a few yards ahead and fell into a sensuous embrace. The man yanked on the neckline of the woman's dress, exposing her shoulder. He planted kisses from there up to her neck and ears.

She giggled and sighed, pawed at his groin. "Willy, my dunny love, the Salon is just there."

"Harmony, my dearest flower," he mumbled against the skin of her neck.

Nico quickened his pace to be out of view and out of hearing before their embrace turned into something more. Another wonder added to the list. Lura had once said such things and acted that way. Had they ever been so young?

Which building housed the Salon? Most buildings in this part of the city were well-built homes. The End of the World looked to be a prosperous place. A good sign. If it supported a salon, someone here would appreciate glass art.

He walked to the center of the city. An expanse of grass lay before an official-looking building with granite columns. Such places were natural gathering spots for the shelterless. Even wealthy cities—particularly the wealthiest—had shelterless. In his experience, there was safety among those who regularly slept in the streets. A few were desperate enough to thieve, but there were others who would help. There was a code among them—mind your business, assist when needed, and no one would bother you.

No one lay in the commons or under its trees. But three

men and two women huddled together beside the officious building at the far end of the commons. Was it the Mayor's Palace? It didn't look like a palace, though the columns were stately and finely wrought. The structure was a little over two stories tall, rectangular, and had a single set of unguarded double doors at the landing at the top of a flight of stone steps which rose between the columns. There were no windows, only steel-grated vents just above the ground.

All five shelterless sat beside or lay against one another and the building. "Good evening," he said to one woman. She was no older than thirty. Street dust smudged her face, and her green cloak was little more than rags. In the dim light her hair looked an unusual shade of blue, as if painted on. A very unnatural shade of blue. There were two silver rings in her nose.

She looked up at him with weary eyes. "It's evening for sure."

"Mind if I snag a spot beside you?"

"Isn't mine to give."

Taking that as permission, he placed his creel against the building and sat with his back against it. The soft weave of the creel had often doubled as a backrest. The city was quiet. It wasn't late, and he wasn't sleepy, but no one spoke. "What realm is this?" he asked no one specifically. "Who rules here?"

"No realm," said a man with a throat full of phlegm. He was much older and wore a long gray coat with its collar high to his ears, hiding most of his wizened face. A shock of pure white hair stood tall on his head like spikes. "No king, queen, or emperor rules here. This is the End of the World. The Mayor handles affairs, such as they are."

"The Mayor would be the one to see about permission to trade?"

"Yes, but the Mayor will have other business with you."

"I see," he said—but he didn't. The man in the mirrored

spectacles hadn't stretched the truth when he said the city was strange. But there also seemed a prosperity to support his claim that it would be a profitable place to sell glass figures. There was no further conversation to share, so he closed his eyes and eventually slept with the occasional bark of a dog, or cough from one of the other shelterless damaging the quiet. He dreamed of the year he met Lura, and of their courtship. They had indeed been so young.

A BREEZE BLEW against his face, and he opened his eyes to the dim light of dawn. He was alone. A new day, and a new plan: get to a money changer and exchange his coin—and anything else they might take for chips. Then see the Mayor for a license. No time for food, and nothing to pay with anyway.

He didn't need the map to find his way to the harbor. Five tiny wooden shacks along the docks bore signs declaring money changing services. He stopped at the first and knocked. A wood panel slid open, revealing a woman who had to be younger than twenty, with wide eyes and long brown hair that tumbled over her exposed brown shoulders in waves. "What do you have or what do you wish?" she asked. Her smile was wide with bright teeth, and her skin smooth as worn stone—almost polished in the early sunlight. Another flaunted display of youth. The man with mirrored spectacles, the couple, the serving girl, the shelterless woman—all so young. The world was infected with them.

"I need to exchange a coin for chips."

She held out a manicured hand with painted nails, and he dropped the coin in it. "The smelters can't do much with a single piece of copper alloy. This will get you two cv—chip-value." She handed him a wooden chip. It appeared well used and faded by age. It was vaguely oval.

"This is worth two chips?"

"It has two chip-value, for now."

He recalled the menu. A half pint of ale was 2cv. "I have something else." He opened his creel and removed a figurine wrapped in scrap linen. He unwrapped it in a dramatic fashion, as if revealing the fourth gift of the Magi. It was a clear glass in the shape of an elephant. He held it out to the changer.

She took it, smiled, then giggled. "What manner of creature is this?"

"An elephant. Have you not heard of such creatures from the wilds of the east and south?"

"East? South? Hmm. I could get maybe 3cv from Pearcy, the glassblower. I'll give you one."

"One?"

That there was no value in the glass's shape was a disappointment and a concern. She pointed at the wooden chip. It was a shade more pink. "Three chip-value now."

"How did that happen?" Half his stock might not be enough for a license to sell the other half. Based on the price of ale, three chip-value wasn't enough. Fifty might not be enough. He changed plans again. He needed paying work. "Do you know—"

"Of anyone hiring? Sure, the harbor warehouses and traders always need laborers. Find Almariss, the dockmaster."

"How did you know that's what I would ask?"

"You're a cropper."

"A what?"

"You know, fallen a-cropper."

"Oh, I haven't fallen into anything."

"Haven't you?" Despite the soft friendliness of her eyes, there was a bite to her words. "Have you visited the Mayor?"

"Not yet."

She stuck her head out the window and looked around,

then beckoned him close. "Sometimes," she whispered, "it's better never visiting the Mayor." Then she closed the blind.

~

AT THE DOCKS he found a tall, slender woman wearing a long black coat with thin gold trim. A narrow-brimmed black hat stood on her wavy black hair like a tree stump. A long, thin pipe drooped from her lips. She held a quill and papers and stood in front of a small wooden building bearing a sign declaring it the Dockmaster's Office.

"Almariss, the dockmaster?" he asked.

"So I'm told."

"How much for a day's work?"

"Depends on the effort." She looked down at him from face to foot. "Your laboring days are well behind you."

"I can manage, but I don't understand the wage."

"Ah, a cropper." She removed her pipe. "Look, earning chips is almost like earning money in your realm. You do something for someone and they pay you. But here, your effort determines how much chip-value you receive. It's how helpful your contribution is to the endeavor that matters most. That means doing your share and doing more, helping others. And know this, I don't determine what you receive. The fates—specifically your fate—measures. Show me your chips."

He pulled the wooden coin from his pocket.

"About three. Well, you are a desperate sop." She returned the pipe to her mouth and scribbled on her papers. "Given the number of laborers and the time I have left to empty that ship, your share of the job is one hundred fifty bales of tea from that ship to that storehouse by sunset. I'll give you another chip worth five. If you work harder—and don't drop dead—that chip in your hand will increase by some amount according to your fate."

"I don't understand."

She took a long draw on her pipe and blew the smoke out of the side of her mouth. It smelled of pine and sage. "Labor is a hard way to earn chips. It's for the young. There are easier ways for someone your age." She hunched down and looked into his eyes. Her cheeks were sun-freckled. "Do something for someone. Do a favor, and you gain a little goodwill you can exchange."

"I'm familiar with favors, but you can't trade in goodwill."

"You can and probably do, you just don't realize it. Here, there is a tangible realization."

"How many favors to earn enough chips to stay at the inn?"

"Hard to say. It isn't just the quantity of what you do, quality determines chip-value too. Save someone's life and you'll be a wealthy man for a while. Lead an elderly woman around a puddle of mud and you'll buy yourself a drink."

HE WORKED under a beating sun and unmoving, sweltering humidity. His heart made its effort known, pumping hard against the wall of his chest and loudly in his ears. Dropping dead was an actual possibility.

At midday, when he stopped to drink tepid water from a black wooden bucket, he asked for his tally. "Twenty-three bales," Almariss said. At this rate, he wouldn't even earn the five on a new chip. He hurried back to the ship for another bale and pushed himself harder. He skipped the afternoon break.

When the sun sank, Almariss arrived with everyone's pay. She held his for last. He was shirtless. His gray-haired chest and paunch dripped with sweat and were red with sunburn.

"Dear uncle, you survived. You've earned your five." She handed him a new chip tinged with pink.

"Thank you."

She leaned close enough to kiss his cheek, but instead she whispered, "If you were really my uncle, I would tell you to see the basket weaver, Shaday." Then she pulled away. Her brows furrowed. "Have you seen the Mayor?"

"Not yet."

A worried look came over her face. "The palace will be closed now, but be sure to see the Mayor in the morning."

"But the money changer told me—"

"Don't listen to them. Some work as money changers because they can't earn chip-value."

"Can't earn?"

"Any chip-value they earn fades. We say they are out-of-their-chips, and sometimes they do desperate things. Remember—the Mayor, then Shaday. You should visit the Salon too. You'll find comfort and advice there." She left him in the dying light of day.

Nico's hunger was the only thing he could focus on. It had risen during the first hour of work to the point it wobbled his legs and dizzied his head, but he had pushed through. Now, hunger was emptiness quickly turning to pain. Eight or nine chip-value would buy a small meal at least, but he'd have to sleep in the streets again.

Why would some people not earn or keep any chip-value? Why had the money changer urged him not to meet with the Mayor? What if his chips lost their value? He pulled the chip from his pocket. It was a darker gray-pink than it had been, almost as dark as the one from Almariss. If it was worth three chip-value before and his new chip was worth five, then the money changer's was now worth four. A total chip-value of nine, maybe. He hadn't lost any, but it was still not enough for shelter. What had he been thinking? Selling glass figurines in this city was madness—and far too much work.

HIS DINNER—ROASTED lamb and herb-dusted potatoes—was small but delicious. Unable to afford a room, he splurged three chip-value on a cup of wine. It was a smooth vintage and stronger than three cups in Budens.

While he ate, people gambled at a nearby table. A simple game of dice called Doubles, in which the highest roll won the bet. Any double roll beat any non-double roll. Ties had to roll again. They wagered each turn. Bystanders could wager on which player would win by betting their wooden chips, but the players themselves did not wager chips. One bet his hearing while the other wagered the breath of his life's final year.

The man wagering his breath was at least ten years older than Nico and wore a dusty, sweat-stained turban. His skin was dark and deeply wrinkled by sun and wind. He rolled a three and a five. The player wagering his hearing was pale and younger, maybe forty, and wore a leather jacket and fingerless gloves. He rolled two ones.

The older man shook his head and left the table.

The younger man laughed. "What's the loss of a year at the End of the World?" Then he looked at Nico. "What about you, cropper?"

"I haven't chips to spare."

"We don't wager chips. I could just sell you something and gain chips. Nah, we wager things we can't sell or buy. You got a wife?"

"I—no, I won't wager my wife."

"But you have one and you'll wager something. Tell you what, if you win I'll give you the last year of breath I just won from old Omesh."

"That's ridiculous. I can't collect that."

"If you stay at the End of the World, you can."

"You're trying to take advantage of a cropper."

"Jarrod's not tricking you," said a short, heavy bystander. "I won Terik's eyesight."

"Gatlin's right, we call him Blind Terik now. Ask anyone. C'mon, it's just a game."

It was just a game. And perhaps good to make contacts. Contacts were a peddler's path forward. Besides, no one could collect on these crazy wagers. "Fine," he said. "I'll wager my best memory."

"And what would that be? How do I know your best memory ain't worse than my worst?"

It was a better memory than most, and he held it carefully in his mind like a newfound treasure, because once he had recalled it, it was a treasure. "The memory is of the year I met and married my Lura. My father tinkered for her family, and one day while my father was hammering a dent out of a ladle, Lura's mother resumed an argument they must have been having. She mentioned how some Antoine would be a fine husband and that Lura was wasting her years of beauty. Lura stepped over to me, looped her arm in mine, and told her mother I was a finer man—and the one she would marry. Just like that. We'd not spoke more than a sentence before that. She chose me when she could have had any man in the village. We were young and quite happy."

"Why did she choose you?" Jarrod asked.

He couldn't answer that. He still couldn't remember. "That's not part of the bargain," he said.

"Fine. It's a wager."

Jarrod handed over the dice, which were well worn and made from the bone or tusk of some animal. Nico shook it and rolled—five and two.

Jarrod took his turn—two and five. "Ties roll again, but you can up the ante."

"I'll not."

"Okay, we reverse. My roll." Jarrod rolled a four and a six.

Sweat beaded on Nico's face. Why was he nervous? This

was a farce. No one could ever really win or lose these bets. He rolled a three and a four.

"Thank you, good sir. But now that I've won the bet, tell me, why did your young gal choose you?"

Nico finished his wine. His head felt lighter than wine could account for. "She—I . . . I don't know." Except he should—he did once. He had asked that very question the night of their wedding and she had told him.

"Well, no matter. I see in my memory she was a lovely bird —luscious brown hair, nice body—I'll dream of her tonight in the most indecent of dreams." Laughter erupted. Nico left the inn. His stomach threatened to heave.

The night was starless and overcast, and the smell of rain clung to the air. Why had Lura chosen him? Had she? He called her his wife, and they had lived together many years, but he could not recall the wedding or if there had even been one. He returned to the building from the previous night, which he'd learned was indeed the Mayor's Palace. The huddle of shelterless clung to its side. Tonight, there were only four.

"Where's Gray Coat—the old man?" he asked.

"You're the old man," said the woman with the odd blue hair.

Too tired for talk, he fell into a deep, muscle-worn sleep.

DAWN CAME COOL AND GRAY. A slight mist soaked Nico's clothes. He rose with a slow, stiff effort, alone again. Where did the shelterless go before sunrise? He hoisted his creel and rounded to the front of the palace. Gray Coat, the man with the white hair, stood at the bottom of the steps. Two men in matching uniforms stood beside the doors, between the columns. They had no weapons and stood silently in finely tailored black trousers and silky red shirts. Each wore a shiny black hat which came to one point over their faces and another behind their heads.

The man took a step.

"Visiting the Mayor?" Nico asked.

The man spun, red-faced. "The Mayor was wrong! I can earn chip-value just like anyone else." He turned back to the uniformed men and took another step, then another until he reached the landing where the men greeted him. "Are you certain?" the left one asked.

"There's no second chance," added the other.

"I either walk through that door and see the Mayor, or I don't. That's a greater chance for a better tomorrow than walking beyond the borders of this forsaken city."

The men each held a key and twisted them in an unlocking motion in the air. The doors opened. The man stepped inside, and the doors closed behind him. Nothing. No sound. No one came out. The doormen stood at silent attention, staring straight over the Commons. Nico shook his head. Meeting the Mayor could wait. He darted away in search of the basket weaver. A basket weaver like Lura.

SHADAY FINDS MAGIC AT THE END OF THE WORLD

Magic will find you here.
It beats beneath the streets.
Not a fire, but warmth.
Not ice, but cold blue silver.
- Notes of a Traveller

$\mathcal{I}$n the main market square, Nico found Shaday's stall squeezed between a cloth merchant's and a potter's. Baskets of all types filled Shaday's stall: small, dainty, artistic-looking bowls woven from a slim, dried, green grass; wide, shallow baskets meant for carrying on one's head. Hanging from the stall's canvas covering were tiny baskets shaped like a variety of animals: rabbits, lions, and horses, each with an opening just big enough for something the size of an egg or two. Despite their lack of size and utility, they were the most beautiful woven objects he'd ever seen. She interlaced something in the weave of reeds that made them shimmer with rainbow colors, like wet grass in the sun. Shaday's hands were far more skilled than Lura's.

No one tended the stall, but there was a canvas and thatch lean-to at the back. He knocked, and no one answered. His curiosity urged him to pull the animal-skin curtain to the side. A narrow pile of fur and wool blankets lay on the ground, a cooking pot hung over a small fire pit, and there were piles of dried grass, strips of wood, and other basketmaking materials. In a corner, on a tiny, three-legged wooden table, sat one of the small baskets—a Moses basket. Inside was a wicker doll. A grown woman with a doll had to represent something; a lost child, perhaps. He closed the lean-to and waited beside the stall.

He didn't wait long. A woman wearing a light green smock and a leather apron approached. She had long, reddish-brown hair that was tied back and a few gray hairs emerging at her temples. Her eyes darted over her inventory.

"Looking for a basket?" she asked.

"Actually, Almariss gave me your name as someone who might need my help."

"How do you know I'm the person who matches the name?"

"Pardon me, you are correct. I made the assumption you are Shaday, the basket weaver."

"That is what they call me."

"And do you need help?"

She walked past him and into the stall, placing her hands on her hips. "Everyone needs help. But you can't give me the help I need."

"I can help with the baskets—deliver them, I mean. I'm guessing you just made a delivery, but your stall was empty, inviting theft."

"Theft is not so common as that. It's usually croppers like you who don't understand."

He lowered his head and said nothing for a moment. When trying to make a sale, it was better to listen than to speak.

"How can I trust that you, a cropper who doesn't understand theft here, won't steal my baskets? Salty good it would do you."

"I'm a merchant, just as you. Even if theft is not your prime concern, perhaps you miss a sale when you're absent." He lowered the creel from his back, opened the lid, and removed a glass ornament in the shape of a swaddled infant. "All I wish to do is sell these. I haven't chips enough for a license, but if I can deliver your baskets and part with a few of these, then I can build up my chip-value."

She looked at him, her green eyes narrowed. "I can't pay you. I barely keep myself fed with fish broth. Most of what I earn goes to materials."

"All I ask is to deliver your baskets and return to sleep in your stall. I have nowhere else to go."

"Sleep here?" Her eyes were wide with alarm.

He said nothing. Instead, he offered her the glass infant. She looked at him and then the infant. "Consider it my payment for shelter," he said. "I won't ask for any of your stew."

The alarm in her eyes faded. She took the infant and held it as if it would break into pieces at her touch. A tear escaped her left eye onto her cheek.

"You were a cropper," he said. "You haven't seen your child or children for a long time."

More tears came. She clasped her hand around the infant and pressed her other hand to her chest. "Ten years," she said. "How did you know?"

"I just—it's in your demeanor." He recalled the amorous couple. Natives seemed to enjoy themselves here. "We croppers are confused, lonely, missing home—all of it. You never intended to stay, yet you did, and now you regret at least part of that choice."

She wiped her tears. "The choices we make here are not what you expect. Take those to the Mayor," she said, pointing to two large brown baskets. "She ordered them a week ago and I should have delivered them yesterday. They cost twenty—ten each."

He recalled Gray Coat entering the Mayor's doors and wondered if he ever came out. Nico wasn't ready to meet the Mayor, but he needed Shaday's trust. He replaced the creel over his back and took the baskets.

THE DOORMEN STOOD AT ATTENTION. Nico climbed the steps. When he reached the landing, each of the men bowed and pulled open a door without using their keys or unlocking motions.

"Thank you," he said.

"Certainly," said the one on the left.

"The Mayor?"

"In the office at the back," said the man on the right. Up close, it was clear they were twins.

Nico took a deep breath and entered.

The inside was brightly lit with shaded lamps of many colors. Red, green, lavender, even copper and yellow. Several low-walled offices lined the right and left sides of the building. Ministers and clerks dressed similarly to the twins, but with colored shirts that matched the lights in their offices, worked at the details of administering a city. No one took notice of him.

The Mayor's office was as wide as the building, taking up the entire back half. There were no doors. The wall was waist high, with a dark wooden balustrade as tall as the top of his head.

A woman, taller even than Almariss, stood behind the desk, an ornate white cane in her left hand. She was light skinned and wore a white fur stole around her neck and shoulders, and she stared directly at him. Beneath the fur was a simple but elegant white gown, and she wore jewels on chains around her neck and wrists. Her black hair was braided, with strands of gray streaking each twist. She was younger than Lura, but not as young as Shaday.

Shelves filled the walls of the room, each of which housed candles in various colors and stages of use. All were lit. At the center of the Mayor's desk spun a colored globe. It flickered— purple, gold, and white—at an entrancing speed. How did it move on its own? On either side of the globe were two open boxes. They were black and richly decorated, engraved with endless knots. The entire room smelled of sage, as if they stood in a garden of it. Nico placed the baskets on the desk beside the spinning globe, unable to take his eyes from it.

"Ah, Shaday's fine work," said the Mayor. "And you must be our latest cropper."

He bowed. "Madam."

When he lifted his head, the Mayor's face was close to his. Her faced had changed. It was that of a younger woman, only about twenty. Her hair was loose and dark but held the two streaks of gray on each side. She sniffed him. "So, will you stay at the End of the World? Or will you venture into the unknown?"

"I just wish to sell my wares, change my chip-value to currency, and return to Budens."

"Budens? I've never heard of it. By the scent of your clothes, I'd say you won't find a path to your home for a very long while, if ever. I can't be sure. It's such an inexact skill."

"Skill?"

"Navigating the End of the World. Here is Shaday's payment." A dark gray-pink wooden chip appeared between two of the Mayor's long fingers. Her voice and face changed again. She was a young teen, still with black hair and gray streaks. "I hope you'll stay. I always fear for those who venture into the places they know cannot lead them home. Be sure to see the Ventals. The Salon serves as a place where croppers can meet and learn about the city. They help with the transition from your time to this."

"My time . . . I just want to sell—"

"Oh yes, your license. You can pick it up in the office to the right of the doors, the one with the lavender light. Commerce Minister Kana."

"But I only have—"

"No charge. You see, that's how I judiciously earn my salary. That was a lovely thing you did for Shaday. She's been inconsolable since coming a-cropper."

"How did—"

"It's my job. Check your chip."

He did, and it was no longer gray-pink but a full light pink.

"Also," the Mayor resumed, "if you hear of anything illegal or dangerous, be sure to let me or my valet, Eristol, know." She pointed to a short, bald man with a ruddy complexion who stepped into the office wearing a simple white shirt and blue-and white-striped pants held up by red suspenders. "There are desperate people who can't earn chips or keep their value. Desperate people sometimes become dangerous people."

"I—well, there was the young money changer—"

"That's Brunella," said Eristol. "She's harmless, just immune to the earning of chip-value." He laughed, a giggle that shook his belly and his pink jowls. "She used to steal chips only to find they were worthless later."

"Why don't people like her leave?"

"Most do," the Mayor said. "But a few remain, particularly more recently. That's what concerns me. We have no captain of the Defense, so we need to be extra careful." The Mayor melted into the older woman.

"Why do you—"

"It's been a pleasure meeting you, Nico. You are a welcome addition to the city, if you stay."

Eristol led him to the lavender-lit licensing desk where Commerce Minister Kana sat. She was very young, possibly still a child, and wore a lavender blouse. Her hair was short and black, her skin pale. She handed him an official scroll sealed with the Mayor's mark. "Your license," she said. Her voice was soft, demure, and she bowed her head. He had seen a few men from the far east, but never a woman. She certainly appeared to be from that part of the world. He bowed slightly in a likewise manner, though he didn't know why, then left the palace.

The map seller had been right. How does anyone fit in here? As soon as he sold his glass, he would head home. What had the Mayor said? Stay or venture into the unknown? He didn't intend to do any venturing. He knew the way home. It was right on the map.

HE DID NOT to return directly to Shaday.

He hurried through the city. It was busy. Hundreds of people circulated the streets, going about their business. The air was still warm, but it drizzled rain. Beneath the bustle of everyday life, a silent hum vibrated in the streets. He felt it in the air and beneath his feet. People carried things, pushed things, walked with purpose and intention. They knew where they were and where they were going. He was confident and shared that certainty. He just needed to verify the map still contained the right landmarks to lead him home.

He passed the last small cottages at the edge of the city and followed the Goresetch. He just needed to see the road leading toward Vila da Luz. Then he would return Shaday's chips and decide if it was worth trying to sell some glass figurines or if he should just return home to Lura. The first thing he would do is ask her why she chose him. He felt an emptiness in his arms. How long had it been since they had truly embraced? He checked the map and headed along the road over the Goresetch Finger.

Under low clouds and rain, a wide, flat plain of sand dunes littered with tufts of grass grew visible in the distance. Where were the low hills and thin forest? This was not the Goresetch Finger. The sea roiled to the east, a thick forest clung to the north and west, and a vast emptiness opened to the south. There should have been sea to the south and hills to the north.

The road was not hardpacked but sandy, and it twisted farther south. This road would not take him home. He checked what he saw against the map. Nothing matched. The map had been useful only once, not because the mapmaker had drawn it inaccurately, but because the land itself had changed. The markings at the edge, familiar towns like Burgau and Vila da Luz, were no longer marked. The edges of the map were clean. Was that magic? He stuffed the map into his jacket and walked back to the End of the World. Was he truly trapped? Was there no way home?

~

HE GAVE Shaday the Mayor's chip.

"Thank you," Shaday said. "There are three small spice baskets beside you. If you'd like to take them to the Scale and Tentacle, it would be a help."

He heard himself say, "Glad to help." But his mind was swirling. He watched her work with her fingers and reed. She was forming a new, small basket. The rainbow filaments were not part of the reed and not something in her hands. They appeared once she made the weave. His head felt light, as if he'd had too much wine. His feet felt as though they might lift from the ground at any moment. No way home?

"Ten years?" he asked, hoping the sound of Shaday's voice might tether him somehow.

She didn't look up from her work. "Ten years, two months, and six days. Evan is fourteen. Who did you leave behind?"

He wiped his face with his hand. "My wife, a few friends." And memories, too, though he didn't say so. "Lura, my wife, also makes baskets."

Shaday looked up. "No children?"

"No, we never—we couldn't afford it."

"But you're staying."

Was he? When he had asked to sleep in her stall, he was thinking it would be just for as long as it took him to sell the glass, but now? Now it seemed there was no decision. He couldn't find his way back. The map was useless. The road was different. Had he forgotten the way? No—but maybe. The map had changed. If there was magic, it was definitely at work here. "I don't know. What will I find if I just walk away from here tomorrow, or next week?"

"Who knows, but chances are against you finding your way home. I've heard some people do, or at least think they've spotted it, but if they make it back to the city, they say they didn't return to their when."

"Their when?"

"They found their place, but everyone they knew was dead, or never born. Seems like we can't get back to our exact place and time."

"So we're stuck for the rest of our lives?"

She set the basket down and stood to face him. "Stuck in

our fate, we say. Those we left behind must think us dead or run away."

"You stayed."

She took his left hand and stroked it gently. "It is a strange place, but what lies beyond the borders of this city is often stranger—and dangerous. I tried to leave and I walked into a place full of steel and machines. There were no mules or oxen, only fast-moving metal wagons that raced about on their own. Thousands of people jammed into streets, jostling against each other but unaware of anyone. It was cold and dangerous. I ran back as quickly as I could, afraid the End of the World would disappear and leave me stranded."

"Why baskets?"

"It's honest work. I thought I could give the baskets away, but people have to need or want them to earn much chip-value, and there's the cost of materials. Selling works best." She pulled down one of the miniature baskets. It was a creel, like his own. She handed it to him. "Thanks for helping. I didn't know I needed it." He took the basket, complete with a small attached lid. The work was so fine, and the shimmering weave tingled when he touched it. "Most of us get by with a simple trade," she said. "But there are other ways to gain wealth. You know who's the wealthiest here?"

"Not the Mayor?"

She laughed. "Hardly. The Ventals. Harmony and Wilcott Vental. You should meet them. They run the Salon and the Ballroom. They help croppers adjust. New croppers and old visit the Salon in the evenings. It's very helpful. They also throw parties. Sometimes in honor of someone they choose, and sometimes just to celebrate a minor thing, such as the sunrise. They host a New Year's Eve Ball for the entire city too. Their work and goodwill to everyone has made them wealthy."

He recalled the young couple on their way to the Salon.

"I've seen them, I think. They were quite . . . infatuated with each other."

"More than infatuated," Shaday said. "I know. I fell in love once."

He had fallen in love too. He had been as infatuated with Lura as the Ventals were with each other, and that passion had ignited a lifelong love. He knew that the same way a stone in a wall is certain of its position, yet like a stone he didn't know how he had gotten there. He would never know. It was over, if Shaday and the Mayor were correct. "I'll never see Lura again." His voice as shaky as his legs. "She joked, told me not to fall off the edge of the world, but I've done just that. I've left her alone."

Shaday closed his hand around the tiny basket and squeezed, then let go and returned to her work. "It's difficult being a cropper, but it's also not so difficult. As near as I can tell, everyone here was once a cropper. There are no natives. Everyone came from elsewhere. Some just fit in and embrace what the city provides."

His mind swirled with this new, desperate reality. Not only was he stranded, cut off from his old life—from Lura—but he needed to survive. If he sold or gave away all of his glass ornaments he might gain some chip-value, but not enough for the rest of his days. People needed what you were selling to maximize the gain. If he ventured far out of the city to peddle, he'd be stranded wherever and whenever and unable to return to the city. He shook his head. With no better alternative, and no remedy to his situation, he stuck the miniature creel into his vest pocket and picked up Shaday's baskets for the Scale and Tentacle.

~

THE TAVERN WAS BUSY, as usual. The Scale and Tentacle had competition, which he saw when he passed other taverns: the Fated Gale, Croppers' Corner, and the Horn of Plenty. But many seemed to favor the Scale and Tentacle. Inside, under a cloud of tobacco pipe smoke, another game was underway. This time the players wagered the attention of their spouses.

"He's a rotten sot," said one player. A woman of middle age, thin and with gray bags under her eyes. She took a long swallow of ale and picked up the yellowed dice. "But he's a hell of a lover."

The other player shook her dark curly head and said, "Well, Darla's a real looker, but she won't share my bed. Guess she doesn't favor heavy women. Maybe she'll like you better."

The dice rolled. A *thunk* and *clack* of ivory against ivory and the wooden table. The sounds of fate.

The middle-aged woman lost. "Well, now you've got Humfred to fill your bed."

The larger woman laughed. "Hope he's got the magic you claim."

"Endowed him with it myself. Been infected with minor magic ever since I fell a-cropper."

"Another wager?"

Infected with magic.

Nico pulled Shaday's creel from his pocket. The weave rippled rainbow colors and tingled the tips of his fingers. It matched the silent hum he felt in his bones. The town crackled with magic. He plucked the glass mule from his pocket. It was cloudy with a lavender-tinted stain. Was it damaged or defective? Had all his glass become stained? He squeezed it in defeat. Everything he did was useless. His plans had failed him, and he'd failed Lura. The thought of never seeing her again was like death, but worse. Knowing she lived but being unable to return to her was purgatory. Could you mourn the living?

He didn't stay to see the next round. He gave the innkeeper

the baskets and collected Shaday's chips. Then he dashed outside and behind the tavern to be alone. In the late afternoon light, the cloudy stain still hung inside his glass mule. It moved, floating in the glass. He stuffed the mule into the tiny creel and shook it at the sky. "Useless." Everything he did was useless. His plans to sell unique items for high profit always failed. *Sorry, Lura.* He prepared to throw the tiny basket and glass mule into the tavern's garden, but Shaday's weave buzzed in his fist. Defective?

Or infected?

He pulled the mule out of the basket. The cloud in the glass solidified into a crystal. Lavender. The color beamed from the inner crystal and into the air before him. Something vibrated in the ground beneath his feet—and deeper in his bones.

Lura stood there in her wedding dress of pale lavender. She wore a crown of lavender and white flowers. She was twenty, and she was the most beautiful woman in the world. She spoke. "I made a bargain—the best bargain. My love for a man who loved me unconditionally. I knew it had to be you. Anyone who loved a mule as tenderly as you did had love in plenty."

Then she was gone. Her scent—floral, full of spring—filled the air of the garden. The crystal was gone, but a lavender cloud remained floating inside the glass. It was warm.

Infected, just as the woman had claimed.

Another memory flooded his mind and vision: the memory of the day he purchased their small house. He had just sold the last of dozens of carts filled with metal scraps: discarded spoons, broken knives, tiny chains bereft of their dangling charms, stained or broken charms freed from lost chains, pots with holes. He had finally earned enough to pay the landlord rent on the tiny cottage, and Lura had fallen in love with it. It had a well and lay nestled at the edge of a grove of carob trees surrounded by wheat fields. Their home for thirty years.

The cloud in the mule crystalized and formed another

beam of light. Lura appeared again, young and wearing the green linen dress she liked best. A smile stretched the edges of her face and lit her polished brown eyes. She hugged him and leaned in to kiss him. He leaned to meet her lips, but he stumbled and dropped the mule and basket. She was unreachable. Clouds descended over the city. A cool drizzle soaked him as he lifted the glass and basket from the ground. The smell of Lura still lingered in his breath, but he was alone. He returned the mule to the basket, and he was dry. Fingers caressed his cheek, and Lura kissed him deeply.

He soaked in the memory and let it wash over him like the rain. He held it tight to the sharp, aching point of knowing he could not return to her. The vision faded.

He smiled. Though it was a bittersweet solution, this was the answer. He didn't have to be poor, and neither did Shaday. She was as infected as he.

He jogged through the drizzle back to Shaday's stall and arrived out of breath. She set aside the basket she was making. "Are you all right?"

"I'm fine—better than fine. I've seen fifty years of this world, but my mind hasn't left me yet. These," he said, pointing at one of the tiny, delicate woven baskets: a small covered box made of a fine black reed that glistened with Shaday's magical sheen. "You give these away, don't you?"

"Yes. Mostly to children."

"And because you do it out of kindness, and the gift is unexpected but desired, you gain a little chip-value."

She narrowed her eyes at him. "And?"

He separated his mule from the small creel. The crystal was cloudy still. Then, he pulled out the basket and placed the mule inside. The lavender-tinted cloud coalesced and crystalized in the glass, and colored light beamed into his face. Lura sat in her chair, weaving a basket.

"What do you see?" he asked.

"I see a soft lavender light coming from my small creel. How did you do that?"

"I'm calling it Memory Glass."

"Memory Glass?"

He covered the creel and his vision of Lura faded with the light. "The mule reminds me of my home, and of Lura. She became real as I recalled a memory. Shaday, you can make the baskets, the glass blower can make more shapes, and I can interview croppers. If we give them something to remember what they left behind, we'll earn more together than separately for as long as croppers fall into the End of the World."

"But how does it work? I won't be part of a scam."

"Not a scam—magic. Let me guess, you were a good weaver back home, but you couldn't make anything like this tiny box. Your baskets didn't shimmer like they do here."

"It's true. I don't know how or why. There's a hum in my bones."

"It's the magic of this place. It's gathered in you. You're infected with it." As he said it, her eyes widened with dawning realization, and she smiled. Nico continued, "You've already placed the little infant into a basket, haven't you?"

She ducked into the lean-to and emerged with the small Moses basket. The glass infant rested inside, as if lying in a little bed. A soft orange cloud hung in the glass.

"I thought I was losing my senses, or growing new ones. Ever since you gave this to me, I see Evan. He even speaks to me like he did ten years ago. I can smell him."

"Memory Glass. Memories experienced, not just recalled in flashes in our minds. Lived again and again."

The crush that had pressed down on his shoulders for years fell away. The weight of failure shifted and lightened. Lura remained in Budens, and though he had lost what he thought was his best memory, there were others—a lifetime of them, equally wonderful. There might be no fresh memories, but at least something still connected him to Lura through the glass which preserved his memories. He wondered, when he recalled them through the glass, would she recall them too? Would she experience them at the same moment—a flash of memory which she wouldn't know the reason for recalling? He would never know for sure, but he believed she must.

MEMORIES AT THE END OF THE WORLD

Whirlwind through time and place
Neither when nor where, pace waves
Tortoise in the sea
\- Notes of a Traveller

*A*nne walked away from the Mayor's Palace with Noble at her heels. She had put the meeting off for months, and the conversation had been short. She wanted to arrange a partnership with the Mayor, because she was getting nowhere on her own. The fucking chips and their inability to remain even slightly pinkish kept her sleeping in a scrap lean-to in the chip-less camp, a place that at least felt safer than the rest of the city because it was full of people like her. She had not wanted to meet the Mayor as a homeless wastrel, rather as an equal and a leader of industry.

But the city had no industry. There were crafters, farmers, herders, butchers, carpenters, wheelwrights, and smiths, and whatever the city needed in quantity it traded for with the

41

stranded ships. Some captains found it best to offload their cargo for a few motley coins; others took their chances and sailed with their cargoes into the unknown. But it was enough for the city. There was no manufacturing, no technology, and nothing she could wrap her head around.

Marta waited for her on the Commons. She had come to the city from New Jersey during World War II. Cherub-stocky with dark wavy hair, she was a welder and a carpenter. It was Marta who had shown her how to build the lean-to. But Marta had the same problem: though she worked in the harbor repairing ships, her chip-value faded. Not as quickly as Anne's, but too quick to save for better shelter.

"What did the Mayor say?" Marta asked.

"The same as she told you. She wasn't interested in any partnership. Warned me not to step into the palace if my fate was barren. What bullshit. If my fate was barren, wouldn't I be dead, with no future?"

"It means not keeping chip-value or even earning it."

"I know what it fucking means. Those damned chips. I worked hard for the Ventals. Just as hard as that Angi kid, but Angi's chips were always a deeper, darker shade of pink— almost red. But we did the same work. Greet and seat people for a performance, serve drinks, and clean up the damn Salon."

"And I work just as hard as the next carpenter, but my chip-value is never as deep as theirs."

"Sure, Angi's younger, pretty in her own way, and she smiles nicer. But we weren't earning tips. And the Ventals didn't have any influence over the value? Horse shit."

They strolled past the edge of the market toward the small chip-less camp near the Finger Light. Despite the unfairness of it all, the situation was real. Going hungry was an actual threat. The direness of it had become clear one afternoon when she was in the market and the potter's purse was open. Inside was a deep red chip. On impulse, she had snatched the chip and slipped away from the stall. Would a deeper red keep its value longer? It fucking didn't. By morning it was as shit gray as the clouds.

"You know, I raised nearly a billion dollars through promises and a kiosk demo," she said.

"A kiosk?"

"But the Mayor didn't listen. She wants me to leave."

"Maybe we should."

"Marta, you would have already if you could. You would have hopped on one of those ships and been in a normal place in a few hours. But you didn't."

"Normal maybe, but what if I sailed into the middle of the war?"

"Exactly. The risk of the unknown is too much. The world is a shitty place and sailing into it blind is just fucking foolish."

"The End of the World's pretty shitty too, for some of us."

"As shitty as it is, the most dangerous thing in it is possibly starving to death through lack of chip-value."

The air was chilly, and a stiff wind blew against them. Anne wore just her sweater and thin Urbletics. She couldn't even buy clothes. There was a gift shop that gave items away to those that needed it, but the owners gained chip-value through the practice and fuck if she would help them earn income by allowing her to be poor. It was a perverse sort of taking advantage. Really, they weren't even very wealthy. The gift shop was a dilapidated cottage at the edge of the city proper, but it was the principle.

Anne pulled her gray chip from her sports bra. "What if we painted the chip to look like one with moderate value—just a little pink stain? How would anyone know?"

Marta stopped and looked at her with wide-eyed surprise. "You mean fake them? Counterfeit?"

"Who's to know? There's a treasury here. We just need a little stain the right shade and some worthless chips. If it works, we can make plenty." Enough to establish herself with wealth. Power and influence would come after.

"I don't know. It seems like stealing."

"Stealing what? It's not fair we're discriminated against. We need to make our own advantage, our own fate."

"Well, there's a red tea that might be the right shade."

"That's the spirit. Now we just need some plain chips."

THE MAYOR'S Palace was cold. How she lived in such frigid air was still a mystery to Almariss. During the day, and if it was hot outside, the ambient air and the series of vents at the bottom of the building warmed the office some. The candles and lamps helped a little too. But the Mayor and Eristol's living quarters were cold even when it was hot outside. Was it related to the city's magic? But Eristol had no connection to the magic. How did he manage the cold?

She climbed the wooden steps, followed the narrow hall to the Mayor's apartment, and knocked.

"Come in, Almariss dear. I tell you every week, after all these years you need not knock."

"Just courtesy." She entered and closed the door. The Mayor sat behind the game table drinking tea. An Affinity Globe spun beside the familiar tea set. Almariss filled a cup for herself.

"Quite a few croppers these past weeks," the Mayor said between sips. She was the bright, nine-year-old version of the Mayor that Almariss was the least familiar with. Almariss loathed and desired a glimpse—however short—of the thirty-year-old Mayor. That always released a flood of emotions. The girl of nine, filled with the age and wisdom of the Mayor spoken in the soft, light voice of a child, was almost comical and difficult to take seriously.

"The ships bring many," Almariss noted.

"I should have tried to avoid that raging sea. Actually, I did try."

"A fair number have come down the Goresetch too." Almariss looked at the board. The carefully drawn lines and images flickered and glittered with their own rainbow light. The images on the tiles, stacked and ready, glimmered similarly. The Mayor called it patolli. The original, she said, was a gambling game, but here they only wagered the six jade stones given to each player. The first to lose all six stones lost the game, and the number of tiles dictated the length of the game between wagers. The goal was to stack tiles that matched an element of the one laid down before until the allotted tiles had each been played, and the first to use all their tiles won the round and the wager stone. The Mayor had laid out at least two dozen tiles each. It would be a long evening.

The Mayor made her first wager and move. "It's not how many arrive, but how many choose to stay."

"Have you met with them all?"

"Nearly. No significant disruptors, and a few helpful ones like that girl Angi a few years ago. You know, Nico surprised me."

Nico was a surprise. The way he had drawn Shaday out of her years-long malaise was amazing and a relief. He'd had an effect not just on Shaday, but herself too—she'd called him uncle, as if somehow he were truly family. She placed her wager stone on the board and found a tile with a shimmering painted sparrow matching the one on the Mayor's tile.

The Mayor's appearance drifted into that of the thirty-year-old woman she had met long ago. The same age she had been. The Mayor's silver-black eyes could mirror the slightest light with a sparkle that lit the lonely edges of her heart. Sensations Almariss thought she had buried long ago surged.

"Almariss, why do you never use my name?"

That was true. In those heated times, the Mayor's name

had burned through every waking thought or breathless dream, but she kept that name at bay now. Some say to know another's name is to have power over them. To let the Mayor's name into your heart gave her power over you. "You never touch me as you once did." That was more than she'd meant to say, if she'd meant to say anything.

"I cannot. You don't understand what it might do to me. I'm so bound to this place I cannot be the one I was, not for more than a moment." She melted into a stately woman of fifty. Still crushingly beautiful.

"A specific form is not what I need from you. You don't understand what these years with you have been like for me. So close and so distant."

The Mayor wagered, then carefully considered her next tile. "I do understand," she said. "I feel everything you feel—and more. I spare you the more."

Did she want sparing? There was a terrifying delight in the thought of being used and consumed by the passion they once shared until there was nothing left of her. The Mayor played her tile. Almariss placed a wager stone on the board and placed a tile matching a gold-painted infinity loop over the Mayor's.

THE GAME ENDED LONG after middle-night. The Mayor won, as she usually did. The walk back to Almariss's small home on the docks was warmer but still left her chilled. She glanced down the road toward the Finger Light, glowing red against the rocks and sea. The same road led to Nico and Shaday's new cottage. If only Nico had been here when she and the Mayor had been so close, she'd have a Memory Glass to relive those moments now. But that might have been worse, to feel the same feelings—better simply to hold her memories, half faded and half hidden from the damage they did. Beyond the red glow of the light, there was a shadow of a ship. More croppers.

NICO WALKED through the descending evening along the winding sandy path that led from the city to the salt marshes and the cottage where he and Shaday lived. What homey touch had she added today? The move from the stall and lean-to came quickly once word of their Memory Glass reached croppers who had chosen, at least for a while, to stay in the city, and their combined chip-value had increased enough to purchase the single-room cottage. Shaday was firm on the location. She wanted to be close to the reeds and grasses that were her materials. He enjoyed being near the ocean and letting the surf lull him to sleep. The proximity to her materials and his operation of the stall gave Shaday time for homely touches, like a reed mat for the doorway that glistened with her magic. It wasn't life with Lura, but it was a life.

His stomach growled in response to the mouthwatering aroma drifting from the meat pie he carried. It was unlike those in Budens. This one held the fragrance of rare spices, and its crust was twisted into a shape like an onion but it was as large as a melon. The Scale and Tentacle didn't make these, but they sold them on behalf of a woman, the sister of Commerce Minister Kana, as it happened. You had to place an order days in advance. He couldn't wait to see the look on Shaday's face.

Darkness was nearly complete by the time he arrived at the cottage. A dim light glowed behind the two small windows, and the doormat glinted slightly, reflecting the light of the stars. Inside, Shaday sat in her chair beside the wooden table where the fish-oil lantern illuminated her work on a tiny basket, the shape of which he could not yet discern.

"Dinner," he said as he placed the cloth-wrapped pie on the table.

"Ooh, one of Asami's?"

"Yes. A small celebration."

Shaday put her work away while he pulled shallow bowls and spoons from the cupboard. "What are we celebrating?"

"Anything you'd like."

She unwrapped the pie and cut it open. Steam rose, filling the cottage with its warm, delicious scent. "How is it still so warm?"

"Perhaps that's Asami's magic," he said, spooning the pie into their bowls.

He wished he'd thought of some wine, but Shaday never drank it anyway. She preferred ale or mead. They ate while he related his day working the stall. There had been little business, but Almariss had stopped by and made an interesting comment, leaving him with a question that burned in his mind the rest of the afternoon. After a few moments of quiet while he and Shaday enjoyed the pie, he asked, "What's the End of the World Brigade?"

Shaday pushed her empty bowl away and cocked her head. "Why?"

"Almariss mentioned that she was late for a meeting with the Mayor and the Brigade. She didn't stay for me to ask her about it."

"The Brigade are volunteers for the city. They put out fires, repair homes damaged by weather, that sort of thing."

"Ah, makes sense. I wonder if they need—"

A soft rapping on the door interrupted him.

"Who is that at this hour?" Shaday said. She pulled her green wool shawl from a hook and draped it over her shoulders.

Nico went to the window and looked out, but it was too dark to see who it was.

Angi.

"It's Angi," he said. *From the Salon.* Odd. He hadn't seen her yet, and he didn't know her; the knowledge simply became present in his mind. "From the Salon."

"Oh," Shaday said.

He opened the door. A woman stood on the mat dressed in a fine white ruffled blouse, elegant black trousers, and shiny black boots. She looked quite young.

"I'm sorry to come so late, but you sell the Memory Glass?"

"We don't sell them, but come in, come in. Would you like some meat pie? It's Asami's."

Angi stepped inside. "No, thank you. I get plenty at the Salon."

"The Nowruz celebration," Shaday said. "But I didn't know that until just—"

"I have a few hours before the party."

"I remember you from the New Year's Eve Ball a couple years ago. You were a greeter, and so young—still young."

"I was seventeen."

"Sit." Shaday pointed to Nico's chair. He cleaned away the bowls and remains of the pie. "So, you would like a Memory Glass?"

"Is it real? I don't know if I believe in magic."

"You must judge for yourself if it's real—if it works for you."

"Do they not work sometimes?"

"Never failed so far," Nico said. Angi had light skin and brown eyes. Her hair was blonde but dark at the roots.

"How does it work? Do I just tell you a memory?"

"Something like that," said Shaday. "Nico, make us some tea."

"Excellent idea." He set about stoking the small fire in the fireplace and checking the water in the pot hanging over it. "You've been a cropper for a few years," he said. Did he know that? *Three*.

"I arrived when I was sixteen."

49

"What was your most cherished thing from your earlier life?"

"Thing?"

"Or place. Maybe start there," added Shaday. "What did you like to do, or where did you like to go?"

"I loved the beach. We lived on an island."

"You and your parents? Siblings?"

"Just me and my parents. We lived in an enormous city, lots of tall buildings and machines. Everything was made of metal or concrete. I enjoyed going to the beach. I was the only person with a natural tan." She stopped and looked down at her hands, which were folded on the table.

"Go on," said Nico. She said nothing, but *I don't know* came to him. He poured the hot water over the tea leaves, which sat a small metal basket Shaday had woven for the purpose. The water glinted rainbow swirls as it passed through the wire mesh. "I know some memories from our former lives can be difficult. It's hard being reminded of what we can never reach again."

"It's not that. I'm not homesick. I mean, I was during the first months I was here, but I adjusted. I think I adjusted too much."

"Too adjusted?" Shaday said.

"I can't really remember my old life. Everything feels very far away, more like a dream that you can't quite remember in the morning."

"You're too young to lose your memory," Nico said. He placed the steaming mug of tea in front of her.

"No," Shaday said. "All memories fade." She reached her hands across the table to cover Angi's. "You loved the beach. What did you see there?"

"The sky. It was blue, so blue. The sand burned my feet. I could smell salt. The beach was always empty. Everyone stayed inside where it was cool, but I liked the sun. I liked how it seeped under my skin and warmed me from the artificial chill of our buildings."

"Were there ships and boats, people fishing?" Nico asked. He placed Shaday's mug beside her outstretched arms.

"No. Our food came by AirTrains. Fish were not safe to eat. I remember lizards in the rocks between the city and the beach. There were palm trees too. I think I made a lizard into a pet, but I wasn't allowed to bring it home." She pulled her hands away from Shaday's and placed them around her mug.

Shaday sipped her own tea. "Did your parents go with you to the beach?"

Nico was still pondering what an air train might be when the question, *Did they?* came into his mind.

"I don't think so," Angi said.

Nico fished through his trunk of glass figurines. There were no lizards. He would have the glass blower make one. Was there something else Angi might feel attached to? He found the elephant he had bought back from Brunella at ten times the chip-value he'd gained by giving it to her. She hadn't wanted it and he would not allow anyone to melt it for a window or jewelry. He placed the elephant on the table. "No lizards," he said.

"There weren't any elephants on the island."

"No, naturally not." He left the elephant on the table.

"Do you like living at the End of the World, Angi?" Shaday asked.

"Like it? Does it matter? I can't leave. I've been to the Lookout a hundred times, and I tried to walk away the first few days, but there's never anything like the world I came from. Mostly it's old like this place, or older. Everything feels dangerous."

"You've settled, but you don't really want to be here."

Angi's eyes widened. "You're right. I don't want to be here

forever. But I can't leave, and I can barely remember what home was like."

I'm losing myself.

"Did anyone important to you die when you were growing up? Why do you think you went to the beach? Was there something besides the cold of your buildings you wanted to get away from?"

Angi was silent. She held her mug tight. Then, "I think Mother was sick."

"The beach was your solace."

"I remember turtle eggs. And turtles. I rescued a turtle!" The excitement in Angi's voice lit Nico's own excitement. He had a turtle in his chest, and he removed the elephant. He placed the turtle in Angi's hands and covered them with his own. The humming in his bones began, like hundreds of migrating geese leaping into the air at once. A swirling cacophony of remembered things.

Angi spewed memory after memory. Shaday began weaving a miniature basket while they listened. There were long afternoons that felt too short, the heat of the sun making her sweat and turning her skin pink. Sand scorched the bottom of her feet in a way that was pleasantly painful—just right. Green-blue waves curled with white foam brows. Birds with wings and beaks of brilliant blues, greens, reds, and yellows. Opposing emotions swirled in confusion—love falling into emptiness. There was fear of the cold buildings. And there were turtles, hundreds of tiny turtles scrambling across the beach.

When Angi finished, Nico placed the glass turtle into the small nest Shaday had made. It vibrated with energy and glimmered in a deep, summer sky blue between the weave. Angi took it gently.

"I tell everyone to wait to try it until they are alone," Nico cautioned. "It works best, and you won't look strange staring into a beam of colored light, which is what anyone around you will see."

"Thank you. I will try, but all my memories are swirling in my head now. It buzzes, and it's so warm."

She thanked them several more times, then left. He and Shaday stood at the doorway, watching her return toward the city. He'd offered to escort her, but she declined. He understood. When the night swallowed her, a green light took her place, then the city's glow swallowed the green as well.

"How did you know to make the nest?" he asked. "She hadn't mentioned it."

"That's her magic."

Then he knew.

I shared with Shaday the memory of the nest I made for a turtle egg I found. I watched daily until it hatched.

It wasn't exactly Angi's voice in his mind, but her words were there like his own thoughts, yet not his own.

STINA DRIVES TO THE END OF THE WORLD

Some say this place is like any other place.
This place is precisely like every other.
It is a place like no other.
Some say it is out of time, but no;
this place is among all times.
- Notes of a Traveller

*S*tina shoved open the chrome and glass door of the club. Hit it so hard the glass shook and threatened to break. Her grandmum's ring clacked against the glass and the heel of her palm vibrated numb. Ignoring the pain and the smirking bouncer, she dashed into the rain and ducked past the drenched valet holding open the door of her restored VW. He smiled a smile reserved for owners of VWs parked at the Whispers night club. *No tip, dude.* His smile melted as she slammed the door. Fuck him. Fuck the club. And fuck Hans.

She threw her purse into the passenger seat, turned the

ignition, and stomped on the accelerator. The wheels spun against the wet pavement.

Fuck the rain.

The VW raced through the sheen-glistened streets of Plymouth. She took the A38 west, got off at Treruelfoot, and took the A374 toward Polbathic. All the while, she sucked on her mum's pearl necklace. The narrow roads of the coast were still unfamiliar, but when a flash of white and blue from the Halfway House pub appeared, she took the right. Not much farther to Downderry and Uncle Jacque's beach house.

Hans had suggested a night at the casinos, saying it would do her good. What a cock-up. He didn't gamble but stood over her, coaching which cards to play, when to bet, and ordering red or black. Too many hard-earned tips disappeared into the dealer's hands. Wages at the inn on Downderry Beach didn't come easy, and tips were small and rare.

Gambling while Hans loomed wasn't fun. Cheap wanker; he wagered none of his own money. Whispers—music, dancing, and a few drinks—was her idea. Better to spend money on drinks than watch a dealer pull it away. At least she could enjoy the buzz for a while. But the club was also a mistake. The worst was, it was money she shouldn't have spent. She'd have to take an extra shift if she could get it.

It was a mistake also because those two blondes knew Hans and knew him in a special way, as if they were hungry. Like they'd been waiting for him to walk in, their blouses cut low to their navels. Of course he was a player. His shy act at the library was just that, an act—and a shabby one. He used charm like makeup, covering the blemishes of his soul.

A sign for Widegates flashed in her headlights. Bloody rot, wrong way—too far west. She turned left at the next intersection and passed through No Man's Land, but the road didn't turn back toward Downderry. She needed to turn around, but the road narrowed to a single lane and then turned into dirt. Stone walls lined both sides.

About a mile beyond No Man's Land, she passed a hand-painted wooden sign for the End of the World. Made sense; what else would come once you passed No Man's Land?

The rain lessened to a drizzle. Finally, at the edge of the so-called End of the World, there was enough room to turn the car around with a multi-point turn. She misjudged backing into the fourth point, though, and the left rear wheel dropped off the road and sank into the mud. The wheel spun an angry whine of rubber on grit.

Bloody hell.

In the rain, a quick look at the tire confirmed her need for a push or a tow. She took off her heels and found an old pair of tennis shoes in the back seat, then she walked toward the first house at the edge of town. What a sight she must have looked. Muddy sneakers, a soaked blue Bardot minidress, and her small matching purse. The house was just a cottage and no lights. Her watch glowed 2:17 a.m. Maybe the village pub.

She splashed into the town. A few lights flickered in some of the buildings. The rain stopped, but the street was mud. Her shoes were soaked and her feet frozen. The place stank of brackish saltwater in stagnant pools. Behind the buildings on the right side of the street were shadows of something that looked like ships. A fishing town, like Downderry. Not too far from home at least.

At one corner, a building cast steady warm light and the sound of voices onto the street. Someone sang a rowdy drinking tune. The Scale and Tentacle Tavern & Inn. Stina ran her hand through her thick, wet curls and tried to present herself as best she could. What did it matter? They'd all be looking at her with beer goggles, as Sara would say.

As soon as she entered the pub, many of the men and some women started looking her over. If not with beer goggles then with hungry eyes like Hans's blondes. If only her dress could unroll into a longer gown. Why hadn't someone invented that?

She approached the barmaid, a hefty woman with a small anchor tattooed on her left cheek like a tear. The barmaid placed a small ceramic cup on the counter, but when she looked at Stina closer, she pulled the cup away.

"Excuse me," Stina said. "I need a push. My car has gotten stuck in the mud just outside town. Is there someone here you trust to help me?"

The barmaid shook her head. Her hair had once been a light brown but was now mostly gray. "Won't do any good. Your whatever probably won't be there. You've 'come a-croppa now."

"Croppa?"

"You've 'come-a-croppa, a saying 'round here."

The phrase sounded vaguely familiar, but she couldn't focus on that. "Well, whatever I may be, my car is stuck and I need to get back to Downderry."

"Like I said, your whatever—your ca'—won't be there. You're here now."

Stina sighed. "Is there a tow service?" She pulled her phone from her purse and woke it. No signal.

"I don't know what you're looking for."

"Is there a phone? Can I make a call on your phone?" She hated to rouse Rusty at the pub, but he'd still be up and would make the trip.

"No idea what sort of call you can make, but shout as much as you like. I can get you some fish stew for free, and a room— well no, not tonight. We're full up."

"No, I need a phone."

"Haven't got anything like that. Look, like I said, you've fallen into the End of the World. You're stuck now."

Stina sighed again, loud, and stomped out of the tavern. No cars in the street. No stop signs at intersections. No wires on poles. No poles. Looking back at the pub, the lights were all lamps—real lamps, not electrical lights made to look like lamps. What the serious hell? She took her phone out again. No signal, and only thirty percent charged. The car. She could charge the phone and maybe catch a signal. She walked back to the VW. It wasn't there.

What the actual fuck? Bloody thieves. Screw the End of the World.

She trotted on the muddy road away from the town, toward No Man's Land. The minidress didn't allow a full run. The sound of the ocean drifted behind her and the smell of brackish water cleared from her nose. She held up her phone. No signal. How far to No Man's Land? Three miles; four?

STINA WALKED AND SHIVERED. No more rain, but she was soaked. Almost 4 a.m. She should have reached No Man's Land by now, but there was no sign of anyone. The road was still dirt, and it was narrower. Where was the paved road? Did she take a wrong turn? No, there had been no turns. The phone still showed no signal. Twenty-eight percent. Something moved in the forest to her right.

Forest? There shouldn't be a forest this near the coast. Not one as dense and ancient as that. The trees were old, tall, and thick. The road was just a trail, a foot path. She was moving away from civilization, not toward it. Hell. Had Hans slipped something into her drink? She should never have been driving.

The darkness thickened. It was like walking through a jelly. She strained her eyes to bring shadows into recognizable shapes, but the shadows resisted. A silent electric buzz shivered across the ground. She took measured, carefully plodded steps. Where was she going? Anything familiar was absent from this nightscape.

Something shambled across her vision. *Shambled* was the only word for the way it moved. It was a shadow bigger than a truck, and it lumbered on four feet. It stopped and appeared to consider her, but what it thought of her, she wouldn't know. It stank of wet fur, like a giant bear rug left in a wet cellar for years. A bear? No, bigger. Much bigger.

It huffed. A deep exhale, followed by a rapid sniffing. In the shadows, the animal appeared to have tusks and a trunk. Not an elephant with bare skin, it was a mammoth. *Hans, you bastard. What did you put in my drink?* Stina backed away slowly. Whatever was underneath this hallucination could still be wild and dangerous. The mammoth shook its enormous head and curved tusks like scimitars slashed the shadows. It bellowed. It was a call that filled the night with the echo of loss. The sheer volume of the noise sent ripples of fear through Stina's muscles.

Cold fog clung to her goose bumped skin. She stepped backward and continued. The mammoth, or whatever, must have decided she wasn't a meal and shambled into the forest. She turned and ran. At least there were people at the End of the World.

WHEN STINA REACHED the spot where the VW should have been, her thighs ached. There were no tire ruts, no sign the car had ever been there. She kept walking.

When she reached the Scale and Tentacle, the sun's glow spilled over the water's horizon. The port at the End of the World was full of ships—sailing ships—and the main street was no longer empty. There were still no cars, no sound of trucks rumbling through the early dawn, but people were starting their day like any small city. Yet, it wasn't. How could a place like this —with no technology—still exist? An official-looking building stood at the far end of the main street. Maybe there was a cop. Should've just asked the barmaid for a cop.

Hans, if I ever—you laced my drink? You could have killed me in a crash. I missed the turn to Downderry. Now this? Drugged. Fuck you, Hans. Maybe one of those blondes who latched herself onto you will give you a VD.

Stina thought of home and her bed, but the desire for a soft bed and sleep was like hunger. Maybe this bad trip would pass if she just lay down for a while.

She reached what she first took for a police station, but up close it clearly was not. There were two guards, or doormen. They didn't have any weapons, so they weren't cops, but they had matching uniforms. Each wore red silk shirts, sharp black pants, and shiny black Napoleon hats. They were at once both elegant and silly looking. But they were officials—maybe. She climbed the steps between thick granite columns. At the landing, the men bowed to her.

"The palace is closed, madam," said the one on the left. They were twins.

"The Mayor can see you in an hour," said the other.

"I don't really need the Mayor. I could use the police."

The men leaned toward each other and discussed something at a whisper. Then the one on the right looked at her and announced, "By police, we assume you mean a civilian military from your time. They do not exist here. There is only the Mayor's Defense, and you will need the Mayor's permission for their help. If it is a real emergency—a fire or missing child—we can call the Brigade."

"No police? Well, who are you?"

"Parla was right, the missing cropper," said the one on the left. "Looks like we've found her."

"Madam, are you hurt?" asked the other. He was looking at her legs.

61

She smoothed and tugged at the hem of her dress. "I'm fine. I just really need a phone. Someone stole my car."

"Slow down, madam. You need to see the Mayor—in an hour."

"No—I don't need to see the Mayor. If you're not cops, what are you? Is there a phone I can use?"

"We are door ministers. The Mayor sees all croppers."

"Croppers—yeah, right. Look, I just took a wrong turn earlier. Several, actually, the first being stepping out of my front door, but really I just need to call someone to pick me up. I'll file a complaint about my car in Downderry."

"You may file a complaint with the Mayor," said the first door minister.

She huffed. "I don't need to see—never mind. Fine, I'll see the Mayor."

"Why didn't you stay at the Scale and Tentacle? Croppers get their first night free."

"They said there were no rooms."

"Oh dear, that many croppers. This will be a long day."

"Is there someplace inside I can wait? It's cold out here, and I've been drenched."

"No. The palace remains locked until the Mayor is in."

"But you have the key and could let me in?"

"No, no keys. Only the Mayor has the keys and hands them to us in the morning."

"What if I go see the Mayor now, where does he live?"

"The Mayor lives inside," the door ministers said in unison.

There was a bench on the landing where she and the men stood. "Fine, I'll wait here."

"If you wish, madam."

She fell onto the bench, grateful to be off her feet, and stabbed her hands into her matted hair. This gave new meaning to the walk of shame. After several minutes of silence, the left door minister said, "I'll never understand why so many croppers show up in their underclothes."

THE SOUND of thumping inside the building woke her. Stina had fallen into an immediate and sound sleep. The door ministers were still at attention and not looking at her but at a point in the distance over the grassy green Commons.

The doors opened inward. A woman in her mid-forties, white, dressed in white fur and a white suit, and carrying an ornate white cane strode through the opening. Her movements were thin and elegant.

"Good morning Tiffet, good morning Taffet."

"Good morning, Your Honor," the door ministers said in unison, without removing their gaze from the distance.

"Ah, our missing cropper." She pointed her cane at Stina. "Come in, come in. We must talk."

The Mayor scanned her, foot to face, with a look that was not just curiosity, nor of a curiosity that made Stina uncomfortable. Still, she felt that yet again the minidress had been another terrible choice. Though she had never done one, this must have been what a walk of shame felt like.

She hoped for a cup of coffee, or even water, but the building had no such things. It didn't seem to have a toilet either. The Mayor led her to an office at the end of the building spanning the structure's entire width. The only wall was low and crowned with a wooden balustrade that rose just above her head. Shelves lined the walls, holding candles—all lit. A spinning gold, purple, and white globe sat on the desk, spinning silently at a moderate speed, and on either side of the globe were two open wooden black boxes, each engraved with endless knots. The scent of sage—a reminder of fields and her mum—came strong.

"Your Honor, I don't wish to bother you with this. I just need to file a stolen car report and make a phone call to my boss. I'll be late for work."

"I imagine so." The Mayor took a seat behind the desk and pulled out a flask and two ceramic mugs. "Have some port, dear. It will warm those thin bones of yours."

Port? Hans and drugs, the mammoth. The Mayor didn't need to roofie her, she was already helpless. She accepted the flask. "Thank you."

The Mayor took a long, noisy sip, then stood before a row of flickering candles at the side of the office. There were no windows; none in the entire building in fact. The port was smooth, and it warmed her throat down to her rumbling belly. She drank the rest. At least it was only a small amount. She still needed a toilet.

"I'm afraid you will be late for a good many things," the Mayor said. Her voice had changed. It was higher pitched, younger, almost sensual. She even looked younger than she had outside.

"No offense, Your Honor, but I would like to leave this place and find my way home."

The Mayor pivoted, bearing the face of a woman younger than she. "You have struck upon it rightly. You must find your way home, but a new home."

What the hell was the Mayor saying, and how did she become so young? The port—Hans's drugs.

The Mayor continued. "You see, every cropper wishes to return to their home. At least, most do. But finding that path is more difficult than just finding the right road. The road must exist at the same time and place as when the person left—a near impossibility. You really have fallen a-cropper."

Fallen a-cropper. Now she recalled the phrase. Her grandmum had used it whenever something went missing. She stood, unsure if she should run or stay and talk. "You're saying I can't leave?"

"You may leave whenever you wish. But you may never find your home, neither its place nor its when."

Its when? The lack of technology. "I've fallen into the past? It's not 2014?" This was like a young adult fantasy she read when she was fifteen.

"The past or the future, or perhaps some time that has never been in your realm."

Her realm. The British Isles; home to enchantments, faeries, and dragons, at least long ago. They all existed in another realm, just at the edge of the real world. Legends and superstitions. "Does anyone leave?"

"Most leave, but they do not return home. What they walk into when they leave here, I can't say. I suspect much of what they find is often more dangerous than anything here at the End of the World."

"If I walk out of this city in any direction, I may never find Downderry, or even any familiar place?"

"Or if you do, it may not contain your family and friends or even be in the same decade or century from which you left. Taking a ship out of the harbor is no different."

Hans, this is a really bad trip. If I ever see you again, I'll drive the heel of my shoe through your eye. She felt nauseous and her knees wobbled. She grabbed the balustrade to hold herself upright.

"You need not decide today, or even tomorrow." The Mayor was again the charming, forty-ish woman. "But you'll need currency for food and shelter."

"I have some money." She dug in her purse.

The Mayor held up a hand. "Your coins are only of value to changers, smelters, and jewelers. Your paper is worthless. You need chips. That ring and that necklace might be of considerable chip-value if they are important to you and you find the right reason and the right person to give them to."

"They are important. My grandmum's ring and my mum's necklace. I could never sell them."

"Selling them won't do you near as much good as giving them away. The trick is finding the right person with the right need to maximize the value of the gift."

The room started a slow spin. If it didn't stop, she would piss the floor or throw up—or both. She squeezed her eyes tight and shook her head. When she opened her eyes, the room had stabilized. She looked at her hands as if they could give her answers. "What do I do now?"

"Whatever you wish. I imagine you are hungry and would not care to spend another night in the elements in that slip of a dress."

"So, earn chips."

The Mayor nodded. "If you find you cannot earn chips—if your fate is barren—I suggest you leave immediately into whatever awaits beyond the city. It's not much of a life earning chips through the measure of work alone. And if you cannot retain chip-value, you'll starve."

"What does that mean—a barren fate?"

"Not everyone accumulates or retains chip-value. They lack empathy and can't contribute to society without taking more than they give. If you can't earn chip-value, it's best you leave immediately."

"I have empathy, I can—"

"I believe you, but ultimately fate—your fate—determines what will happen. If you can earn, then by all means stay. Fall in love, build a life here."

"I'm not likely to fall in love here." She fondled her necklace.

"Love is unlikely anywhere, yet we find it everywhere."

66

OUTSIDE, in the center of the strange, quaint city, there were dozens of people going about their business. Business. How were they earning chips?

Her mum had given her the pearl necklace, and it was her mum's before that. There was no meaning beyond its heritage, but that was something. The ring was different. Her father's mum, from Antigua, had given it to her when she was fourteen. "You are a woman now," she had said. "This gold worn around your finger will keep you safe." For years, she'd regarded the gift as a cultural belief, but later it turned out to be something her grandmum had invented. Grandmum magic.

Chips. Work. Gifts.

The Scale and Tentacle. She knew how to serve drinks and food; she could try there.

THE TAVERN WAS busy with customers finishing their breakfast. The barmaid was not there, but a young blonde woman wearing a gray wimple and smock and a long, stained apron was busy picking up plates. Stina stepped in to help. In the kitchen, the woman gave her a close look. "You're not dressed for it, but you know how to tuck tables."

"I've done my share. Mind if I help? My name's Stina."

"Stina the cropper, I've heard. I'm Hallea. You'll need more of an outfit, dearest, if you're going to work here." Hallea's eyes were like a bright sky, and she had an easy smile. She led Stina to a room behind the kitchen, which was a pantry full of potatoes with a side of pork hanging from the rafters. She found a stained tan smock and handed it to Stina, who slipped it over her head. A little too large, but at least it was better than just her minidress. "Before I start, I really need to piss."

Hallea smiled and jabbed her thumb at the door to the rear of the pantry. Stina darted outside and found a small wooden privy across the yard and garden. Less than twenty-four hours ago she'd pissed in the red, black, and gold faux luxury of the restroom of Whispers night club. This somehow felt better—more relaxing, if a little too rustic. When she returned, Hallea was speaking to a burly man with a bright red beard that reached below his belly. He was bald and wore a gold earring in his left ear.

"This is Padrok, the owner. Padrok, this is Stina."

Stina reached out her hand, but Padrok waved at it with his own. "Hallea says you know what you're doing. You better. If I hired every cropper that offered to work here, it would be chaos. Everyone thinks it's easy."

"I work in a pub in Downd—in my old home."

"Good. I'll start you off at half Hallea's wage, but if you're good, I'll match it." He left them, then from the dining room called, "Tables, ladies."

"He's not really so gruff," said Hallea.

"Not to sound greedy, but can I live on half of what you make?"

"Barely, maybe. The trick is to do a little more than expected."

"Tips, I'm used to that. If they like my service, or my smile."

"Customers won't give you anything normally, but your fate may increase your chip-value. I don't know if a smile helps, but it won't hurt."

THE DAY PASSED QUICKLY. At the end of the evening, Stina collapsed on the creaking wooden steps that led to the rooms above. She watched two men gamble with yellowed dice. They declared a ridiculous wager between one man's taste and the other's touch. Was it any more ridiculous than wagering your savings to visit your mum on red? Her stomach growled. All she'd eaten were a few untouched nibbles she'd snuck from customers' plates while returning them to the kitchen. Hopefully Padrok hadn't seen. He didn't spend much time in the kitchen. He seemed to prefer talking with the customers.

"How's your chip-value looking?" asked Hallea, joining her on the stairs.

"I don't know. I think I've done solid work."

"Well, let's see it and find out."

"It—oh, a chip is an actual thing?"

Hallea shook her head. "I thought you knew. You need at least one wooden chip to display your chip-value."

"Where do I find one of those?"

"Well, you could trade today's work for one from Padrok. It won't be worth as much as the work you've done, but tomorrow it'll catch full value."

Stina rose to find Padrok.

"One other thing," Hallea said. "Padrok said he doesn't hire many croppers, but that's not true. Many people come here knowing how to tuck tables. There could be competition tomorrow, but the good news is they don't last long. I've seen ten like you in the last two months."

"Where did they go?"

"They left the End of the World."

"Into the unknown?"

"Into their fates, we say."

Bloody hell.

Padrok gave her a wooden coin that had a hint of pink color. He told her she could spend the night in a room with another cropper. Of course he would. That would gain him a little extra chip-value. She saw how this worked.

∾

HER ROOMMATE WAS a slight girl of just nineteen—a year younger than Stina. She had short blonde hair that might have once been dyed blue or green. Her skin was light, and her eyes were brown.

There's no 'e' at the end of Angi. The 'e' is old-style.

How did she know that? Angi hadn't told her, but the knowledge was in her mind the moment they met.

"I came here three years ago from an island city called Trufo," Angi said.

"Where's Trufo?"

"Built in the middle of the Panatlantis Ocean. All I have of it are some clothes, three worthless gadgets like yours, and memories. My batteries lasted three months, but I could never get on the cloud."

"Mine died today."

The room was narrow and low, with a single round window. A converted attic. They each lay on narrow cots covered with stale-smelling furs. It reminded Stina of the beast in the forest. The more she thought about it, the more certain she was that it had, in fact, been a mammoth. But that had to be a hallucination, didn't it? "What do you do for chips?" she asked, staring at the rafters.

"At first, anything. Even tucking tables and serving drinks like you. I got bored with that. There's a couple—the Ventals, Harmony and Wilcott. They gave me work in the Salon and the Ballroom. I meet and greet, serve food and drinks, clean up, all that."

"That pays enough?"

"Enough. But I gain a little extra in the Salon simply by talking with croppers. The Ventals call it Tea and Conversation. We're all confused and lonely. Mostly we end up crying on each other's shoulders."

I fell in love a few times too. Sometimes it was just shared homesickness, but at least once—well, you'll find love if you stay.

Angi hadn't spoken that, but Stina knew it—like a memory, but it was Angi's and not her own. How was that possible? How many croppers were there, and did they all just wander into the city or was there something more sinister? Was something drawing people to the End of the World? Was it even real? Had she tested her walk far enough to be certain there was no way back to Downderry? She watched Angi fidget with one of her gadgets, a palm-sized disk of iridescent blue.

"You should visit the Salon," Angi said. "The people there will help you understand this place and how to get by if you choose to stay. And there are some cute tools at the End of the World."

"Tools?"

"Men."

Stina laughed. "Where I'm from, we call the ridiculous men tools."

Angi laughed too. "You mean some aren't? Look, the Salon's a decent place to share your loneliness. And I bet the Ventals would hire you for their parties and balls."

Stina stared at the oil lamp hanging by the door. Nothing about this place reminded her of home except the proximity to the ocean. "How did you end up here, if you lived on an island?"

Angi shrugged. "I was curious. I'd spent my entire life on Trufo. Despite all the technology connecting us to the rest of the world—the InstaComs, FarViewers, and InstaTrans—we were still on an island. There was a physical limit to what we could see and where we could walk. I hated it.

"There was a narrow beach I walked every day. Nothing but sea and sky in front of me and the towering glass and steel buildings behind. One day, the beach just kept going. I was listening to my Pods, not paying attention. Before I knew it, the city had receded to just an outline of glimmering steel. I was curious, so I kept walking, thinking maybe they had extended the beach. Maybe they would build another city. Then I walked by the sign for the End of the World."

She grew quiet, then got up and checked a pack at the foot of her cot. It was full. She removed two other electronic devices, which both looked much like Stina's phone. Angi placed all three devices on the table beside the washbasin. "Won't be needing those," she said.

"You don't think you'll ever find your way back to Trufo?"

I know I won't. "I'm leaving tomorrow and walking into whatever lies beyond that wooden sign." Angi took out a small purse and began counting coins. "I spent most of my chips buying coins and jewelry from croppers. I need cash and gold when I walk out of here." She put the purse away. "So how did you end up here?"

Stina was disappointed Angi was leaving so soon, and she suddenly missed the beat-up VW. "I drove here in my car."

Angi's eyes grew wide. "You drove a car? What I'd give to do that. We learned about those old days—the manual driving cars, trucks, busses. It sounded like a chill, all that chaos on the roads."

"I suppose. The car disappeared."

"Bet you walked back to see if you could get to some place familiar. We've all done it."

"I walked for over an hour in the middle of the night."

Angi whistled. "You're lucky the city was still here when you got back."

"Lucky? Bloody hell."

"That far out, you could have walked into another realm."

"It was heavily forested and I couldn't find any sign of a town. The road just disappeared, then it was just a path. There was this creature. I think it was a mammoth, so I bolted."

"You could have been anywhere, and any spot in time. There is a legend of a mammoth around here, or the ghost of one that lurks in the forests. But mammoth or hippo, wolves or people. You could have walked into Sherwood Forest and caught Robin Hood's arrow in your chest."

They were quiet again. She would miss Angi. She missed her friends: Sara, Lola, and Macky. Missed her father. If all this were true and real, she would never visit her mum in Canada. She'd see none of them again. She missed the comforting glow of her phone notifying her of something one of them did. Hundreds of pictures were in there, or in the cloud, but with her battery dead they no longer existed. Memories gone before she'd had the chance to recall them. "Do you miss Trufo? I mean your parents and friends?"

Angi held a small wicker nest that shimmered in the dim lantern light. *I miss blue sky and sunburned sand.* A glass turtle with a green cloud inside sat in the nest. "Yeah. I had a pet gecko, and I miss him too. But I'm stuck here. I had been ready to leave Trufo, but then I ended up here. The End of the World is just another damn island. I want to live in a world connected with other lands and other people. I don't care where or when it is."

Stina wiped a tear from her own cheek.

"It's hard," Angi said. "Your parents?"

"My father's a diplomat. He's based in London but travels all over the world—that's how he met my mum. Now I'm out of university and we were to meet for the holidays. My mum lives in Canada. I'm trying—I was trying—to save enough to visit her. Fucking Hans. There's a proper tool."

"Canada. London. I remember those names from our history wares. They were important places before the oceans changed." Angi lowered the lamplight and crawled onto her cot. "Too bad you didn't arrive sooner. We could have really done some damage in this city. I'm leaving at first light, as they say. You can come with me."

Could she just walk into a new, unknown world? She was just starting to understand where she was and how she might survive. Wherever she and Angi ended up, they would have to start over. She thought of the deep forest and lonely, angry mammoths, the hungry wolves and fierce bears, and Robin Hood's arrow—so many ways to die.

SHE DIDN'T SLEEP, and given the fitful shifting she heard from Angi's cot, it seemed she wasn't alone. Angi rose before the first light and turned up the lamp.

"You up?" Angi asked.

"I'm up."

Angi placed the glass turtle and wicker nest into her pack, but before she did, she held it up as an exhibit. "Get one of these, if you stay. They call it Memory Glass. This guy, Nico, and a basket weaver named Shaday place your best memories into it—or at least that's what they say. Seems to work. I can feel the sun and smell my mother's perfume—even speak with her when I need to. My gecko jabs his tongue against my fingers." She placed the turtle into the pack and lifted it onto her back. "Are you staying?"

Stina put on her tennis shoes and threw on her smock. She took her purse from the floor beside her cot. "I'll walk with you for a while, at least. I don't know if I'm ready."

"I know. Despite its weirdness, the End of the World has a kind of safety to it. It took me a long time to decide I had to leave."

NO ONE WAS in the streets yet, and the sun was not visible over the sea. They walked out of the city and beyond the sign. No forest—only a wide expanse of sand and dunes. The pale green ocean receded into the distance. As the sun lifted into view, the sand took on a red-orange glow.

Angi stopped. "Have you decided? Soon your decision will be made. Look." She pointed to a distant silhouette over the dunes. Shimmering like a mirage were red towers and golden domes.

The distant city had no pull for Stina. Rather, the pull she felt was back to the End of the World. Was that an instinct she could trust? With Angi, she wouldn't be alone. But even together they would be in a much larger city every bit as strange, in its own way, as the End of the World. It might be possibly more dangerous for two young women. Yet, she also didn't want to leave Angi to face that alone.

After several breaths she said, "I can't. I'm not ready."

Angi smiled, but it was not a smile of happiness. *We could do some real damage together.* They stared at one another. Stina pulled her grandmum's ring from her hand and held it out to Angi. "Take this. Remember me and remember that this has been real, or at least prove to me this is real by taking it."

"But you should—"

"Take it. I want a part of me to travel with you into whatever future you find."

Angi took the ring and placed it on her finger, then she took the pack from her back and removed the turtle. "You take this. Have Nico add another memory to it. I doubt it will work where I'm headed."

Stina took the wicker and glass turtle, then she embraced Angi. They squeezed and wept together. "Goodbye," Angi said, and she waved as she turned and walked across the red sands, fading into a blur of windblown sand and haze. Soon, she melted into the mirage.

∾

ANOTHER MIDDAY CROWD filled the Scale and Tentacle. Despite other taverns and the Ventals' salon, the Scale was always full. For the first time, Stina looked closely at the faces of the people she now shared her life with. Hallea and Padrok were fixtures, and she had traveled across the city several times to Asami's home and bakery to pick up and place orders. She thought Asami could become a friend. They shared an age and this fate, but Asami was a dowdy—shy. That would take some time. Asami had a sister, Kana, but they'd not met yet.

Then there were the usual patrons and new croppers. Not much to say to the croppers other than to seek the Mayor and the Ventals. She was still too much a cropper herself to offer any wisdom, and she probably always would be. They were easy to spot, though. They looked bewildered, shocked, and sad all at once.

She noticed a man sitting in the back with long, graying hair and a short beard streaked with gray on his brown face. There were crow's feet at the edges of his eyes; her grandmum said that was a sign of a lucky person, someone who had smiled or laughed a lot. Hallea had pointed him out as Nico. Stina served him eggs and warm cider. A covered basket rested on the floor beside him. While he ate, he stared at a small wicker nest similar to the basket at his feet; this one had a clear glass mule poking out. The mule glowed lavender in the lamplight.

"How much to add another memory to Memory Glass?" she asked. She showed him the turtle in her left hand. In her right, she held out her single wooden chip. It was a scarlet red.

Nico smiled behind his gray whiskers. "Nothing. Nothing at all. That's the beauty of it."

KING SEBASTIÃO BATTLES TO THE END
OF THE WORLD

One will say this is the land of sleeping kings.
Another will declare this a place of loss.
A place of incongruity. A place well-ordered.
This is a hell; this is heaven.
- Notes of a Traveller

*D*ust swirled in choking clouds from beneath horses'
hooves and soldiers' feet. Lieutenant João Carmine
Alejo coughed and spat dust and phlegm. He hated the chaos.
Hated watching his men—the Urso de Batalha—die. Emir Al-
Malik was succeeding at that with alarming ease.

João steered his horse to the middle of what remained of
his men. Twenty, at best. He urged his horse forward, searching
for Commander Stukley. The commander was at the center of
a melee, encouraging the men. They needed it, surrounded by
Al-Malik's orderly yet seething infantry.

King Sebastião rode past him in a flurry and tried to negotiate his horse close to Commander Stukley. He was as dust-and blood-covered as the rest of them.

A musket blast exploded near João's right ear. There was a deafening silence, followed by a shrill ringing. The commander fell from his horse and the infantry held a collective breath just long enough for Al-Malik's soldiers to rush against them. This would be the perfect time for King Sebastião's ally, Abu Abdullah Mohammed, to swoop in, but he and his army were engaged closer to Alcàsser and would not be coming.

João watched the Portuguese cavalry fall into disarray, stunned by the loss of the commander and in desperate hand-to-hand brawls with the enemy. They'd be overrun in moments.

King Sebastião raised his sword and shouted, "To me! To your king!"

João yanked his horse to the king's side and his men fell into order. He raced around them as they reformed their lines at the edge of the fray. The king emboldened them with the words of God.

Robbed of their easy victory, Al-Malik's infantry pulled back and regrouped. The Portuguese were outnumbered, but in this campaign when had they not been? Every battle fought in Morocco's interior against Emir Al-Malik's Jihad had been disadvantaged, and yet somehow, after weeks of blood and dust, they were on the verge of rendering the Jihad a failure. They needed just one more victory.

King Sebastião made the sign of the cross and kissed his fingers, which he then touched to the book of Aquinas at his belt. Sword held high, he shouted, "For God and Christ!" and he rushed Al-Malik's line. João followed, the remaining few hundred infantry and cavalry of the Portuguese line following with him.

~

SILENCE COVERED João like a fog and blanketed his ears. He strained for an opening, a sound—the clank of a sword, a jangle of harness buckle. More ringing would inevitably follow.

But there was no ringing. Birds called and a breeze rustled through the pine boughs. Pine? He lay on his back in the middle of a sandy gravel road. A serene forest looked down on him from above. He felt at his chest, head, stomach, legs—all there. Only a minor cut on his left leg and a pain in his left ankle. He stood. Where was the plain, the battle? The trees were wrong for this part of Morocco.

Someone grunted.

He found his bearskin-decorated scabbard on the ground, covered in dust. He grabbed it and drew his sword. The grunting sounded again. Close. "Who's there?" he asked.

"King Sebastião. Dear God, my Aquinas! I have lost my book—Isabella's letter! Where did they—where is Commander Stukley?"

"He fell."

"Ah, I remember now. God protect his soul."

The king struggled to stand near a large pine. João darted over to assist, and once the king was upright, he bowed. "Your Highness."

King Sebastião gripped his sword, ready to cut down Al-Malik's men. But there were none, and he sheathed it. "You are Lieutenant . . ."

"Lieutenant João Carmine Alejo, Sire."

"Ah, the Urso de Batalha, I remember. Come, let us find our way back to the field. There's time yet, the sun is only three hours over Alcàsser. I think that way." The king pointed to what João agreed was east.

~

THEY WALKED for close to an hour but found nothing familiar. The scent of the ocean drifted to them on the breeze. How could that be this far inland? They were both certain of the direction. The sun was clear through the trees and it was just midmorning. It was cooler than it had been earlier. The trees thinned as they walked, and the road narrowed. They didn't pass a single farmhouse or sheepfold. Not a carob or olive tree anywhere.

João spotted the city first. As they neared, he saw a sign. "Some jest," he said. "The End of the World, written in Portuguese."

"Indeed," the king said.

STINA HAD LEARNED to recognize croppers instantly. A few new ones every day, and most found their way to the Scale and Tentacle. They all had that confused and shocked expression, like they had just learned their best friend was a murderer.

Two men in ancient, dust-caked military uniforms walked in and planted themselves at a table near the door. They had that cropper look. They were young. One was pale and had short reddish-brown hair and a pursed, upturned mouth, as if he were sucking on something. The other was dark and handsome, with longer black hair, and he stood nearly a foot taller than the other. Besides dust, there were ruddy stains on their uniforms. Blood? The tall one sat facing the door and looked around the room as if he were looking for an escape. The other banged his gloved fist on the table and spoke sharply to her. "Young Moor. You there, garçonete, we are in a hurry."

Sure you are—in a hurry to go bloody nowhere, if you only knew. She held an armload of plates and mugs but approached the man. "What can I fetch you?"

"A light repast—ale, cheese, and bread. We must return quickly." He placed two silver coins on the table.

"Your coins are no good here," she said. "Nor your weapons." She pointed to the comely man's sword. Now that she could see his face, she recognized that besides that cropper look he was alert for danger. His black eyes darted around the room and at the door. His broad right hand worked the hilt of his sword.

She dropped her armload in the kitchen and returned with their food and drink. As she served them, she explained the meal was free, but the dude in a hurry interrupted. "I thank you for showing your king his due courtesy, but I insist. I'll not have the people of Morocco sniping that their new sovereign is cheap." He placed the coins directly into her hand.

"Morocco? No, I meant all croppers get—"

"Lieutenant Alejo, ask those men there what town we've drifted into and what road there is to lead us back. I fear the battle has not gone well."

The lieutenant stepped to a table with three men and did as commanded. Typical, they wouldn't ask a woman even though she knew there was no way back. She watched from behind the bar as the lieutenant returned to the shorter man and related what he learned. Then he took a mouthful of cheese and bread as if he hadn't eaten in days.

"Preposterous," said the shorter man. A king? "Come Lieutenant, we must get back."

Stina shook her head and returned to clear their table. The lieutenant stopped in the doorway and turned to her, bowing his head. "Good day, garçonete." Then he strode out behind his king. *They'll be back*, she thought. *We always come back, at first.*

THE ROAD WAS LESS FORESTED than João remembered. He pointed to a low row of hills they had not descended on the way into the city. "Sire, look."

Thick forest covered the hills with hardwoods, oak and

maple. No pines. The road twisted up the rise. Seeing no alternative, they followed it. On the summit was an expanse for many leagues to the south, east, and west. There was nothing below the treeline but dunes in all directions.

"What, in the name of all that is holy . . . ?" The king felt for his Aquinas, and not finding it, he crossed himself. "I do not know what to say, Lieutenant. My bearings fail me."

"Sire, there is no place in Morocco where hardwood hills such as these meet vast stretches of sand such as those. My bearings are no better."

They stared at the vista for a few moments, but nothing moved except the clouds and whirlwinds of sand. The sun was well past midafternoon.

"We have no rations," the king said. "And I do not wish to meet the devil in this wilderness. The day is passing quickly. There is no choice but to return to that city for the night."

BY THE TIME they reached the burgh, it was dark. The End of the World might not be a jest. João crossed himself. Was this a purgatory between heaven and hell? "Pardon, my lord, but could we be dead—killed in the battle—and this is part of the afterlife?"

"That is not within reason. Though I wonder what dear Pedro Nunes, my cosmography instructor, would think of this."

"But there are legends. Legends of sleeping kings like the British Arthur, and Charlemagne, Emperor Barbarossa in his cave in the Alps, and King Olaf. Perhaps—"

"I am no legend, Lieutenant. I am a devout defender of Christ, and God willing, warden of the monarchy." The king rubbed his hand against his chest where his Aquinas should have been. "And Isabella willing, progenitor of the next king of Portugal."

. . .

STINA AND HALLEA struggled to keep up. There were few croppers but plenty of regulars. Something in the air made everyone seek out a meal. Stina wondered if the other taverns were as busy. "Tonight I totally wish one of the new croppers had experience serving," she said.

"Your friends are back." Hallea pointed to two men with Padrok by the door. The king and his lieutenant.

"You must wait for a table," Padrok told them. "And I've just a single cot."

The lieutenant rubbed his face with his hand and shook his head. The king pointed a finger up at Padrok. "I thought this establishment a fair and welcoming place with the offer of a free meal to your king, but this? What is this?"

"Look, I've no problem providing another meal. I just don't have a table, nor a room to give you."

"We are used to campaigning in the open. I shall pay you for a meal. Wrap it in a sack and we will be on our way."

Padrok motioned to Stina and told her to fetch and sack a meal for them. She did as was bid and returned to hear Padrok ask, "King, is it?"

"Yes. Sebastião, King of Portugal and liberator of Morocco. This is Lieutenant João Carmine Alejo of the Urso de Batalha, one of my best cavalry units."

"The End of the World has no use for kings or soldiers. If you stay, you must visit the Mayor, then find an occupation. Your lieutenant might fit in with the Mayor's Defense."

"Occupation? I am your overlord until I can push the false Emir Al-Malik back into the desert and return Abu Abdullah Mohammed to his rightful rule."

Padrok sighed. "You're unknown here. You've fallen a-cropper. You're not where you think you are, and the sooner you accept that the better it will be for you. If you go around acting like you're king of this place, you'll end up in a worse fate."

"A cropper?" João asked.

"Visit the Mayor in the morning. She meets all new croppers. She'll explain."

"The Mayor—she? Finally, something almost sensible," said the king.

Stina handed the satchel of food to João. He met her eyes for a heartbeat, then looked away.

"Come, Lieutenant. We don't have time for Moor mistresses."

"Yes, Sire."

"Might just be the oddest croppers today," Padrok said.

She didn't agree. The king wasn't odd; he was dangerous if he stayed. If João was alert for danger, he'd missed it because he was too close to it and didn't understand his circumstances.

João and the king ate in silence on the docks. The only sound came from the slap of waves against the hulls of ships and the creaking of their wood. None of the banners were familiar. One ship had a design João knew to be from the orient. There were also two vast steel vessels without masts. How could steel float? Their gray bows had white numbers painted on them and what looked like small mounted cannons on their decks. One had white a prayer dome. What devil had Emir Al-Malik sold his soul to?

The king led them through a series of prayers, and they settled to sleep. But João could not find sleep in the darkness or the repetition of creaks and splashes. What had happened in the battle? Had any of his men survived? Did Al-Malik win all? He'd always known there was a chance, a near likelihood, that he would never return to his home to his parents, brothers, and sister. Now he was certain. If he was dead, which seemed most likely, that was all there was to it. If he was not dead, he and the king were lost beyond finding.

This liminal place was not of the world. Yet somehow it was immeasurably safer than the world. No war scarred this town. Was it under God's protection, or the devil's? All the more reason to believe it purgatory. He finally slept while unfamiliar stars wheeled through the slow morass of time above him.

ALMARISS FINISHED REVIEWING the manifest of the barque. There was whale oil and sugar in good measure. They needed more ships like that—and captains willing to trade once they understood their circumstances. The steel ships were useless, full of sailors who couldn't wield a sword but would wave a gun all too readily. At least both those ships were leaving today.

She packed her pipe with piñon and sage. At the first puff, she felt the comforting hum beneath her feet. What was it about the city's nature that she felt connected to? Years ago, she had asked the Mayor questions about the city, but she'd never asked that question. She had to answer it herself. So many years later and she still didn't know.

The two men she'd watched make a picnic and sleep near her office the previous night approached. "Croppers," she announced to them. "You've had one night's rest on my docks, but if you expect another you better lose those swords and get your hides over to that line and report for work. You have your chips?"

"Madam," said the taller of the two, with his hands held out as if he were presenting the shorter, paler man beside him as a glorious prize. "You are addressing King Sebastião of Portugal."

"Am I?" She looked at the king. He was dressed as a soldier. His armor might once have been fine, but it was now battered and stained with blood, and his face was streaked with sweat and dust. "Well, nice to meet you, King Sebastião. Since you don't have any chip-value, I suggest you visit the Mayor and then the changers or the smelters."

"We are already on our way to see the Mayor," the king said.

"Changers?" João asked.

"The Mayor will explain. That stone building over there is the Mayor's Palace." She pointed to a block of a building with columns she knew looked no more like a palace to them than a farm. The banner flying above—a field of red with a circle made of interconnected gold strands in endless knots—stretched in a breeze no one felt.

The king marched in that direction and motioned for his man to follow.

"Good day, madam," the man said.

"Maybe." A king, or anyone who came from a place of great privilege, usually found the city to be a tough place to exist. They never stayed long, and it was probably for the best. The city didn't need a king.

KING SEBASTIÃO LED João directly back to the docks after storming out of the Mayor's Palace. "No role for a monarch? What a ridiculous thing to say. What a ridiculous and heathen mayor. The devil was in there, Lieutenant Alejo. I could feel his breath at the nape of my neck. We must find a ship to take us down the coast and away from this place."

"Sire." He meant the word as agreement, but doubt crept into his mind. Would a ship fare any better in this city? The steel ships—the devil's war machines in service to Al-Malik—were now moving swiftly away without sails. Evil magic.

The king approached a small wooden vessel with Knossos painted on its bow. A crew was unloading bales of tea and sacks of spices. The captain, dressed in a green skull cap, white and gold embroidered tunic, and knee-length hose, oversaw the work of his crew and helped roll barrels down the gangway.

King Sebastião strode to the captain. "I, King Sebastião of Portugal, commission this ship to Larache."

"I don't know where that is," the captain said. "Or who the king of Portugal is. You're not commissioning my ship anywhere."

"How does the captain of a Mediterranean ship not know the coast of Morocco?"

"I don't know what your Mediterranean is. I know there is room aboard, if you've a few gold coins. That's all it will take to leave this goddess-forsaken place. A motley collection of gold and silver currencies is all I profited from this journey, and I'll travel empty for it."

"I can guide you along the Moroccan coast."

"No doubt you could, but we aren't on that coast. We're leaving on a one-way trip to who-knows-where, or when, and it's the only trip any ship in this harbor will take."

"Nonsense and witchery." The king marched away from the captain and the port. João followed, back toward the city's main street. "It's no use, Lieutenant Alejo. They all play the devil's game."

João wasn't sure what they should do. They were captive, contained, restrained from Morocco, perhaps from life itself. Had they really tried, though? Had they traveled far enough to know where they weren't? "Sire, perhaps we could try the road again. It might eventually lead us somewhere familiar, if we follow it long enough."

"Yes. Yes, that is as good a plan as any."

As they passed the Scale and Tentacle, the young garçonete swept the stones at the doorway. He waved, and she waved in return. A slight smile graced her face, but she shook her head as if knowing something they didn't, or thinking them fools, or both.

"João," said the king. "We've duty."

THE FARTHER THEY WALKED, the less sure he was of his plan. The road bent away from the sea and to the north. The line of hills was no longer visible, and no trees crowded the road. A short way outside the village, the road became paved with stone.

"Ah," said the king. "We've come to civilization now."

Soon there were people and ox-drawn carts along the road. The people wore long wraps and turbans.

"At least we've returned to Moorish territory," said the king.

João stopped a man carrying a basket upon his shoulder. "Which way to Alcàsser?"

The man shrugged and kept walking.

"The King of Portugal, your liberator, demands to know."

The man said something in response, but it was not in Arabic, Berber, or Portuguese. "Morocco?" João tried. The man shook his head. João asked three other people and tried all three languages but received the same response.

The sun burned overhead, searing the paved stones and sand.

Finally, the king dropped to his knees and began praying. João joined him. "Heavenly Father, in the name of Christ I, your humble servant on Earth, am lost. Please guide me. Deliver a sign. Inform my heart what to do."

Nothing but silence, heat, and wind. The people walked out of sight, leaving the road empty. João thought again, this could only be a purgatory. "Perhaps we really have died and this is the realm of sleeping kings."

"Forgive me, Isabella," said the king, squeezing his eyes shut and pressing his hands together. "Dear God, are we to sleep forever at the End of the World, or to roam until we find our way?"

Nothing.

João felt an urgency growing within. The garçonete's knowing head shake had foretold this moment. He was running out of time. What was the reason for it? There were still several hours until dark. Were his war-trained senses warning him of an ambush? He looked around at nothing but sand and dunes. Still, something tugged at him like an insistent, begging street urchin. A certainty he was on the wrong side of the time remaining to him.

The breeze grew into a wind, then to a gale. It flung stinging sand across the pavers and into their eyes and blew away from the town, toward the greater emptiness where the people had traveled.

"God has answered," the king said, rising. He followed the road into the sandy wastes.

João trudged behind, but each step felt wrong. After climbing several gentle rises, a smooth black pavement replaced the pavers. Trees crowded the road, and poles stood regularly beside it with black ropes strung between them. In the distance rose a silhouette of an enormous city. At its center, the spire of a great cathedral pierced the sky.

Something like a giant insect flew overhead, making a deafening, shuddering noise. It glinted blue-black, like heated and cooled metal, and a dull roar reached them from ahead. Many covered metal carts—oxless, horseless—moved swiftly on other roads.

"This is the future, Lieutenant Alejo," the king said, sweeping his arm across the scene. "It lies there with machines and science, yet it still has one foot in the past. That glorious house of God remains central and tethered to our time—to eternity. God has delivered us a path. From this future I shall return to Isabella. From this future we might even return to the days of Christ and his disciples walking the earth."

"Forgive me, my lord," João said. "But is that a miracle, or magic?"

"It is a pathway to Christ, through that glorious house of the Lord. It is a miracle. Let us go." The king adjusted his sword and strode forward.

João remained. He looked back along the road toward the End of the World. His time was running out, but what time? His present? The thought of machines, like the one flying overhead, being used for war chilled him—and it was a machine of war, there was no mistaking it for anything else. A soldier of any era could see that. It was hard enough watching men die at the hands of other men; how much worse to watch mindless machines slaughter them? Despite the cathedral, this was a soulless, godless place.

The Mayor had mentioned her Defense—but there was peace at the End of the World, a distinct lack of war. It was also closer to his world than this future. His time, what remained of his present, existed there.

"Come along, Lieutenant Alejo," King Sebastião called.

"I am less certain, Sire. In that world, I believe science has replaced their belief in kings and has a different, lesser view of God. If you enter that city, you may find a way home, but you may not. Your own time might run out, catching you in that future forever."

The king stopped and stared at him. "The House of God calls to me. There is no such place at the End of the World."

True, there was no great cathedral. But there was peace and perhaps love. Weren't those God? His time was running out faster the closer he stepped toward the unknown city. "Perhaps that grand city of sleeping kings and the house of God is meant for you. My fate is not yours. I will remain at the End of the World."

The king frowned. Then a smile grew upon his dust-streaked face. "Ah, the young garçonete. As you wish, my loyal Lieutenant Alejo. I go."

He didn't watch the king shrink into the distance, nor as the steel city swallowed the diminutive man. He ran toward the End of the World. Would it still be there? He wanted it to be— needed it to be. It was a place where one could live and not just survive.

IT WAS THERE, and when he arrived João no longer felt out of time. As he passed the sign and entered the city, he felt at home for the first time in years. Not with his family, but safe from the call of war, and that was home enough.

CROYDON RIDES TO THE END OF THE WORLD

This place of city, forest, harbor, and road contains those
who never asked to arrive but find reason to stay.
It allows others to pass through.
Neither may return.

This place is destined not to revisit
any instant of time and place;
there are too many—infinitely too many.
- Notes of a Traveller

*A*lmariss tallied the bales of cotton offloaded from the
Precious. All there. She scribbled her signature at the
bottom of the list while the captain waited. She was diminutive,
with short silver hair and sea-rough hands and weather wrinkles
on her forehead. "There's your coin," Almariss said, pointing to
a small covered basket. She exchanged chips with the changers
for croppers' worthless coins, so it was an odd collection of
gold, silver, bronze, brass, and copper. But ship captains often

found it enticing enough to leave at least some of their cargo behind.

"Going to be damned hard explaining this if we ever get back to Savanah," the captain said.

"You won't."

The captain fixed her gaze up at Almariss. "You know where we'll end up, don't you?"

"I don't. I just know you won't end up in Savanah in 1922." She'd felt that before, and what the city connected to now didn't feel the same. The silent vibration beneath her feet hummed a different rhythm.

The captain shook her head and lifted the basket with both hands.

Almariss was about to light her pipe when she heard a boyish voice, one too young for the docks. Captain Slagrett, who had given her a rough deal earlier, yelled at his crew from the same direction.

"Get moving, you seal lizards. There's nothing for us in this hell port." Slagrett pointed to a boy. "You! You looking for work?"

The boy shook his head.

"How old?"

"Twelve," the boy said.

"Well," Slagrett said. "I've got decks that need stain, and there's nothing like a little sea venture for a young boy."

The boy was obviously a cropper. She hurried to them. Slagrett approached the boy, and before the boy could slip away he had one arm draped over his shoulder and his face close. "There's nothing like the sea to make a boy into a man. I can see you've been whitewashing—there's splatter in your hair. You can stain decks. The sea calls us. Where to, who knows, and it don't matter. All that matters is the salt spray on your lips and the sea under your feet."

Almariss placed a hand on the boy's head and ruffled his

brown hair. "He works for me, Slagrett." She was several inches taller than the captain. He removed his arm from the boy's shoulders, and Almariss put her own over them and pulled the boy away.

"Does he?" Slagrett said. "You hire him out to whitewash?"

"He earns his keep honestly."

"Honest? Nothing honest about this place. Can't pick up a decent manifest, can't even sell half of what I have—hell, I can't even visit the Mayor without getting magicked."

"Which is why it's best you put out and go where your fate leads you."

"Gladly, but I can't do that with half a crew."

"Then I suggest recruiting grown sailors. There are plenty of newly arrived adult croppers."

Slagrett spat, then he counted the crew who were just finishing their walk up the gangway.

She turned the boy by his shoulders to face her. Tears threatened to burst from behind his brown eyes, and his pale chin shivered. "My name's Almariss. Don't worry, I won't let anything bad happen to you. Did you say you were twelve?"

"Yes, and I'm not scared. I'll be thirteen next week." His voice cracked.

"Hmm. And your name?"

"Croydon. Croydon White."

"Young croppers are the most difficult," she said, but not to him. She looked toward the city. "Everyone wants one, but few know how to take care of them." She bent level with his face. "You hungry?"

"Well—"

"I know you are. You're a twelve-year-old boy."

∾

SHE TOOK him to her small wooden office, which also served as her home. The calm black water of the harbor surrounded it on three sides and a long quay extended along the north. Inside, her blackened stew pot simmered over the small mortared stone pit with low burning coals. A hole in the roof above the pit let smoke out, and there was a lever to close it, which she did now. She ladled a bowl from the pot.

The boy's eyes fixed on her Affinity Globe, spinning between two candles resting on her small table. He was curious, no doubt, but there was too much to explain before addressing the globe.

She handed him the bowl. "Fish stew."

She sat in one of two three-legged chairs. He sat in the other, sniffed the stew, and began eating.

"Where am I?" he asked between spoonfuls. "Is this Shamptown on Potters Road? I can walk back if it is."

"No. This is the End of the World."

"Don't make fun."

"Make fun? No, I'm not doing that."

"I've never heard of the End of the World, except sailors used to believe they might fall off it."

"They don't believe that now?"

"Of course not. Everybody knows the world's round."

"Round will get you back, unless you fall into a hole."

"A hole?"

She pulled her pipe from her vest pocket and concentrated on lighting it with a stick lit from the coals. "I have to tell you something important, Croydon."

"Okay." He drew the word out slowly, clearly suspicious of what she had to say—as he should be.

"You're a long way from home. I don't know how or why. I just know you won't find your way back. Your parents won't be able to find you here."

He stopped eating. "I only crossed the bridge. I was going

fishing. My pole and bike are right there. My house is just on the other side of the bridge—"

"Was there anything strange about the bridge?"

"Well I mean, it shouldn't have been there. The covered bridge washed out years ago. This one wasn't covered."

"You crossed a bridge that shouldn't be there? Well, that's how you ended up at the End of the World. Like falling into a hole."

"Does the name mean the actual end of the world, like we're all dead?"

"No, we're not dead. You just aren't in the same place in the world as when you woke up."

"There's no way back?"

She puffed at the pipe. "There are many who try. I suppose, over the centuries, there may have been a few lucky enough to find their time and place. But most folks—we call you croppers—most find a new home somewhere else. Some stay here."

He stopped eating, and his eyes had a glassy gaze. Was he about to cry?

"You want to lie down? You're pale as a fish."

He thrust the bowl at her, ran outside, then threw up into the water. She brought a blanket and wrapped him in it and took him back inside. His shuddering eased. He hadn't cried. She wasn't sure what she would do if he had; she had no experience with children. She gave him her bed and told him she would be back later.

She walked along the long quay, which was empty of people. The Finger Light pulsed its red glow over the sea. Almariss inhaled deeply from her pipe. The thrum beneath her feet was there as expected, comforting. All was right at the End of the World. It was only herself that was out of place. Responsibility for an adolescent boy was disturbing. She could not do it for long.

. . .

IT WAS STILL dark outside when he woke. Almariss kneeled in front of a lit candle repeating, "Yameh so-alev." When she saw he was awake, she stopped. "Feeling better?"

"A little." The small rainbow-colored globe continued to spin.

"There's fresh bread in the chair. Thought it might go better than the stew and settle your stomach." She stood and pinched out the candle.

His stomach was empty and the smell of bread reminded him of his grandmother's homemade holiday bread. He wanted to go home, to his own room and bed. But he didn't know how to get away. Almariss was intent that he couldn't leave. He picked up the small loaf and started eating. "Were you praying?" he asked.

"It's called a mantra. It helps me relax." She leaned against the door. "Sit, there's more I have to tell you."

He sat and kept a steady stream of bread pulled from loaf to mouth.

"First, I hope you understand. Like it or not, you're here with no real chance of ever going home."

He kept eating the bread. He wasn't sure if he believed her or not. It might just be something she said to keep kids from running away.

"Second, people don't use money here. What you do to work and help or please others will show in wooden chips. We call it chip-value." She pulled a pinkish wooden coin from her vest pocket. "This is worth about fifteen chips. It was only worth two this morning. It was as gray as fog, but now it's pink. I suspect by tomorrow it will be a deeper pink and worth fifty or more."

"How does it do that?"

"I'm looking after you. I fed and sheltered you and saved you from getting pressed by Slagrett. There are many people here who love to find young croppers, think they can give you food and a place to sleep and they'll get rich. They see only chip-value, not the responsibility of raising a child. They're soon disappointed to find they don't earn as much chip-value as they hoped. Providing food and shelter is a bare minimum of care. Then they give up caring at all about the child. That makes them poorer and more resentful."

Almariss cleaned her pipe with a metal pick. "There are other people who can't earn chips at all. They—well, they just aren't very helpful or nice people. Those people won't try to take you in. They know it wouldn't do them any good, but they might try to convince you the rest of us are crazy and to work with them to trick other croppers." He had eaten all but the last heel of bread and held it out to Almariss. She shook her head. "Finish it."

"Why do they want to trick croppers?"

"Because they can't get ahead here. Most come from places where they achieved power and privilege by taking advantage of others. Here, taking advantage of someone makes you poorer. Some now use fake chips and trick croppers into handing over genuine ones or other valuables. The real chips lose their value quickly in their possession. The city works against them that way."

"The city? How does it work?"

"The only one who understands is the Mayor. She's the guardian of the secrets left by the Wandering Master. He found this place—called it an oasis and learned its magic. That knowledge has passed to each mayor. Without the Mayor, the chips wouldn't work and the End of the World would be just like everywhere else. It would lose its power."

Why was she telling him all of this? Shouldn't she at least be trying to get him home? If they couldn't find the way, then maybe he would believe her. "Can we look for the bridge?" he asked.

"Look for it?"

"If I could see it, I could cross and go home."

Almariss sighed. "You aren't understanding me. The city has moved. The bridge isn't there."

"The city moves?" He didn't believe that. This was some trap. Nice as Almariss seemed, he remembered that his father led ants to traps with a trail of sugar.

"That's what the city does. It moves through time and place. It bounces off most of the time, but now and again it catches for a few hours or a day."

It had been more than a few hours, but it had to be less than a day. All hope was not lost, despite what she said.

"So, I'm afraid you're stuck at the End of the World."

"If I'm stuck here, will you look after me until I'm older?"

Almariss smiled what seemed a sad smile. "Don't you think this house is a little small for two? And the docks are no place for kids. There are a lot worse than Slagrett out there."

"You'll put me in an orphanage." Pressure built behind his eyes, but he refused to cry. Thirteen in a week. He would not cry like a little kid.

"An orphanage?"

"A home for kids with no parents."

"Oh no, we have nothing like that. We try to sort out among ourselves who should look after the young croppers. There's a couple who help with that. The Ventals."

"So you'll give me to them?"

She placed a hand on his arm. "You're not mine to give. I think you're old enough to decide for yourself. I have some others in mind and you can meet them tomorrow. If you don't like them, we can try the Ventals or someone else. You can stay here until you find the right place."

She didn't want him, and she didn't want to help him find his way home. He didn't know what she wanted. But he wasn't staying just because someone said there wasn't another choice. He had to try.

LATER, Almariss reclined in her chair in front of the door. When he was certain she breathed deep, sleeping breaths, he cried. Tears came, then breath-stealing sobs. The last time he had cried like that he was six or seven and he'd been punished for hurting his little sister. But what had he done to deserve this punishment? Why couldn't he just walk back home? There had to be a way back. If only he hadn't left the bike on the far side of the bridge. He'd finished painting for his father, and he'd just wanted a little fishing for an hour before the other kids came to the swimming hole. Now he was stuck in a weird city with weird-looking people. What was with Almariss and her pine-smelly pipe and Lincoln hat? She seemed nice, but all of this talk about being stuck in another place and time, that wasn't for him. In the morning, when there was light, he'd return home.

THE MORNING WAS GRAY, windy, and cold. Almariss didn't have a coat that fit him. "It's fine," he said. "I don't need it. I'm used to cold weather back home."

Almariss led him into the city. It was like walking through a museum. All the houses were old and the people dressed like the old days, like long before the Revolution. There was no electricity and no cars or trucks, just people walking and carts drawn by oxen or mules. There was a market with many tiny shops, which Almariss called stalls. Weavers, potters, oil-sellers, candlemakers; every crafter he'd heard of sold their work.

He wondered about Almariss's chips. "Why do they sell things?" he asked. "Wouldn't they gain more chip-value if they just gave it away?"

"They would, and that was the Wandering Master's intent. But once he'd given people a tangible measure—the chips—

they began hoarding them and then trading to gain more. It seems to be people's nature to keep as much of something they value as they can, even if the value of the thing would increase if they gave some away."

She led him to the basketweaver's stall. Inside was a woman with reddish-brown hair about his mother's age and an older man with hair like a hippie and a gray-streaked beard. They were talking but stopped when they saw Almariss. The woman looked at him, and he thought she might cry or reach out to hug him—or both. Instead, she averted her eyes and stepped behind the hippie.

"Morning, Shaday. Nico," Almariss said.

"Good day," Nico said. "Who's that with you?"

Almariss said nothing for a breath, then, "A cropper. Twelve, almost thirteen."

"Well, luck's with you today."

"He's only with me until he finds the right place."

"No," Shaday said from behind Nico. "You can't ask me."

"I trust you most." Almariss looked back at him. "His name's Croydon. He fell a-cropper yesterday."

"No," Shaday said.

"What's going on?" Nico asked.

"She wants to give the boy to me."

"Oh—"

"Not give. He's old enough to decide."

Shaday stepped forward. She was a slight and short woman with bright green eyes. "You know what happens when they get older," she said. "They leave."

"Yes, that's the way," Almariss agreed.

"I don't think I can manage that."

"You're the one person I know in this town who can manage it. I know you'll care for him honestly."

"That's just the problem, I'll care too much, and when he's fifteen or sixteen, he'll walk away into whatever lies beyond the road." She pointed at Almariss. "Why not you? You took him in."

"The docks aren't safe. He can help you and Nico and learn the business."

Nico stepped from behind the stall and tugged on Croydon's shirt. "Let's have a chat and leave the ladies to themselves."

Though he wanted to leave the town, Croydon wasn't sure he was ready to leave Almariss. Despite her oddness, and something nagging him that she might be dangerous, he trusted her. She felt like a much older sister. But Nico was insistent.

They walked to the edge of the market, where a broad green lawn spread out in the middle of the city. They leaned against one of the ancient oaks that rimmed the grass.

"Do you understand what's happened to you?" Nico asked.

"Almariss said I've come to a place where my parents can't find me. And I can't find them."

"That's right."

"So I'm lost. I can't go back to them."

"I'm sure your parents will say so, but do you feel lost?"

"A little, but I—"

"You will grow homesick. We all did."

"You were lost too—a cropper?"

Nico smiled. "I didn't think so at first. I came here on purpose, to make a lot of money."

"But you couldn't leave?"

"Nor could I make any money. The End of the World is a strange city where you can become very wealthy and still have no money."

"So you're rich?"

"Not in coins, but in other ways, yes, very wealthy. Shaday has been—well, she's helped me make a minor magic."

A strange feeling fell over Croydon. It was the certainty of death—his death. He'd had the same feeling the time he climbed the face of the destroyed bridge abutment in winter. Two-thirds of the way up, he lost the strength to continue. He knew he would fall and die, alone and frozen on the river. Somehow, after what seemed like an hour, he found the strength to finish, but that moment of certain death came to him now. Panic gripped his chest and squeezed his breath into quick gasps. "How did I find this city at the edge of my neighborhood?" He looked at the museum-like town, the tall ships with furled sails, the people dressed from history. "It was never on that road before. I was just going to the swimming hole, then there was this strange bridge—how did that happen?"

"I don't know. I've been here just a few months and all I know is that the Mayor somehow helps guides the city as it snags on place to place and time to time. They say keeping the city moving maintains the magic."

"I don't believe in magic. That's for little kids." No way home, chips, now magic? The panic gained strength.

Nico gazed up at the tree as if trying to remember something. "Where I'm from, anyone who could do magic was a witch. If you were a good witch like a hedge witch and made things grow or got a horse to foal, then that was fine, but if you put curses on people or made their luck spoil, then you could be in real trouble—stoned, or whipped. But magic is different here. More powerful, in a strange way."

Croydon tried to exhale slowly. "You believe in it?"

"Like I said, Shaday and I make some. I couldn't live here without believing in magic. How do you think we talk and understand each other? Few of us share the same language. Magic is the easiest thing in the world to believe."

He pulled a small shiny basket made of wicker containing a little glass bear from his pocket. "It's called Memory Glass. This glass is clear, but when there's a memory in it, it gets cloudy with whatever color the memory is. The memory owner can then experience it again and again as if it were really happening."

Croydon jumped up and stepped back. He couldn't catch air—forgot how to breathe. "Almariss said not to let anyone try to give me anything. I might owe them something bad."

"Fine advice, but I'm not offering this to you, just showing you what we do. Shaday makes the baskets that hold the glass. Would you like to learn how to do this magic?"

Learn magic? Maybe back home, where magic was just a trick, he would have said yes. In this place? No. It was too real. He just wanted to breathe and to go home. There was no one between him and the road. It still had not been a full day since crossing the bridge. This was his chance.

He ran.

"Wait!" Nico called. But he was leaving and wasn't looking back. He ran past the market, into Main Street, and to the edge of the city.

ALMARISS SAW Nico running toward them. He was alone.

"He's gone." Nico gasped for breath. "That way—out of the city."

"What did you say to him?" Shaday asked, her hands on her hips.

"I asked him if he wanted to learn magic."

"He's trying to find his way home," Almariss said. She darted in the direction Nico pointed. Shaday followed.

They ran beyond the last houses of the city and onto a sandy beach. The sea was wide against the long beach, with green waves gently sliding against the shore. The Goresetch road ended at a dune. A deep blue filled the sky. No people, no road, no ships. No Croydon.

"He's gone," Shaday said, panting.

"How did he get so far so quickly?"

"The Goresetch is short today. The city must be moving."

"But if Croydon ran into this we'd still see him—at least, I would," Almariss said. "But I see nothing for leagues."

Shaday hooked her arm in Almariss's. "It's for the best. I couldn't bear to take him. You don't know what it's like being a mother and losing your children. It's the worst pain you can imagine."

"I'm imagining."

They scanned the horizon a final time, but there was only sand and waves so they followed the stub of the Goresetch back. Nico met them with the barmaid, Stina, and João, the new commander of the Mayor's Defense.

"João knew Croydon was missing," Nico said. "He knew he was running away from us."

"You knew he was missing?" Almariss asked João.

"Yes. I've discovered I know and can count all of the people at the End of the World at any moment. I know when anyone arrives or leaves. When he ran from you, I figured that could not be good."

"You what?" Stina said.

"I knew the boy had left the boundary—beyond the sign— and then Shaday and Almariss after that."

"What the fuck? So you—oh, never mind." Stina made a wiping motion with her hand before her face, as if clearing away what she had just learned. "Twelve is too young to be outside the town. There are machines, armies, a beast . . ."

"He's not here," Shaday said. She looked over the sand again and wept. "The world's already changed. The city's left him."

"Not good." Stina held her hand over her brow to block the sun and she searched the sands. "No telling what he'll find."

"Or what will find him," said Almariss. She didn't want to give up, but when the city moved, there was no going back.

THEY STROLLED BACK to the city in silence. João and Stina walked side by side, while Almariss remained entwined with Shaday's arm. Nico walked beside her. The chip-value system had its benefits, but there was a cost rendered in loss and guilt. The tax of caring. Shaday wasn't the only one burdened with it.

When they drew close to the city, near the sign, Stina darted away from João. "Do you hear it?" she asked. She ran behind the sign and disappeared into the surrounding bushes.

"Wait," João said. "He's—"

"Here, what's this?" Stina said from behind the bushes. Almariss joined her.

Croydon was curled into a tight ball, sobbing.

"I DON'T WANT to be at the end of the world. I want to go home." Croydon didn't want to be crying, but it was too late. He sniffed and wiped his tears on his sleeve like a frigging eight-year-old. Almariss offered her hand, but he didn't take it.

A girl stooped over him. Black-skinned, darker than Nico. "None of us wanted to come here, and for the first few days none of us wanted to stay." She spoke with an accent—British. Not a girl, a woman. Her eyes were big and brown, her hair black and in tight curls. Her smile eased the panic away a little. "But you know what, my dude? We all stay here, because out there—whatever appears out there every day—it's dangerous. You just might find the end of your world."

He sat up, sniffed back the last tears, and felt his face grow warm. It must have been red with shame.

"My name is Stina. I've only been here a few months."

She extended her hand. Croydon took it and stood up. Almariss stayed close. Shaday and Nico were nearby, along with a soldier wearing a sword. Did they all come looking for him? Stina and a soldier—people he hadn't met?

"How did you know he was there?" Almariss asked Stina.

"I . . . I heard him. I mean, I guess I heard his heartbeat. Hearing isn't right, but I can hear all of your hearts. It's like feeling them inside along with my own."

"He must have just reached the sign," the soldier said. "I counted him returned just as Stina heard him," He was tall and had black hair clasped behind his head. He was darker than Nico, but not as dark as Stina. He looked important.

"I never knew I could do that, nor that João could do his thing. What's happening to us?"

"It's the city," Nico said. "Magic infects us."

Stina still held Croydon's hand, and he didn't let go. She led him away from the bushes and walked beside the soldier. The three of them walked past the sign together.

"Croydon," Stina said. "Do you see the angle of the sign?"

"What do you mean?"

"It doesn't face directly out to those entering the city, nor does it face directly into the city for those leaving. It faces both ways. If you enter, you've come to the end of your old world, and if you leave, you go to another world. I stay because I don't know what's out there. I've seen places in the future and in the past. I saw a place full of wild beasts. I even saw a mammoth— but I never saw a place for me. This is my place now."

"But I want to go home. I don't want to be dead."

She smiled, "You're not dead. You're here, alive with us."

"I'm dead to my parents, and my sister, and my friends."

No one said anything to that. Then Shaday reached for him and wrapped him in a tight hug, the kind his grandmother gave on Easter and Thanksgiving. Stina let go of his hand and he found himself enveloped in Shaday's soft warmth. She smelled like sweet grass and flowers.

"Somewhere there's a boy, just a few years older than you,

who thinks me dead. He's certain he's lost his mother, but I send him my love each day. Your mother will do the same. You're alive to me and you'll always be alive to her."

Maybe that was true, but it didn't make him feel different. None of it was real, yet at the same time it was all too real. "I have no place to live."

"Many people will gladly take you into their homes," Stina said.

"Will you?" She seemed even more like an older sister than Almariss, even though he'd just met her.

Stina's eyes widened. "I . . . I don't have a place. I live at the inn."

"You'll stay with me and Nico," Shaday said. "That's if you want. We have a little one-room cottage, but we'll find space. Right, Nico?"

"Plenty of space." He produced a wooden chip from his shirt pocket. It was deep red. "I think we can afford to expand a little."

Shaday smiled and squeezed him harder.

"Don't forget to take him to see the Mayor, now that it's settled," said Almariss. She walked into the city, fiddling with her pipe.

Settled. From the miles of sand Croydon had seen, there was no way home. There was no home here either. Just strangers in a strange town. But it was settled. For now.

PART II

THE COMPANY GOES PUBLIC AT THE END OF THE WORLD

Awash in tides green
I saw clouds sinking, stars rising
Time receding
- Notes of a Traveller

*A*nne stood at the front of a room that could be any boardroom she had commanded during the startup of Project E266. Except it wasn't. That world had left her. Maggie, the company, the board, her parents, her sister—all gone. She was at the End of the World, in a shack of a cottage with Noble and six others like her: abandoned and unable to earn chip-value. She worked a faded gray chip through her fingers. Always gray.

She swallowed to get her voice to a lower tone, the one she knew commanded respect. Then she looked across the faces of the others, registering nothing about them beyond their presence. "The Company is entering a new phase."

"About time," grumbled Father Al.

She ignored him. He'd been useless in the manufacture and distribution of her Red Chips. He just hung around for the small bits of food they bought with them. "The Red Chips established us, but we need to go beyond."

"Beyond the chips?" Juli asked. She was a pale, solid girl with blue hair and rings in her nose.

"Red Chips, my ass," Truly huffed. She had blonde hair so bright it was nearly white. She had been a teacher. "Should call them Black Chips."

"The Red Chips work," Anne said. She didn't care for the defensive tone of her voice, so she relaxed and exhaled. "You just need to get better at making the switch and choosing who to trade with."

"What's this next phase?" Marta asked.

"Our problem is not about the chips. It's the phenomena. Some call it magic, but I'm a woman of science." She was registering their faces now and noted she finally had some of their attention. "There are natural but strange phenomena working in this town. Some barrier that holds us in." She had them deeper. She made full use of her form-fitting Urbletics and her blue-eyed, unblinking gaze. This was how to control a boardroom and captivate men and women alike. "If we can learn how these phenomena work, we can turn it to our advantage."

"How do we do that?" Frank asked. He was bald and burly, an ex-soldier of the First World War.

"A two-part strategy. I'll need some of you to continue to work the Red Chips, but only on croppers. Trade them for the last of their coins, jewels, anything. They won't know until it's too late. Once we have control, we'll be the wealthiest, and the ones with power."

"Won't that draw the Mayor's attention?" Frank asked.

"I don't give a damn about the Mayor."

"What is the other strategy?" Jacob asked. He was tall,

muscular, fit, and quiet. He claimed to have walked out of the Hague. His accent was French with a Dutch dialect, or maybe it was the other way around. His clothes were eighteenth-century vintage and impeccable, and Anne couldn't imagine how, in this place, he kept the whites white and ruffles ruffled.

"Yeah," Juli said, snapping a piece of gum in her mouth. "What's the second part?"

Anne delivered her best silent stare to each of them. Then she said, "We infiltrate the Mayor's Palace."

Anne glanced up at the moonless sky laden with thick clouds. Perfect. Noble sat beside her in the shadows of the wide oaks of the Commons. She watched her team. It had grown over the three weeks since she announced the plan. John was a lanky man of forty who said he'd led a group from the Roanoke colony. He'd arrived with a sword and musket, but without powder to replenish the gun it was useless. How many croppers might have more modern guns? It would be helpful to know that, but she'd seen none, and neither had Jacob.

Besides John, there was Amber from 1980s California. She had shoulder-length blonde curls and wore bubblegum-pink lipstick; an original valley girl who became the caricature. Then there was Jeff, whom Jacob had caught trying to steal cheese in the marketplace. Jeff apparently walked out of New Jersey at the turn of the millennium. A hefty white kid who wore black combat boots and a long black army coat, but he'd never served. Anne wasn't sure what he would be useful for, but when Jacob gave Jeff the choice of staying with them or being turned over to the Mayor, he stayed.

Frank and John had scouted the Mayor's Defense for a week to learn their rounds and duties. The Defense wasn't much of a threat. A single pair of members strode through the town during daylight and evening hours, and by midnight they returned to the barracks behind the Mayor's Palace to join the other two members. Two more off-duty guards were in their own homes. Six guards total; four men and two women. Each carried only swords, no guns. The new commander of the Defense also patrolled the city and slept in the barracks, but he was still really a cropper and not a threat.

The plan was to have Frank and Jeff watch the barracks after midnight while the guards slept. Then she would lead Juli and John to the palace doors. The rest of the team was to spread out across the Commons to the streets beside and behind the palace and give a warning if anyone approached. Juli would pick the lock. John carried his sword.

Noble lay at her side, panting softly.

Anne knew a little of the inside of the palace from her visit with the Mayor. The Mayor's threat against entering the building again unless she could gain and hold some pink in her faded gray chip was an annoying mote that grew daily. Never once had the chip revealed the slightest tint of any color. What form of trap did the Mayor have? Why did the Mayor dislike her so? Why discriminate just because her chip-value faded and wouldn't grow? That was a double penalty. To be poor and then ostracized because you were poor. No different from her own time, and the reason why she'd vowed to never be poor. No matter. She would be inside soon and would learn the Mayor's secrets.

Juli worked the lock with a pick set she'd created out of trinkets carried by croppers in trade for Red Chips.

"Is it working?"

"Yes," whispered Juli.

"How much longer?"

"It's done."

"John."

"Wait," Juli said. "That was way too easy. Like it wasn't locked at all. This has to be a trap."

"I know it's a trap. She's got to back up her threats against us with something. That's why we have John."

Juli stepped to the side, and John pressed his shoulder against the door. He lifted the latch, and Juli traded her pick set for a knife. John held his sword ready, then shoved the door open. It was black inside. Anne lifted the shade on the small lantern she carried. It was still too dark to see anything. She handed the lantern to Juli.

John stepped into the darkness. "There be nothing to my eyes, or ears, or nose."

Juli looked back. Anne waved her forward, and Juli stepped through the door. It immediately swung shut, catching her hand with the lantern. She yelped, then shouted, "Oh my god!" and dropped the lantern. Noble whined and fled. Anne watched the door press against Juli's pale fingers. Then they slipped inside and the door sealed.

The night was as silent as it was dark. Anne shivered. Marta, Truly, and Amber joined her on the steps of the palace.

"What happened?" Marta asked.

"They're . . . they're in," she said.

"What was Juli shouting about?"

"Juli—she was scared, that's all."

"So like, now what?" Amber nibbled at her nails.

"We wait." Anne noticed Truly standing silently with her arms crossed, and she made a mental note to have Frank do something about her attitude.

THEY WAITED until the pale gray light of predawn glowed beyond the harbor. Noble had returned and laid at her feet while she sat on the bench between the columns of the landing. No sounds came from within the building.

"They aren't coming out," Marta said.

"Why?" Amber looked from Marta to Anne.

"The Mayor's trap."

"Trap? Why does she have a trap?"

"You haven't seen the Mayor, have you?"

"No. Didn't see the point. She sent some dude from the Defense to get me to see her or to leave."

"But you stayed. Good for us."

"It's, like, way too scary out there." Amber flung her arm at the world.

"Yes, dear . . . I have a job for you later this morning."

"What job?" Amber crossed her arms and frowned.

"It's time you had that meeting with the Mayor."

THE SUN WAS WARM, and Anne, along with Amber and Jacob, stayed in the shadows. Marta and Truly had returned to HQ. Noble sniffed the grounds of the Commons and the bottom steps of the palace.

"You sure I won't, like, get thrown in jail?" Amber asked.

"Absolutely. The Mayor will talk to you and urge you to leave. Then she'll warn you not to return to the palace."

"Precisely how do you know?" Jacob asked.

"That's her pattern, and I'm certain she cannot do otherwise."

"Certain?"

"It's related to the phenomena."

Amber blew a bubble with her gum, then sucked it in. "If she captures me, like, I'm counting on you to get me out."

"Don't worry. Now go on. The Mayor is in, the doormen are outside, the doors are unlocked."

Amber stepped slowly up the steps between the columns. The doormen bowed in greeting and held the doors open for her.

"Have you thought about those stairs?" Jacob asked. "If there is a prison in this town, I would wager it is under the first floor. Those vents lead to something."

"I've never heard mention of a prison. The Mayor lives above the offices with her valet. I don't know what's underneath."

"Then what does the Mayor's Defense do with real criminals?"

"They escort them out of town and prevent them from returning," Anne said. "They're banished."

AMBER EMERGED through the doors a few minutes later. She scurried down the steps and joined them. "It was like you said, but weird. Some, like, smelly candles and a stupid spinning globe. Ooh, and that valet dude was creepy." She hugged herself and shivered despite her sweater and the warmth of the sun.

"Any sign of John and Juli?"

"Nope."

"Did you ask?"

"Nope." She turned and walked away.

"Where are you going?"

"Like, I don't know, okay?"

"There must be a dungeon," Jacob said. "Under the office. If we can chip those vents wider—"

"Even if there is a dungeon, I don't think that's where Juli and John are."

"Then where?"

"I don't know, but I'm certain it's related to the phenomena."

"You seem certain of many things."

"Fuck you, Jacob."

There had to be a way to understand the phenomena and how the Mayor used it. Anne walked toward HQ and Noble walked with her.

"Where are you going?" Jacob asked. "What about John and the young lady?"

She ignored his whining. What force of nature could move a town through both place and time, connect it for a brief time, then disconnect again? What propelled it? She pulled the dull gray chip from her sports bra. It sat between her fingers as faded and colorless as the day she'd lifted it from the potter's purse, its secrets locked in the absence of color.

NEW YEAR'S EVE AT THE END OF THE WORLD

Aberration and oasis
The city moves unmoored, and unencumbered
There are tomorrows behind and yesterdays ahead.
- Notes of a Traveller

*S*tina found Shaday and Almariss already seated with a pot of tea, wine, and mead on a table between them. Their corner of the Salon occupied the smallest of three fireplaces. At the other two, men roared in shared storytelling, lying and embellishing as men do. New croppers sat the center of the room around a long oval table. Harmony and Wilcott Vental sat at each end. The scene reminded Stina of her own Tea and Conversation sessions. The Ventals had a way of welcoming that, despite appearing silly, put you at ease enough so you could really consider what you faced. What to expect from life at the bloody End of the World. The Ventals' food and drink and a pay-what-you-feel-and-only-what-you-can-afford attitude went a long way in those early days.

The room filled her with beating hearts, a strange warmth and rhythmic sensation—a loosely organized cacophony she was just begging to accept. When she reached Shaday and Almariss, Shaday patted the chair beside her and Almariss handed her a cup of wine. Almariss drank the tea and Shaday the mead. The fire was lit and cast a warm glow over their little corner. Monday evening out with the ladies was nice despite the feeling she had become a grandmum. Without this regular event, she would have forgotten the days and missed the passing of weeks. Without the disruptions of modern life, the rhythm of days, weeks, and months at the End of the World was smooth and strange, like a pond without ripples. No matter where the city landed, time moved forward. Today could have been a day in an October like any northern hemisphere October. Leaves changed color and fell. The nights and mornings were chill. Farmers outside the city gathered a harvest. The city might land anywhere and in any time, but inside, change poured like treacle.

Stina sat beside Shaday. "What are you girls chittering over?"

Almariss passed a furtive glance at Shaday, but Shaday beamed. "You," she said. "You and that handsome commander of the Mayor's Defense."

Stina scowled. She lifted her wine and sipped. "Hardly interesting enough for this corner."

"Precisely this corner's interest. He eats often at the Scale, and you're the only one who serves him."

"What can I say? The man has to eat and I'm good at tucking tables."

Shaday laughed. "He hasn't asked you out, has he?"

It was no use. Shaday wouldn't drop this. "No. He's a devout Catholic soldier from sixteenth-century Portugal. Dating wasn't invented then."

"Not dating, courting. I'm sure he knows how to court. The question is, do you?"

"Probably not." Did she even want to be courted? Courting implied a lot of things she wasn't interested in being to any man.

"You don't have to *be* courted," Almariss said. "You can *do* the courting."

"That's right," Shaday said. "Subtle though. The act of courting is the art of letting your lover think they are in control."

So nothing had changed between courting and dating, and the acting and manipulation was still what she hated about it all. Why couldn't people just like each other and be together and skip going on the pull? She must have displayed some expression and Shaday reacted by placing a freckled hand on Stina's knee.

"Just buy a sweet dress," she said. "The rest will take care of itself. Do what comes natural. If it's meant to be, he'll recognize it."

"Why would I need a dress?"

"For the New Year's Eve Ball. The Ventals throw one every year. They invite everyone in the city."

"I'll think about it." Almariss stared at the fireplace. Her unlit pipe drooped from her lips. "What's chewing at you, Almariss?"

"Nothing. Just thinking."

"About?"

"The Mayor." She looked at her tea. "She's withdrawn lately."

"She never leaves the palace, how much more—"

"In what way?" Shaday asked, squeezing Stina's knee.

"Last night was our regular patolli tiles and tea night, but during the whole evening, through the entire game, she said nothing. All she spoke was 'come in' and 'good night.'"

"Do you think something's wrong with the city?" Shaday asked.

"What could be wrong with the city?" Stina added.

Almariss considered them for a moment, as if deciding if she could trust them with a secret. Almariss had been in the city the longest and revealed the least about herself. Stina knew she was close to the Mayor, probably the only person close enough to call her a friend.

"Disruption," Almariss said. "Like a bad one. Disruptions happen all the time. She says they're what enable croppers to arrive or leave, but she's always worried about a big one that might stop the city permanently. Leave us stuck somewhere."

"Bloody hell."

"That would be terrible," Shaday said. She sipped her mead. "We've seen some pretty dangerous places. Landed in the middle of wars a few times."

"And the Mayor tries to avoid those places as much as she can and to disconnect as soon as possible. But she's always worried she won't be able to disconnect."

"But maybe if the place were just a regular place," Stina suggested. "A place with no war—"

"What place is without war?" Shaday asked. She shook her head and sighed. "The magic would end. The city would become just another city."

"People would die," Almariss added.

Stina was about to ask why that would be if the place were safe, but Almariss continued.

"I think it's worse than just her normal worries. Or it's nothing at all to do with the city. Maybe she's just bored with me. We've had the same routine for . . . a long time. The previous week she didn't say much more."

Shaday refilled Almariss's tea. "I doubt that. She needs you."

"She hasn't needed me for years. I just go because I need . . . I need to play the game, to see her."

"We could play," Stina said. "Bring it here. Teach us."

Almariss gave her a look that didn't seem to belong on her face. Sadness and a little anger. Shaday looked back at each of them. "Right," Stina added. "We could play the game—even add a second night to our schedules."

"Maybe," Almariss said. "But if it's not me—if she's learned of something dangerous—what if the city is coming to some crisis only she can see? It would be like her to try to solve it herself."

"Have you asked her directly?"

"No. I fear all answers."

"Maybe there's another possibility you haven't considered," Stina said. "I don't know what, but usually if I see only two choices and neither is right, there's a third I didn't see at first."

Almariss returned to silence and Shaday appeared not to know what to say or do. Time to change the subject. Stina had always wondered about the Japanese sisters—had hoped to get to know them, since their ages were similar. "Do either of you know anything about the girl Asami? The one that makes the meat pies—those huge dumplings? She never brings them to the tavern. I pick them up at her house, but I only see her for just a few minutes. She doesn't really engage."

"Asami does stay at home mostly, but she makes an appearance now and then." Shady finished her mead. "She cooks for the New Year's Eve Ball and other events."

"So she's just a dowdy—an introvert?"

"Maybe," Almariss said. "The Mayor thinks the magic might have touched her and her sister more than the rest of us. Who knows what that might do?"

Stina sipped her wine. "Speaking of—how has magic affected you? I've never heard you mention it."

Almariss hesitated. "In a few ways. I can see for many miles. I see ships just as they enter the reach of the city, a few hours before they arrive."

"That's incredible. And the others?"

"Feelings, really. Sometimes I think I can sense things happening without knowing they're happening. Not so useful as the vision thing, especially when I can't understand what I'm sensing. But the worst thing is reading the memories behind someone's emotions. Why they do what they do. Often they don't know themselves because they've forgotten, but I know."

"That's pants. I wouldn't like that either. How do you deal with it?"

"Mostly ignore it, try to let it fade into the background. But then they mix with my own and sometimes I don't know what I'm feeling."

Stina sipped more wine and allowed herself to feel the heartbeats in the room. The slight electric hum under her skin. She understood Almariss. The rhythm of a room full of heartbeats that weren't your own was a fucking riot. But sometimes she found herself just drifting along the trails of their beats like footpaths and suddenly feeling wrapped in a blanket that wasn't entirely uneasy. Doing this now, she felt connected to everyone in the Salon. Among the croppers at the table were a couple and a child—and a fourth heartbeat. Do women hear the heartbeats of their unborn? She had never asked her mum or grandmums. She would hear hers, if she ever had a child. The Ventals could do little to help anyone grow accustomed to living with their magic. It was such an individual thing. She was just settling in with hers and she doubted she would ever grow comfortable with it. Living at the End of the World was such a strange fate.

The rest of the evening passed quietly. When they left, Shaday reminded her, "Don't forget that dress. Laraine is the best."

A custom dress. She'd never had one. Since coming to the city, she'd only bought used clothes, like thrift store shopping back home. She preferred clothes from her own time. Jeans and a simple blouse or t-shirt, mostly. And warm sweats for the nights in her room. A dress—a formal one—that was something else. And would it help? João was very much a Catholic soldier of the sixteenth century.

LARAINE'S SHOP SAT—LEANED, actually—against an ancient home of stained black shingles nestled under the forest at the far end of town, near Durgo's goat pasture. Stina had only traveled this far once, when she'd visited Lookout Hill. She and a handful of croppers had climbed up to glimpse what place and time the town might attach itself to next. That time, it was a smoky European mill village in the mid-1800s. She almost went for it, but villages in that time treated Blacks harshly and women had a hard lot. She couldn't bring herself to walk into that. The End of the World was safer.

Today, she didn't want to leave. A dress in a very specific style sat foremost in her mind. The Ventals' New Year's Eve Ball was only four weeks away, and hopefully Laraine could finish the dress in time. Shaday's suggestion had come weeks ago, but a custom dress would take a pissload of chip-value, so she had delayed her request in order to save.

The door creaked like the side door of her uncle Jacque's beach house—a pinching, elongated cracking sound. The wood floor inside creaked as well with a shallow hollowness. Bolts of cloth, jars of beads and buttons, and streamers of lace and frills jammed every available space. The shop was a single square room with a low ceiling that made Stina feel the need to stoop. Laraine sat in a rocking chair beside a small iron stove which radiated a comfortable heat.

Laraine looked up from her sewing. "Hello, Miss Stina. I wondered when I might see you." Laraine's accent was thick French, but if Stina had to guess, it sounded country, not Parisian.

"You did?"

"Yes, and forgive me, I do not know your last name."

"Oh, it's Maurice."

"Lovely French name, like the saint."

"I guess. Why did you expect me?"

"It was only a matter of time before you needed something better than those faded trousers. You're such a lovely young lady, and the commander of the Mayor's Defense is devilishly handsome."

"I—thank you. He—"

"So what will it be? A long gown for the New Year's Eve Ball?"

"Sort of, but from a specific time period. Can you do something like that?"

"Easy. Croppers want what's familiar to them and I do my best to make that. Even dresses from your party-crazy London of 2014, or Searise Los Angeles of 2030, though I admit I need sketches for those. What time period and locale?"

"Portugal, in the mid-1550s."

"Ah, yes. Lovely dresses, lots of color, and some lovely exposed shoulders."

"I—um—no exposed shoulders, I think. But yes, color. A blue-green, described to me as what I think of as teal, with gold embroidery. I know there isn't too much time and I'm sure you have other orders, so something fairly simple is fine."

"Plenty of time. Come, let me take your measure."

Laraine measured and noted every detail of Stina's body, and Stina wondered when she should address the cost. Laraine sketched a dress on a parchment. It was perfect, exactly the way João had described the noblewomen who seemed to have impressed him so. He had mentioned them to her each of the first three times they'd spoken alone. "Excuse me, but how much will this cost?"

"The materials are not especially costly, as we get ships with fine cloth quite regularly. About seventy chip-value."

Almariss's ability to utilize the changers and trade some of the croppers' useless valuables for the contents of ships was a magical ability Almariss had neglected to count that evening in the Salon. "And your labor?"

"Seventy-one."

"So one hundred forty-one?"

"No, just seventy-one."

"Your labor's worth more than a single chip."

"I'm sure, but you needn't worry. This dress is for a good cause."

"A cause? I'm no charity—"

"The only cause for which anything should be done—for love."

Fine. Older people always said rubbish like that when she had a new boyfriend. Even just mentioning a dude was cute would elicit something. They said she had a look. Well, whatever silly look people thought she had was just infatuation. João was devilishly handsome, and he'd been delicately kind in a way most men couldn't muster even for their sisters. But love? Unlikely. There were literally centuries between them.

CHRISTMAS at the End of the World was unlike anything Croydon had experienced. First, his family—sister, mother, father, grandmother, and great-aunt—weren't there. And there was very little emphasis on the holiday. Even the Christians of João's church did little to mark its coming. There was a Mass, and João took him to it. He'd never been to one, because his family wasn't Catholic. Mass was just as long and boring as church at home. Even Father Al seemed bored.

But Nico had insisted on a dinner and invited Stina and João. Shaday didn't celebrate Christmas and knew little about it, but she was all for what she called Yuletide Dinner, especially since Nico promised it would end with one of Asami's chocolate chiffon cake rolls. Chocolate was rare and Shaday chided Nico for spending so much, but she ate at least as much as anyone else. It was Croydon's first chocolate since arriving in the city and his memories surged. Christmas meant chocolate coins, bells, and boxed assortments.

There were few gifts. Gift sharing was something only he and Stina knew as a tradition, but João did give him a wooden practice sword.

"And, if Shaday agrees, I'll teach you the *artes marciais.*"

He looked immediately to Shaday, who frowned. "If you must. But mind you, teach him to protect himself first."

"Defense is the first and most important lesson."

"Thank you," Croydon said. He must have gushed like a little kid, but he didn't care. He shook João's hand, and João pulled and embraced him in a soldier's hug.

Stina smiled brightly, Shaday huffed, and Nico let out a lengthy breath. "A sword is a weapon. If you attack, you're forced to defend. If you defend only, you may never need to attack."

"Is that from a book?"

"No, I just made it up. But it seems reasonable."

"He is not wrong," João said.

AFTER DINNER, Croydon told João and the others about Christmas in New England. João's only memory of snow was of a miserable march with the army through some mountains.

"There was snow on the Lookout yesterday—only a dusting," Croydon added.

"You went to the Lookout?" Shaday looked at him with dismay and anger.

He'd never considered it a secret, but suddenly he wished he'd said nothing. "Yes. It was cold on the hill." He'd followed the muddy track with three or four other croppers, hoping to get a glimpse of something familiar. There wasn't. There never was.

"Do you go there often?"

"Just sometimes." At least twice a week, but he wasn't about to reveal that.

"I was hoping to see snow again, with my mother in Canada," Stina said. "We hiked in the mountains of Wales when I was eighteen. There were patches on the ground even though it was spring, and there were flurries."

"My sister and I used to go sledding on the hill behind our house," Croydon said. "I miss that."

"More cake?" Shaday offered. But only he and Shaday had more. They sat together, eating the miraculous confection while everyone else retreated to the fireplace. A quiet holiday. Too quiet, and too full of memories. It was probably like the holidays his grandparents and great-grandparents experienced. "I used to eat chocolate every day," he said. He squashed the crumbs with his fingers and licked them.

"I never had it before I came here, and only a few times since." Shaday cleared the table. "But if there's magic outside this city, it's in chocolate."

He retrieved his sword and ran his fingers across the wooden blade, imagining it was steel. Swords were as rare as chocolate. Only the Mayor's Defense needed them. A few others came to the city from times where swords were common, but even they dropped the habit of carrying them if they stayed.

"I don't know why you want a real one of those," Shaday said.

She had developed the ability to read his thoughts better than his own mother. Maybe that was more of her magic. "I don't know. I guess it just seems neat, or maybe that having one means I'm grown up. João looks good wearing his. Important."

"João would look good without one too."

He put the sword away and pulled his chair to the others at the fire. "Tell us a story, Nico. Christmas is the perfect time for stories."

Nico smiled, wrinkling the corners of his eyes. "What story would be fitting?"

"Any. It doesn't have to be Christmas related. How about the one with the six-fingered man?"

"Not much of a story to that."

Nico's stories always started with that note. They weren't much, but then he told them and he weaved in others, and before you knew it an hour had passed. Without TV or many books, this was the most entertainment he'd get. Music and plays on the Commons in summer or at the Salon were better, but those didn't happen every day.

The evening passed. João shared some of his own stories, mostly of long marches and seasick voyages with the army. Stina added the story of her father giving her a restored VW on her eighteenth birthday. Shaday added the tale of the Wild Hunt, though she said it wasn't a tale. He wished he could tell a story, but he hadn't lived a long or interesting enough life. Too young to have any interesting stories, too young to own a sword. Being caught at the End of the World wasn't the only way he was stuck. Life as a teenager was its own trap.

~

A WEEK LATER, Croydon sat on a rock overlooking the marshes, honing his wooden sword. The sky was a deep gray, almost blue, and the sun made the marsh grass and reeds glow in a bright golden light. João had said sword practice included taking care of his weapon—even if it was only wood. "Practice in everything makes one good at anything," he had said, or something like it. Croydon wanted to be good with an actual sword, though. If he had to live at the End of the World, he wanted to be a member of the Mayor's Defense and know how to wield one. Shaday forbade João to let him use a metal sword until he was fourteen—next August. How did they count years at the End of the World? New Year's Eve was in two days, but what year did they call it now? No one ever said. It was always just this year, last year, or next year. That made sense enough for a city that appeared and disappeared through time.

"Croydon," Shaday called from the cottage. "There's an errand for you."

Swords were expensive and odd jobs were the only way he could save enough. He put away his stone and sword and joined her.

"Kana, the baker's sister, came by the stall this morning and asked if you would pick up two sacks of flour from the mill and deliver it to their house. Do you know where they live?"

"No."

"It's a cottage like this on Gift Street, beyond the barracks behind the palace. They have a large Japanese maple in front with lots of flowers. You'll know it."

"Flowers in winter?"

"Kana's an extraordinary gardener."

AVALON THE MILLER might have been British like Stina. Or maybe not—her accent wasn't quite the same. She wore a canvas smock over her short, round stature and a wide-brimmed hat sat cocked to one side on her head. Croydon couldn't tell how old she might be. She had a dark complexion, and her hair might have been gray or just a silvery blonde. She poured out the measure of flour from a large wooden bin into two sacks.

He tied the sacks of flour to a leather harness Nico had helped him make and slung the harness across his shoulders. The sacks must have been twenty pounds each.

"Asami seems to do all the cooking for the New Year's Eve Ball," Avalon said. "As usual."

"I guess." He worked to steady his balance. He had to hold the strings to still the swinging sacks.

"How are you doing, Croydon?"

"Fine, why?"

"Some young get home-fearin' somethin' awful."

"Home-fearing? Why would I be afraid of my home? Not that I'll ever see it again." That was the first time he'd said it out loud since the summer. It still didn't sound right.

"Not afraid of your home," Avalon said. "Missing your home to the point of gettin' sick. People who get like that are afraid to live their fate, we say. Bad melancholy."

"Melon color?" Did she mean they turned pale, sickly yellow like a mush-melon, or green like a watermelon?

She must have seen his confusion on his face. "Sadness so bad you can't get out of bed."

"Oh. No, not that. Besides, João's teaching me to use a sword. I will be a member of Mayor's Defense."

"Oh good. Shaday's heart would absolutely break if you left."

"I have to get to Asami's."

"Yes, yes, on with ya."

∿

KANA'S WINTER flowers were bright blossoms of white, blue, and red tulips, and petunias were arranged neatly along the walkway. Large lilac bushes partially obscured the house on either side of the door. They bloomed purple, white, and blue. He was familiar with purple lilacs in late spring, but it was strange to see them in December. The maple tree was less welcoming. It hunched over the cottage with long, sharp limbs reaching out from a black trunk. Leafless for the winter, it looked like it might reach out and crush the tiny cottage.

He'd met Kana a few times, when she purchased baskets. He'd never paid attention to girls before—and Kana was not really a girl, she was Stina's age. But Kana was the prettiest he'd ever seen. Short, perfectly smooth black hair, clear black eyes, and a pale, fragile-looking face. She was smaller than he was, too, making her seem very fragile, like her flowers. He'd never met Asami, though. She never seemed to leave their house.

Croydon knocked on the rich, blue-stained door. Movement caught his eye at one window, but he couldn't see through. Then the door opened. While Kana was beautiful, Asami—as this woman must be—was something delicate. The sisterly resemblance was unmistakable. Asami did not meet his eyes; she kept them lowered as she beckoned him in with a hand that might have floated of its own will. He seemed to have forgotten to breathe, and he gasped.

"Heavy," Asami said. Her voice was so soft she might have willed the words into his ears.

"Not really," he managed. "Just a long walk."

"Here, here, in the kitchen."

He placed the sacks on a counter that was more pristine than any he'd seen. Every utensil, knife, pot, and bowl was in a specific place, and the entire kitchen looked newly built and never used. But he could smell spiced cakes, meat pies, and sweet apples.

"I do not have a chip," she said. "But let me hold one of yours."

She held out her small, perfect hand, and he placed one of his chips in it. Instantly it was a shade darker. At least ten chip-value. She handed the chip back, and the tips of her fingers touched his palm. Nothing was as soft or had made him feel the way he was feeling. Was this normal? It wasn't like touching Shaday or Stina, or his mother and sister. He'd have to ask João.

"Thank you," she said. She bowed her head slightly as she did so.

He bowed as well and struggled to form the words, "Thank you."

THE AIR OUTSIDE was crisp and cold. He might have skipped back to Shaday's if he were nine. But if he were nine and not thirteen, he wouldn't have felt like this. He had intended to stop at the barracks to see João, but it was getting dark and Shaday would worry so he stuck to Main Street.

He met Kana as he neared the Mayor's Palace.

"Did you bring Asami her flour?" Kana asked. Her cheeks were pink from the cool air.

"I did. Your sister does a lot of cooking, but I've never seen such a clean kitchen."

"Asami is a magician in there. Consider yourself fortunate to have seen her shrine. I have never stepped foot in there since we moved in."

"She doesn't let you in?"

"Oh, she would, but it feels like trespassing, like tramping in someone else's garden."

"I'm sorry." He lowered his eyes.

"I did not mean to find fault. It is fine. She invited you in with a delivery, a practical thing. She trusted you."

That was a relief. It must have been okay. She'd paid him well and didn't rush him out. He lifted his eyes again and smiled at the memory of her touch. The light was fading quickly.

"I must go," Kana said.

"Me too."

She bowed her head slightly and he did the same. As he turned the corner toward Marsh Road, he saw a man, well dressed in the style of the 1700s. He'd seen the man before but didn't know his name. The man saw him, gave a pointed wave, and walked toward the center of the city.

STINA LIFTED the hem of her new dress above her ankles and tried desperately not to let it touch the muddy street. The walk from the Scale and Tentacle to the Ballroom was not far, only a few blocks, but rain earlier in the day turned it into a journey of gown-imperiling, cart-track mud rivers and puddles.

Attending the ball had not been a firm decision in her mind until she purchased the dress. Her last night on the town had been filled with hallucinations and a nightmare dream that had landed her in this bloody city. Passed straight through No Man's Land proper and into the End of the World. Maybe any night out was a terrible idea. But this was different. That night was bloody Hans's fault, but this was a party with people she knew and trusted. She had won the argument with herself and now defeated the mud. She stepped onto the stone steps in front of the Ballroom, where Harmony Vental stood at the door greeting guests.

If ever there was one, Harmony was the absurdly perfect-dimensioned doll in living flesh. Her golden hair was quaffed in a gentle bun with strategic curls dangling to touch her perfectly smooth, pale shoulders.

Stina reached the landing and doorway, and Harmony curtsied before her. "Madam Maurice, welcome." Her voice was so sincerely friendly, Stina found no energy for jealousy. "I dare say, Madam Maurice, you look lovely. You will be the center of attention this evening."

"Thank you, Harmony. You look stunning, as usual. The attention will be all yours."

"Thank you, dear. Go on inside and enjoy yourself."

THEY HAD DECORATED the Ballroom in red, green, gold, and silver streamers and bows. Lamps covered in colored shades glowed against the walls around the room, and a candlelit chandelier shed an umbrella of light over the center. So many hearts beat together. Strong ones, weak ones, even a couple that were irregular. She would have made an excellent doctor. She made a note to try isolating the weaker and irregular ones. Though what could they do without modern medicine? Still, they deserved to know and take care of themselves as best as they could. Maybe she should set up a screening.

People, nearly everyone she knew and many she did not, filled the Ballroom. They mingled, drank, laughed, and talked. A band played soft jigs.

Jigs. There was a term she'd never expected to use.

Shaday stepped beside her holding a blue drink in a crystal tumbler. She had done her hair in an artfully coiled long braid that was trussed on the top of her head. "You look wonderful," she said. "Let's get you one of these." She raised the drink. "They taste like what I imagine nectar tastes to a butterfly." Shaday steered her to a table with a gigantic bowl of the blue liquid and ladled a tumbler full. It did taste wonderful. Not sweet exactly, but with the promise of sweetness; not fruity or flowery, yet again with hints and promises of both. Stina looked around the room.

"He's not here," Shaday said.

"Who, Nico?"

Shaday scowled at her. "Nico's home with his glass, remembering other years. You know who I mean. You didn't buy that dress for me."

"How do you know I didn't? I don't see you with a date."

Shaday laughed. "If I stay close to you and that dress, I'm bound to have my pick of your cast-offs." She sipped her drink, which left a slight blue stain on her lips. "Actually, I brought Croydon, though that might have been a mistake."

"Why?"

"I thought it would be good for him to meet more people, but he's hiding in the kitchen."

"Hiding?"

"He's just in there talking a storm with Asami. She's got enough to do without him distracting her so he can steal sweets."

"Shaday." Stina pulled her close and whispered into her freckled ear. "He's thirteen. He's not in the kitchen for that kind of sweet."

Shaday pulled away, then popped her hand over her mouth. "Oh dear. I hadn't thought of that."

"He's fine. Let's see who we know."

WILCOTT VENTAL STEPPED onto the stage in front of the musicians. "Attention! Attention everyone!" He was dressed as stunningly as Harmony, with a long white tail coat and top hat. His golden hair and bronze face glowed under the lights. "The Mayor sends us her New Year's message." He stepped to the side, and the Mayor's valet, Eristol, stepped forward. Behind him stood João. He caught Stina's eye and smiled. So he was working, guarding the little valet. Why did the valet need guarding, or was it just ceremonial?

"Her Honor wishes fortune and good fate to all!" Eristol made up for his lack of size with an excess in voice. "Welcome to our new neighbors who chose to stay. Best fortunes to those who chose to leave. Glad tidings to all as we enter another year!"

The crowd applauded and cheered.

That was it, wasn't it—entering another year, another time and place? At the End of the World there weren't any new years, just other years. Years belonging to some other time. She left Shaday and worked her way through the throng until she reached the stage as João escorted Eristol off. "João, do you have to leave now?" Shit. Try not to sound bloody desperate.

João looked at Eristol. "Don't mind me," said the valet. "I'm going to stuff my face with Asami's delicacies. Her squid rolls are not to be missed."

The band reassembled themselves and started a gentle waltz. Couples began dancing.

"Dance with me, João." She held her hand out to him. He looked around the room and his face darkened a shade. He took her hand and stepped close.

"I'm not very good. I'm a soldier."

"You're an officer. I'm sure you've danced. What about those noble ladies you mentioned? I'm sure you danced with them." Idiot. Why did she bring them up? And wearing a dress to remind him. This was a dodgy idea.

He shook his head. "No, not with them. But you are right, I have danced a little—at my sister's wedding and the weddings of a few cousins."

He put his arm around her waist and guided her to the floor. There, they danced. He wasn't good, but neither was she.

She could burn down a club with all the popular moves, but she'd only waltzed two or three times. It didn't matter. They were close, they were touching, and she was so aware of his heart. Not only was it inside his chest, but it nestled beside her own, pulsing together. It was shockingly intimate. There might be magic at the End of the World, but there was electricity too.

When the music stopped and the applause died. Harmony swooped in and whispered something to João, then she vanished as quickly as she had arrived.

"What did she say?" Stina asked.

"I have to leave. They Mayor has requested a meeting of the Brigade and I must attend."

"Now? In the middle of the party?"

"Yes. My orders." She reached for his hands and tried to pull him close, but he stood still. They held hands. "You . . . you look—" he stammered. "I have to go." He released her hands and turned away. "Eristol," he called. "The Mayor requests our presence. Now."

Shaday appeared at her side and leaned against her. "What's all that?"

"I don't know. The Mayor has some kind of emergency meeting with the Brigade."

The band resumed playing.

"Oh. Well, maybe that's good. That'll get Nico out of the house. I wonder what the emergency is. If it's not a fire or a flood, just a meeting. . . . Oh well, it's New Year's. Come dance with me."

Stina looked down at Shaday. Her freckled cheeks were flushed and her carefully piled hair had fallen and was just a long braid now. "How many of those have you had?" she asked, pointing to Shaday's nearly empty drink.

She grinned. "Two, last I counted."

"And how many since you counted?"

"I don't know, I didn't count them." She giggled.

Stina shook her head, took Shaday's hand, and they danced.

A FEW HOURS LATER, a bell peeled twelve times, heralding the passing of one set of months, weeks, and days for the promise of another. Another set of times and places borrowed from somewhere, and some when.

FAMILY AT THE END OF THE WORLD

Once an oasis, blue; free from the tug of the world.
A place caught in an eddy of places;
unaligned with but instances of time,
it bumps against the walls of yesterday and tomorrow.
This place has come and is going.
- Notes of a Traveller

*A*nne's room opened onto the veranda Marta had built. When she woke, she saw Marta standing there, looking at the harbor under a warm, late spring sun. Anne and Noble walked out and Anne put her arm around Marta's shoulders. "I never thanked you for building this veranda. The view is stunning." Marta said nothing. She worked a wood splinter that served as a toothpick between her teeth and continued watching the harbor. "Are you thinking of leaving?"

"It wouldn't be the first time."

Anne allowed silence.

Marta added, "It all seems so impossible. I wanted the war

to end so badly—I was so afraid the Germans would reach New Jersey. I must have wished so hard I wished myself away."

"They didn't reach New Jersey. The Germans lost the war."

"In your time, but I'm not so sure for my time. The world is an impossible place, no matter where or when."

"Nothing is impossible. You just have to have the right tools and leverage. Look at this veranda and the rest of the improvements you've made to this place. Anything is possible, dear Marta, even getting a dandy like Jacob to roll up his sleeves or acquiring building materials without chip-value."

"Anything is possible if you don't care how you achieve it."

"We didn't steal the lumber. The *Maybrand's* captain sold it for actual money."

"But we stole the money."

"We traded Red Chips for coins."

"Red Chips that turn black and can't be used. Might as well have sold rocks."

"If you look deep enough, you'll find everything is stolen. The metaphor for love is stealing hearts. Are you getting sentimental on me?"

"No. I just never thought I'd end up a thief."

Anne turned Marta to face her. "You're not a thief. You're part of something new. Come, gather the others in the boardroom. I have something that will change the world."

THERE WERE ONLY four of them now. Marta, Jacob, Frank, and Anne herself. Truly had left her, the group, and the city, abandoning them for whatever nightmare waited outside the End of the World. Good riddance. Amber, too, had walked away, and Jeff had followed. Failures. Father Al was a different story. She couldn't trust him. She found him talking with the new commander of the Defense one day, and though he claimed they were just discussing religion, he had to go. Frank took him for a drink at the Fated Gale and she had not seen Father Al since.

She stood at the end of a long table in the newly remodeled building she'd named Galaxy. The HQ for Project E266 never had a name, just an address: Rosewood Court. A stupid name. Despite the planted roses, or because of them, it failed to inspire. This converted cottage overlooking the harbor was a smaller, better iteration.

"This is no den of thieves," she declared. "This is a movement!" Marta and Jacob looked at each other. "And this movement has one goal: control the phenomena and thus our fates. No longer will we be subject to the arbitrary rules of the fucking Mayor and the perceived power of chip-value. No, we will repair this broken part of the world, and we will ensure it connects to a safe time and place where we can come and go freely. No more discrimination."

She gazed at each of them. Few could ever meet her wide, unblinking gaze. Everyone always flinched. "Are you ready to change the world?" she asked. "Are you ready to make a connection? A permanent, safe connection? Because if you aren't, leave now. Get the fuck out of my sight. Take your fucking disloyalty out of this city."

Marta looked puzzled, and Jacob grinned. Frank stood expressionless by the door with his arms crossed.

"No one wants to leave? You're all in on this? Good, because this is no longer the Company. You're all part of the Connectionist Movement." Anne paced and let the news soak in. "Now, we know the Mayor 'navigates' the city, and I've worked out how." She again waited for the information to penetrate. Only Jacob seemed to consider it deeply. She continued, "The Mayor doesn't steer us on some master-planned journey. Given the random and often dangerous locations the city appears near, she can't intentionally be seeking them. No, she steers the city away after it connects. It is her goal to keep the city disconnected from the world."

"She keeps us prisoners," Jacob said. This brought Marta and Frank's full attention. "Why would she do that?"

"Remember, she doesn't want us. We're of no value to her and she wants us to leave because we represent a disruption to the order of her world. She wants the others, the ones she can control with chip-value. The ones affected by the phenomena."

"The ones with magic," Marta said.

"Phenomena."

"Dendron, down at the Fated Gale, can make pine cones glow," Frank said. "Says he doesn't need candles or lamps."

"But you see, the pine cones are part of the land, part of the phenomena. Not fucking magic. What we need is a way to use the phenomena to bring this city to a stable, connected place. Then we can walk away safely, or we can stay. We could even come and go. Either way, when we're connected to the rest of the world chip-value will no longer be valuable. People will naturally gravitate toward gold."

"If we controlled the phenomena, we could determine where and when to remain connected," Jacob said. "It would be us deciding whether to disconnect and connect somewhere else."

"That's it exactly. We are the Connectionists. What do we say? Fuck the Mayor! Repeat after me, fuck the Mayor!"

The three others joined her chant, half-heartedly at first, then more fully, and finally with conviction. "Fuck the Mayor!"

When the enthusiasm subsided, Marta asked, "How do we control the phenomena? How do we get connected where we want to be?"

"I need a spy on the inside."

"Inside the palace?"

"Inside. We just need to find the most vulnerable clerk or minister."

"There is a candidate," Jacob said. He wore a sly grin on his face. "A minister very attached to an even more vulnerable sister."

That was what she needed to hear. "Tell me more."

THE INTERIOR of the minister's home was spare but comfortable. Anne found it very Japanese. They should have removed their shoes. The place was perfectly ordered, maybe according to the rules of feng shui—no, that was Chinese. Still, there was an order, a purpose that was not unlike the Dogon mythology she'd borrowed for Project E266. An alignment with the 266 signs that embraced the essence of all things. Mythology was as fluid across cultures as this city was through time and place.

She sat on a comfortable couch, something like a futon, and scratched Noble's head. She could live in this comfortable, simple elegance. Freshly cut lilacs of purple, white, and blue adorned a simple white porcelain vase painted with the scene of a rushing river. There was something about the backdrop of trees and the raucous foam over jagged rocks that felt dangerous and foreboding—disturbing, and not at all fitting to the lovely flowers. She turned her attention to the door. Jacob stood beside the minister's younger sister, Asami. The door opened a few moments later and a woman wearing a lavender blouse entered. Her small mouth gaped into a tiny 'o' as she gasped. So young. Twenty-one according to her sister, though they each could have been fifteen. "Join us, Kana," Anne said. "Asami makes the best tea and biscuits, but you know that already."

"What . . . what are you doing in our home?"

"Having tea and biscuits."

"Why?"

"We have business to discuss."

"We do?"

"Why don't you change out of that ridiculous uniform and join us?"

Kana glanced at the wolfhound and Jacob, and then to her sister who was holding a tray with more biscuits. Her sister shook her head slowly as Kana passed and stepped behind a beaded curtain. Jacob drew closer to Asami. Kana returned a few minutes later, wearing a loose-fitting green sweater and simple black trousers. She sat opposite Anne and left her cup of tea untouched.

"You've chosen to stay at the End of the World," Anne said. "I don't blame you. As strange as this place is, what often lies outside—well, I wouldn't wish that on anyone. I know you and your sister arrived as teenagers from Japan."

"How do you—"

"What I don't know is when you left Japan. What year, who was your prime minister, your leader?"

Kana glanced at Asami, who kept her head bowed. "Our leader was Lord Tokugawa Ieyasu, honorable shōgun."

"I see. I'm from a country you've never heard of. I speak a different language. How do you think you can understand me?"

"The city's magic."

"Phenomena. Do you know that word?"

"Something like magic, but not. Something natural."

Anne sipped her tea. It was very good. She looked forward to having it every afternoon. "Magic is just phenomena."

"Why speak of this?"

"Because I need details on the phenomena, and you work close to its source." Kana's eyes widened. Anne continued. "The Mayor's Palace is the source."

"I am not privy to what the Mayor does."

"You are, if you allow yourself to notice. You haven't noticed because you think it isn't proper for you to watch your superior. I'm telling you it is now both proper and necessary."

"Why? Why would that be?"

"Because if you don't, Jacob will escort Asami out of the End of the World and you'll never see her again."

Kana's eyes flashed to her sister. Jacob was already walking her out of the house with her arm twisted hard behind her back and the blade of a knife against her side. Kana jumped to her feet and started after them, but Anne jerked on Noble's collar and the wolfhound growled and sniffed at Kana's legs. Kana stopped.

"Don't worry," Anne said, finishing her tea. "Asami will be fine. She will be my cook, and you will tell me everything the Mayor does. Who she sees, what she says, everything." She stood and placed a hand on Kana's shoulder. The girl shuddered. "You will tell no one of me, your sister, or your mission. Otherwise, you will be separated from her forever."

She left. The closing of the door muffled the trembling sobs behind it. Frank leaned against the hideous tree that loomed over the cottage and yard. "Make sure she does nothing stupid," Anne said.

"Ma'am."

JOÃO DISLODGED Croydon's wooden sword from his hand for the third time in five minutes. Croydon grabbed his wrist. It was sore and tired. The sun was blistering for the first time this year. He retrieved the sword and looked up at João, who appeared not to sweat. They were practicing on the Commons to the cheers and jeers of onlookers. Stina had watched for a few moments before moving on, but Shaday remained, though she wasn't really watching.

"Am I getting any better?" he asked João.

"Yes, though you need to practice more. Practice in everything makes anything possible."

"I practice."

"Not enough if you wish to become a member of the Defense."

"I haven't had time to practice. I still have to earn chips for a steel sword, so I've been working."

"You think you will practice more once you have the sword? That you will suddenly have more time?"

"Well, yeah—"

"That could be another year. Practice now, while your muscles still grow. Train your muscles to move without thinking. That's what will make you quick. And the most important things in sword fighting are balance and quickness. Quickness is the most important factor, and good balance leads to quickness."

"Did you practice when you were young?"

"Yes. My father, brother, and I were part of the King's Reserves. We had to be ready to defend our farm or march to war at any moment. And I still had to work the farm and orchards."

Other than handwriting, Croydon couldn't remember ever practicing anything. He didn't play an instrument like some kids. All he did were chores, fishing, swimming, running, sledding, and biking.

The thought of his bike pulled a memory into view. Not just of the bike, but a deeper memory of Mariah, who had lived a few houses down the road. She was the same age. They'd known each other since their first day of school. He remembered her long blonde hair flowing behind her as she rode up to him on a blue bike that was the same shade as his. She told him she'd bought it, blue just like his, so they could ride together. He had wanted nothing to do with her or her bike then, not her nor any girl. But now, suddenly, he wanted to do that more than sword fight. "João?" he asked. "Are you and Stina going to get married?"

João looked startled, as if someone had snuck up behind him and pinched him. "Why, no. We haven't properly courted."

"What does that mean? You spent Christmas with her. I saw you dance with her at the New Year's Eve Ball, and you see her every day at the tavern."

"That dance was improper—on all counts. Courting is a chaste process for getting to know one another and allowing the Lord to bless a couple. If the couple believes they have that blessing, they will then seek the advice of a priest who will guide and test the couple and decide if a marriage should proceed. Then the potential groom must ask the father of the bride for permission to marry."

"Sounds complicated." That word again, *chaste*. João had used it when he asked about the feelings he'd experienced from Asami's touch. He'd said boys and girls, men and women, must remain *chaste* until marriage and not touch, but it seemed to Croydon that João was being unfair. He'd seen him hold Stina's hand. Nico turned out to be a better listener and understood his feelings; he said such feelings were normal and part of growing up. João just had a lot of rules. Soldier rules, church rules.

"I take it proper courting is not so well defined in your time," João said.

"I don't think so, but I was so young when I left, so I don't know."

"Selecting one's partner for life should be a little demanding —like practice."

"Stina has no father here. How will you get permission?"

João did not reply.

Croydon stared at his battered sneakers. Mariah's gold hair danced in his mind. "I think Stina is the only one who can give you permission, and if you don't start seriously courting, you may never have the chance."

João looked at him with his head tilted and brow lifted. "Such wisdom from a thirteen-year-old boy."

"I'll be fourteen soon. But I think I lost a chance when I came here. Maybe my only chance. There are no girls here my age."

"There will be someday. Croppers arrive nearly every day."

"But no girls lately. Just like no horses."

"What?"

"Why are there no horses here?"

"I, well . . . some people do arrive with horses, but I suppose there really isn't any need for them. The farmers and herders have their oxen and mules. Horses are for traveling great distances, and there just isn't the need for them. Horses are used to carry away those wishing to leave the city."

"I guess." Croydon sheathed his sword. The sun was low behind the hills. "I just wish there were more kids my age—and maybe an actual girlfriend."

"Remember, courting is not about acting quickly, and it is not about getting a girlfriend like you get a pet. It's about revealing love and becoming one. Building love to fill a lifetime as something more than just yourself. You may have girls as friends, but you will also find one that is more."

They sat in silence as the sun descended behind Lookout Hill. Then João stood. "I have to go. You should too. Don't keep Shaday waiting."

"Say hello to Stina for me."

João nodded.

"STINA!" Padrok called. "Message for you."

She dropped her armful of plates and mugs on the counter and met Padrok behind the bar. He handed her a small, thick folded paper with her name in an elegant, slanted script. Definitely written with quill and ink.

"Lieutenant Tabray of the Defense delivered it."

"Thanks." Her stomach lurched. Letters were never good, even when they carried good news. They changed your life. Like the letter her mother sent her when she was at school. She could have bloody called, but she'd sent a letter to say she was moving to Canada. Stina stepped outside behind the tavern to read. It opened stiffly, and the page was jammed with the elegant cursive—every space used. Only two words—her name at the top, and João's signature at the bottom—were familiar. It was in Portuguese, and she had no way to make sense of the words without context.

But she didn't need context. She knew the context. She'd pushed him too far and made him uncomfortable at the ball. She'd acted like a lost, nagging puppy ever since. Bugger—she put him off. Of course he was put off. Their dinners together most nights had become just a habit between friends. He'd grown quiet, almost sullen. Last night, he refused and went home at her suggestion they go to the Salon. He'd barely acknowledged her presence two days ago when she watched him and Croydon. Now this. A lengthy, rambling letter. A break-up letter. She'd written a few herself when she was very young and had also received some when she was older.

Bloody fine.

It would never have worked. Too many centuries and too much culture between them. Too much fate. She folded it and stuffed it into her apron's pocket, then returned to work. Her stomach roiled. Life had changed. It shifted like sand washing away under her bare feet at the beach.

JOÃO WATCHED the reflection of the setting sun behind him strike golden ripples on the sea. The Finger Light pulsed like a silent heartbeat. He heard footsteps but did not turn. It was Almariss. The sensation of knowing everyone arriving in or leaving the town had grown into knowing who approached him even when he couldn't see them. It made his head feel as though it were filled with water, like an unbalanced bladder.

"No dinner with Stina?" Almariss asked. She stood beside him and lit her pipe.

"Not tonight."

"Duty? Is there a ship approaching I should be concerned with? I see nothing."

"No."

"Oh, thinking then. I should let you be."

"No. Stay a moment, if you can."

She blew smoke softly into the breeze. "I'm not the one you should trust for council of the heart."

"Is there really anyone who can give such council? I've alienated her, Almariss."

"How?"

"I wrote a letter. I tried to explain how I felt at the ball and since, and how my duty and my church seem at odds with my feelings for her. I tried to explain everything, yet something must have offended."

"Wait, you wrote to her?"

"Yes. I'm afraid I can face death in a charged battle, but I cannot face Stina."

Almariss laughed.

"I suppose it is fun—"

"No, I'm sorry." Almariss put her arm over his shoulders. "I must remind the Ventals to go over the difference between speaking and writing. You see, I can understand you when you speak, even the words that aren't changed in my ears if I know the context, like when you first referred to Stina as *garçonete*. The magic that drives the city makes that happen. But if you hand me a note, I won't be able to read it. The only written words everyone understands are on the sign outside the city. Another part of the magic is at work there."

He looked at her, and the imbalance in his head became a swirl in his belly. "So . . . she doesn't know what I wrote?"

"Unless she's fluent in your language, no."

"Then why did she not ask me to read it to her? She must know it is from me."

"You'll have to ask her that yourself. Like I said, I'm not good at romance."

He was about to leave, but the mirth had left Almariss's face. She looked older than her thirty-odd years. Something other than time had worn grim lines at the edge of her mouth. "I'm sure whatever happened was not your blame," he said. "I cannot imagine you causing someone else heartbreak."

She shook her head. "Apparently I can, and my own along with it. It was a long time ago. Buried memories."

"I am no expert either, but I do know the scars of the heart last longer than those of battle. And battle scars last a lifetime."

"Tell Stina what you wrote."

He turned and jogged toward the Scale and Tentacle.

THE DINNER CROWD HAD LEFT. Only those who usually stayed for the evening remained. The night drinkers would soon filter in, and until then there was a short breather for Stina and Hallea. They sat at a table, each with a small mug: hers of wine, Hallea's of ale.

"I've missed having you around at dinner," Hallea said.

Not going to discuss him. Nope. Leave that shit behind. Steer her away. "I've seen plenty of men watching you, Hallea. Why no dates?"

"Oh, I've had dates, just not since you've been here. I don't know. No one strikes my fancy."

"The last one stung, didn't it?"

Hallea took a long drink. "Stung like a bee the size of a bear. Thought he was a good man. Came in on a ship. We met and became inseparable. We were to be married. I should have seen that impetuous attachment as a problem."

"He found someone else?"

"Took off with a blue-eyed, buxom woman in fancy clothes from some fancy time. Walked straight down the Goresetch without a word."

"Well, obviously you're better without the tool."

"I tell myself that all the time, but that don't change the way I feel. Not one lick."

Stina felt his pounding heart just before João rushed into the common room. Oh god, what's this now? Coming to take back the letter? Or more like he needs something. *They always do, especially after they've broken up with you.*

"Stina," he was a little out of breath and he strode to their table. "I would like to—" He looked at Hallea then back at Stina. "Could we go for a walk?"

"I'll just tap a new keg," Hallea said as she rose. "Don't feel the need to rush back. I can handle it."

Stina remained seated. A walk? What on earth for? Couldn't they just let your heart break without prying it apart?

"It's about the letter. Almariss explained that you couldn't read it."

Oh, so now he wants to explain the letter. Wankers in any century were the same. "I didn't need to read it. I know a break-up letter when I see one." She took it out of her pocket, tossed it onto the table, and stood to leave.

"A break-up letter? What?"

"A long letter apologizing for being a cad, that it's not my fault but yours, and that in the end we can't see each other. That, or you've decided you're better with someone else." Her eyes stung; she was nearly shouting.

"It's not that at all. It's every bit the opposite."

"Sure, well I'll be fine." She stepped away. What had he said? The opposite of a break-up letter? She grabbed the letter and shoved it into his hand. "We're walking all right, and you're reading this to me."

THEY WALKED A LONG WAY, nearly to the Lookout, and he told her what he'd written. A list of the reasons he couldn't respond to her overtures and gestures. He claimed he desperately wanted to, but he was bound to duty. He was trying to live a godly life, and she was like a temptress, though he wanted to give in, et cetera, et cetera, et cetera. All those centuries and cultural differences had gotten him into a proper tangle.

They left the path to the Lookout and followed a narrower one into the forest. João helped her across a stream. She had never ventured into the forest. A mammoth sniffing her up close had put her off that. Even climbing the Lookout path with others in daylight had been nerve-racking. Yet despite the dark, she feared what João was telling her more than what might surprise them from the forest. Besides, he had a sword.

He led her to a pool, where the water was black with silver moonlit ripples radiating from the stream as it filled the basin. They were so far from the city that none of its light or sound penetrated the forest.

"So you see, the letter was an explanation, but not as you thought," he said.

She sat beside him on a stone under the moonlight. The lady of the lake was likely to push a sword out of the water, or there was some tentacled creature waiting to pull them under.

"My king, my family, and I were devout in our belief in the Lord. I based my service to the king upon it and lived my life by it. I still believe, don't mistake me. But I am less certain of the Church's teachings. This place is real and the only thing like it ever preached to me was the Tower of Babel and speaking in tongues. Yet there is magic here not taught by the Church. I believe it still to be God's work, but I question how much the Church really knows or understands about what God really is. They claim our fate is with God, yet He gave us the free will not to believe. So while I may worry about what is proper or godly, I no longer believe so strongly in the dictums of repentance and chastity. I have never courted a woman before and never imagined courting one from the future, one so removed from my experience."

The truth of that was an understatement. This required a fresh approach. But was it worth the effort? João was kind, handsome, and loyal to his beliefs. But to what end? What if she just ended it now? No strings, no trying to make things work. She closed her eyes and tried to feel what that would be like, seeing João around the city but not speaking to him. His heart pulsed inside her chest now in a way that had become comforting and made her feel safe, and more. She was part of something that was not just herself. He'd probably never step foot in the tavern again, but she'd see him and she'd feel his heart. And each time she did she'd feel the same tug, the same pull she felt right now—the need to wrap her arms around him and fall into that strange warmth that enveloped her when they were close. That would tear open a wound nearly every day until maybe someday she'd grow numb to the pain or learn to ignore his heart's beat next to hers.

But wasn't that what entering into a new relationship was? You either gave yourself to it until it ran its course and you came out the other side—hurt or whole—or you avoided it and guaranteed yourself the hurt immediately.

What the hell, it had to be worth a try—a real try. "I never expected to date—to be courted—by someone from the past." It was too dark to see anything but a sparkle of moon glancing off his eyes, but she felt their presence on her. Despite his religion, she knew she could tell him anything, even things his church wouldn't approve of. *Temptress.* He would still look at her the same. Was that true? Or did she just hope it was true? *Fuck it.* "Would it be proper in your time, for a man courting a woman . . . for the man to hold the woman's hand as they sit in the moonlight beside a lovely pool?"

"It would." He reached for her hand. His was warm. She felt his pulse and listened to his heart inside herself. An intimacy she hadn't expected, and couldn't imagine living without, wrapped together inside herself. If the city's magic infected people uniquely, as it appeared, then no human had ever experienced such a feeling. It was hers alone. Her stomach had flutters not of butterflies, but of a squadron of eagles.

TWO AT THE END OF THE WORLD

Sun, stars, and moon linger in the sky,
not fixed in orbits but random
at the start of each day and night.
Sometimes these landmarks of the sky
float hidden behind a veil,
in swirling tides made of time.
- Notes of a Traveller

Now, a sun is lowering, casting long shadows among clutching trees.

Two beings, one large and one very much smaller, approach a pool of dried bones. The large one senses the small first and holds back. She has seen the small one before but remains wary. It was such small ones—those of many skins—who slew the one who fills the pool with her bones and desiccated flesh.

The small one carries flowers. Winter flowers of blue and white. Blue asters, the most difficult to garden and the last touched by frost. She kneels before the bones and places the flowers beside the empty skull. She speaks delicate, simple words—the same words, repeating. A mantra. She bows her head low and water spills from her eyes.

The large one knows. She knows what the small one is thinking, what she's feeling. It surprises her. The slayers are not all alike. Their kind is rash and independent— sisterless and motherless despite their relations. The slayers are shallow of memory and emotion, but this little one is deep and considered. Her sadness and anger are for sisters.

The large one moves forward slowly, as softly as her kind can. The small one lifts her head. She hears the large one before she can see her, but she does not flee. She is not afraid of what comes. She fears only other slayers. She fears them greatly. The smell of slayer fear and sister love surrounds her.

They watch each other as the large one emerges from behind a hill. The small one stands and waits. The large approaches until they stand face to face. Water, salted, falls from the large one's eyes. The small one lifts an arm, her palm slanted upward. The large one lifts her trunk and wraps it gently around the small one's arm.

*C*roydon parried quick, then darted low and in with a jab. The air was humid. He pushed back and raised his sword en guarde. The haystack didn't move. His wooden point barely reached the hay's 'belly' and he placed his right foot wrong, twisting his ankle. He dropped onto a stump beside a pile of wood waiting to be split. Pain pierced his ankle and he rubbed it. He didn't feel the energy for practice or splitting wood.

It was late. The sun was already behind the hills and forest, making long shadows of the tall pines. He drank from the waterskin the farmer's sister, Elana, had brought him. Elana and her brother Mando, short for Armando, were old—much older than Nico. Their farm was one of several that raised food for the city and produced other goods. But while Elana and Mando could herd sheep, collect hens' eggs, and grow crops, they weren't up to cutting and splitting wood.

Croydon checked his chips. He was still less than halfway to the price of the steel sword the smith had quoted him.

Something cracked in the woods behind him. He turned and saw Kana stepping into the field from the forest. When she saw him, she froze. He stood gently and picked up the ax and a piece of wood. "I didn't see you there," he said. "You surprised me." He took a mighty swing at the wood, but his aim was off and he chipped a piece rather than split it in the middle. His ankle refused his weight.

"I . . . I did not see you either," she said. She stepped forward slowly, looking side to side like she had lost something.

He swung at the wood again with better results. "I was just taking a breather after practicing with the sword. João says I have to practice my footwork every day. 'Practice everything,' he says."

Kana stopped looking around and stepped closer to him, her hands held behind her back. "Ritual is good," she said. She looked up at him. Her eyes were perfect black pearls. "I medi-tate every evening to . . . to find my focus. We lose focus so easily. We get distracted."

"Do you meditate in the forest?"

"No . . . well, maybe."

"I was just wondering if that's why you were in the woods." He set the ax down. His ankle pinched with a stab of pain.

"Oh, I . . . I enjoy being in the forest. Being with nature helps me regain my strength. There is great power in the forest."

"There is?"

She looked around again and put her hand on his arm. "Croydon, would you walk with me back to the city?"

"Sure." Reluctantly, he broke the contact, picked up the waterskin and slung it over his shoulder, and then stuck the ax in the stump. By the time he had retrieved his sword and slung it in his sheath, she was already walking on the road. His ankle tightened with each step, but he was not about to limp. He caught up with her and fell into step. "How did you end up here?"

"I walked after work."

"No, I meant at the End of the World."

"Oh." She looked up at him. He couldn't find a word for her expression, but maybe relief? They continued walking. "When I was fifteen and Asami was thirteen, my uncle came to take us to the Royal City from our family home in the Green Province. Everything in our home was green. The hills, the yards, the village center, everything. It was lush and the forest was deep. Deep with magic, Uncle used to say.

"It was a lengthy journey to the Royal City. Our father and mother were already there. Our father performed some official duty for the shōgun, but I never knew what. We traveled by foot, and it rained steadily. Uncle carried most of our belong-ings. Asami and I carried only light packs, but we complained.

We were miserable girls. Uncle was furious at our spoiled nature.

"Then we came to a swollen freshet. Asami and I managed to cross, but Uncle, carrying most of our belongings, slipped. He vanished into the fog and rushing water. He called once or twice, but the sound of the water covered his voice. We were on a high bank of the stream and never saw him again, though we shouted to him."

She was silent for a moment, and he dared not break it. Then she continued. "We cried and wailed for hours. I knew Uncle wasn't coming back. I didn't know the way to the Royal City, but someone would, so I led Asami up the steep bank over wet leaves and then to the top of a rise and a wide forest. We did not know it then, but we had entered the forest here."

She looked around them as she spoke, as if expecting someone.

"What are you looking for?"

"Nothing, just looking."

"That's quite a story. I just walked across a bridge that shouldn't have been there."

"I have told no one," she said. "I have probably spoken more words to you now than I have ever said to anyone other than Asami." She stopped and looked up at him again. "Like Asami told me the first day you brought flour and she let you into the kitchen. I don't know why, but she trusted you. I trust you."

Nico had warned the feelings a teenage boy experiences sometimes are just raw things mixed in a pot that makes a bad stew. Listen more and talk less, wait for things to settle. He tried to heed that advice, but his breath came in short, ugly huffs.

"Have you found your magic?" she asked as they resumed walking.

"Uh . . . no, no magic."

"Well, I think it's your trustworthiness."

"That isn't magic."

"Sure it is. It is a rare gift."

He needed to think about that. And he didn't want her to stop talking. "When you arrived, who took you in?"

"We stayed at the Scale and Tentacle and worked there, then at the Salon and the Ballroom. One night, the Mayor's valet told me the Mayor wanted to see me about a job. She made me a clerk, then Minister of Commerce."

"And Asami cooks."

"Yes. She did."

He wanted to ask what Asami did now. He missed delivering flour and their brief talks, although the talking was all him. "I remember meeting the Mayor. Her office smelled like the woods and the fields. And she kept changing." They neared the city proper. Kana still looked around. He looked, too, but didn't know what they were searching for. There were so many questions he wanted to ask. Why did Asami stop cooking? What did they do for fun? Instead, he said, "I haven't been in the forest much. Just the path up to the Lookout. Are there many animals?"

She might have taken a half step instead of a full. "All kinds. Animals get stuck at the End of the World too."

"Are there monkeys?"

She smiled. "There are. We call them Nihonzaru and they come from my time, or at least from Japan."

"I'd like to see them," he said.

The man he'd seen before, wearing the 1700s clothing, stepped from between two houses and walked toward them. Kana slowed, looked down, and curled her fists. The man greeted them, removed his broad-brimmed hat and nodded to Kana then Croydon. "It's time for your meeting," he said to Kana. "I was afraid you might have gotten lost in the forest."

Kana said nothing but walked forward. The man fell in beside her.

Feeling uninvited to whatever grown-up meeting Kana had and obviously didn't want to attend, Croydon drifted behind them. He pretended to adjust his sword. "I would like to see those monkeys," he said.

Kana turned, but there was no smile. She shook her head. She looked sad and frightened, and something fell loose in his chest. Whatever trust she had didn't include inviting a fourteen-year-old boy to a meeting. But still, she clearly didn't want to attend. Why did she feel she had to? Adults had too much seriousness—and too many rules. At least he was free to limp the rest of the way home, although it was better not to let Shaday see. He'd have to ask Nico who the man was.

SEVERAL DAYS after his walk with Kana, Croydon's back ached from a new move João taught him. Nico had not known the man with Kana, but João did. Jacob van Neck, a Connectionist. The strangeness of Kana's reaction to Jacob stayed with Croydon. He and João took a rest against an oak under a bright mid-October sun.

"She didn't seem to want to go to the meeting."

"I'm sure she didn't. But as Minister of Commerce she has to meet with all sorts, even Connectionists if they have legitimate business."

"I guess."

"There's a new cropper about your age. You should meet him tonight at the Ventals'."

He should, and he supposed he would. But he couldn't shake the look on Kana's face that day. She was angry and frightened at the same time. Who was this Jacob, and what business was he in? "Do you know much about Jacob? What he's like?"

"I only know he and those he spends his time with cannot

earn or hold chip-value. They often try to pass fake chips. Chips painted to look like they have value."

"So he's a criminal?"

"If I catch him passing fake chips, yes. Otherwise, he is just another man, out-of-his-chips and harmless. He may have wanted something from the Mayor, or to get a message to her. He isn't allowed inside the palace without severe consequences."

"Consequences?"

"Those out-of-their-chips suffer a fate if they visit the palace a second time. It's the magic."

"I'm not sure he's so harmless. Kana looked upset. You should watch him a little closer."

João squeezed Croydon's neck. "I will, and I'll mention it to the Defense. We won't let anything happen to Kana."

"Thanks."

ANNE'S LAWS OF END OF THE WORLD PHENOMENA

There is a weaving between oasis and hearts
A cloth made to protect both
A single act may bring the unravelling.
- Notes of a Traveller

*S*he'd been free of the fools and traitors for six months now. They'd abandoned her and didn't deserve a place in the Connectionists. They were fucking liabilities. If you looked at any events that changed the world, small groups managed them. Often a single person. Brilliant individuals like Tesla and Edison started by themselves then moved forward with small teams, and like them the Connectionists were better off as a small, nimble group. Just herself, Jacob, Marta, and Frank. They would change the world; at least, the End of the World.

Anne sipped at her cold green tea. Better than home and that health concoction Maggie always made. Asami made everything better. Marta had finished a few touches on the veranda just a few weeks ago, and it had quickly become Anne's favorite place to ideate, especially with the unusual early November warmth. The months had been lean on opportunity and food since the escapade with John and Juli. Her spy had delivered useful information but no great secrets yet. The secret to the phenomena was so close, but was she getting any closer? She was thirty now. At thirty, she was supposed to be CEO of the hottest company in Silicon Valley. There had been no question.

The E266 breathalyzer was a miracle of technology and science. It performed up to 266 separate tests nearly instantly and indicated if you needed medical attention. The idea came to her while studying at Cal. It was Maggie, a professor of ancient mythology, who suggested 266 tests. She'd referenced the Dogon belief that within a cosmic egg was the material and structure of the universe and the 266 signs that embraced the essence of all things. It was perfect.

Anne envisioned an egg-shaped kiosk in every pharmacy, urgent care clinic, and medical office. Even on naval ships and army bases. People would blow into the breathalyzer and on-site tests would be performed on the composition of the water droplets, the amount of oxygen and other gasses present, and even the DNA inside the water droplets themselves.

It was a brilliant, world-changing idea worth billions. There were still issues to work out: there wasn't enough DNA in a breath for testing, breath collection was fraught with potential contamination, and the size and shape of the test equipment refused to adhere to the egg shape of the kiosk. The prototype's samples had to be analyzed in a lab, and the results were wildly inaccurate. But she was close, and investors, particularly the military, were lining up.

All gone.

At least she left a juicy mystery behind. The press must have loved the strange disappearance of the startup's founder.

∾

A VARIETY of ships and boats anchored in the harbor at the End of the World. Some unloaded cargo. They all eventually sailed away to the unknown. Anne could do that too. Start over in a place where she could use her intelligence and skills to build a new, and better, enterprise.

She could, but she wouldn't. There were beasts in the forest. There were storms and probably pirates at sea. The road leading in or out of town ended in places too deep in time, where there were dangers even historians had failed to report. She'd followed other croppers to the Lookout, high on the hill behind the farms above the forest. From there she'd seen a mushroom cloud in the distance and a squadron of buzzing drones dusting soldiers crawling across dunes with a sickening orange-pink haze. Distant cities and villagescapes appeared daily, but none of them brought a view of anything from the twentieth or twenty-first century. Time expanded. There were more moments, always more for the city to rub against.

No. The answer had to be here, inside the End of the World. Controlling the phenomena was the only way, and the Mayor was the key.

And there it was. It was so simple. How had she not seen it before?

"Jacob," she called.

He emerged at the doorway a moment later. "Yes?"

"Get your papers and quill. I have a proposal for the Mayor."

"A proposal? What sort of proposal?"

"There are rules that bind this town to the phenomena, wouldn't you agree?"

"I suppose. There is something beneath the palace, something no one is meant to see."

"And we know the Mayor navigates the town away from places."

"But what does she mean by that? It's not like the city is a ship."

"Yes it is, Jacob. It's just like one of your East India trading ships. Time is a river, and normally we're on a ship sailing straight with the flow toward an endless ocean. But this city is a faulty ship. It gets caught in eddies and whirlpools, and when the tide comes in from the universe's vast ocean, it pushes the city backward. The Mayor navigates away from the places the city gets caught in. I don't know how she does it yet, but have you noticed we've gone from winter to spring and now summer?"

"I have."

"But why should we? If she only moves the city away from places, there would be no seasons. Each day's weather would be random."

"But the farms couldn't grow crops and manage the live-stock if there weren't seasons."

"Exactly. That means the Mayor is directing the town toward places that match the seasons the town needs."

"You make her sound like a witch."

"If you believe in magic, isn't she? And didn't she tell us both when she met with us that she had to meet with each cropper?"

"That it was her duty to look out for all citizens of the city and to protect it from disruptive forces, presumably us."

"Well, we've stayed. We're citizens. It's time she looked out for our interests. I believe the phenomena binds her to do so, or she'll lose some control. Take this down."

She relayed her request to meet the Mayor. Jacob then folded and sealed the parchment and left to deliver it to the Mayor via her valet.

Anne sipped the tea and scratched Noble's head. Progress, at last.

ALMARISS ADJUSTED her hat and descended the steps of the Mayor's Palace. The first thing she noticed was Jacob van Neck striding toward her, regal and cool in his elegant, ruffled white blouse, trim black trousers, brimmed hat, and long boots. She sweated drops of the sun after being outside for just a moment, yet he looked as though he'd stepped out of a mid-spring morning.

"Ah, good Dockmaster," he said tipping his hat to her.

"Van Neck. Are you visiting the palace?"

"Not to enter, as that would be a rather final choice on my part."

"I was thinking so."

"I am delivering an official message for the Mayor from the Connectionists—to the Mayor's valet, if the door ministers will fetch him."

"I'll deliver the message."

Van Neck considered her for a moment. His eyes twitched in a side glance as he thought. "Very well. The Connectionists, represented by citizen Anne Fields, requests to meet the Mayor in the Commons tomorrow at midday." He handed her the parchment.

"You know the Mayor does not leave the palace."

"Yes, but that is the request nonetheless. Anne is in the same situation as I regarding entering the palace."

"Yes, I know her. And the purpose of this meeting?"

"To discuss terms of safe departure from the End of the World."

"Interesting." Almariss crossed her arms. "I'll inform the Mayor, but tell Anne it will be me she meets with."

Van Neck bowed in a flourish, donned his hat, and left.

ALMARISS RETURNED to the palace and found the Mayor behind her desk, staring at the Affinity Globe. She handed her the parchment and related van Neck's message.

The Mayor opened the parchment and glanced at it quickly.

"Can you read it—van Neck's Dutch?"

"I can. It requests only what he told you—a meeting to hear the demands of a citizen."

"What are they up to?" Almariss asked. "I mean, besides trying to lure you outside."

"Claiming citizenship means Anne believes my control of the magic connects to my duty to protect the citizens, and that this protection extends to her."

"Does it?"

"Yes, while she's here."

"But she doesn't want to be here. Shouldn't we encourage her to leave? She's been disruptive enough."

The Mayor pushed her cane against the floor and stood. "Minor disruptions. Her threat is no worse than many others before, but yes, we should again encourage her and her friends to leave. However, given the name of her group—the Connectionists—I don't think that's her true purpose. She's figured something out and has a design. Leaving on her own terms is a goal, but I fear it is not her plan."

"So what will you do?"

"Meet her demands as best I can."

THE NEXT MIDDAY was cold and rainy, like November should be. Almariss wore her hat and her long oil-slicked coat and waited in the Commons with Eristol and Lieutenant Tabray of the

Mayor's Defense. If Anne expected witnesses for this public meeting, there weren't any others than those they brought with them. The rain saw to that, but Anne would likely think it a conspiracy. Almariss watched as Anne, van Neck, and Frank Accosta strode onto the Commons.

"Lovely weather," Anne said. She wore a foul-looking beaver-hide shawl and her clinging trousers. Her low neon-green and orange shoes were mud stained. Her wolfhound tried to hide from the rain between her legs.

"The rain is fair enough. Your proposal?"

"The Mayor is bound to protect the people of the End of the World, correct?"

"She is."

"Then the Connectionists petition her to navigate—I believe that's her term—to navigate the city to a place of our choosing. A place we know will be safe for us."

"Unfortunately, she cannot do that."

"Why not? If she's navigating, she gets to decide where and when the city connects. That's how she manipulates the seasons and weather like today's. Don't deny."

"The Mayor's ability to navigate does not work as precisely as you believe. I will deliver your petition, but do not hope to receive the answer you require."

"Fuck you," Anne said, and she and her men left.

"And you." Almariss returned to the palace.

THE NEXT MORNING, Anne sat stewing on the veranda. It was cool, almost cold, but at least the air was clean. The previous day's rain had left the city smelling refreshed. The smell of sweat and dung was washed away for now, but with time and sun the stench would rise again, as would her desire to leave. She watched a ship sail away from the harbor with a full belly of something the End of the World didn't need. Where would it emerge once it left the city's reach? What would happen to it if it sailed into the sights of a fucking German U-boat?

"Excuse me," Jacob said. He approached from the steps, fresh from the city. "I have the Mayor's response."

"Tell me."

"She says she cannot agree to our request. She cannot choose precisely where the city ends up. She can, however, give us a few moments' notice if the next place fits a description of what we are looking for. Better than Lookout Hill, and we can leave as soon as the city stops."

Clever. She fulfilled her duty to the city and remained bound to the phenomena while not meeting the demand. A few moments' notice—of a place similar to what Anne describes? What would she describe?

"Miss Fields?"

"What?"

"It has not escaped my notice, or Marta's or Frank's, that you intend us to leave as a group to a place likely of your choosing, regardless of whether that choice is best for all of us. The issue is, you promised us control of the phenomena to depart as we each saw fit. Has this just been an exercise in learning more about the phenomena and the Mayor? Or do you intend us all to leave on your terms?"

If she described San Francisco in 2017 or 2020, or even Vancouver in 2021, could she manage? Could she find Maggie again? Or would she remain abandoned in some variation of the world that only looked familiar? Each time she looked at the horizon, dread chilled her like a cruel wind. It shivered her bones until they felt brittle. "What did you say, Jacob?"

"I asked what the purpose of this exercise has been. Are you giving up seeking control of the phenomena and trying to get us all to leave with you to wherever you wish to go, or are you manipulating the Mayor to reveal more about the phenomena?"

She lifted her tea to take a sip, but her stomach soured. She wanted to fucking leave. She glanced at the harbor. The ship had disappeared. She shivered and wanted to vomit. "The latter, Jacob. I need to understand more about the phenomena. I haven't learned enough yet, but I know some things for certain."

"What is our next move?"

"I'm uncertain. I need to ideate on it."

"Ideate?"

"Brainstorm."

"That doesn't sound at all pleasant."

She shook her head. Whatever she did next, she needed a few more people. Not a large group, but fucking quality people.

IT CAME FROM THE FUTURE TO THE END OF THE WORLD

We all have magic.
We carry with us the seeds of great power.
When planted in the oasis, it grows into something more than ourselves.
- Notes of a Traveller

João smelled the spring air, a scent laced with daffodils, tulips, and fresh grass . . . and a tug of bittersweet memory. If he closed his eyes, he could find himself in the village of Santiago da Guarda near his family home. But he didn't close his eyes, and he kept that memory at bay. Instead, he watched Lieutenant Tabray drill the Defense on the chill, sunlit Commons. She had them progressing nicely. They had not been well trained before he arrived, all of them raw recruits assembled from soldiers of various times and places. Now, they were at least organized and knew how to fight as a group. But were they ready if pressed to face a genuine threat? Soldiers lost their fighting abilities when they idled in peace too long; they lost their ability to set aside daily cares and have the courage to take a life. He'd longed for such peace, and now that he had it all he could do was worry about wars he wasn't fighting. Peace was a war, one soldiers couldn't win or even fight.

The hair on his nape bristled, making him shiver. The rhythm of the city pulsing through his feet and legs skipped a beat. A new cropper—three of them—stepped past the sign on the Goresetch road. The vision of new arrivals was normally a painting-perfect image, but this image was obscured by swirling rays of rainbow-hued light. He saw a tall man in tight clothing, and the one in the middle appeared male in form but he was obscured by a light that glowed as red and bright as the Finger Light. He could not see their faces.

João left the Commons and hurried to Main Street. Despite not having seen his face, the stranger was easy to spot. He was taller than his two companions, and everyone else for that matter. He wore a shiny red skull cap and a tight, single piece of clothing of darker red from neck to black boot top. The cropper scanned everything around him rapidly and grinned. The two walking with him were dressed similarly, but one was in blue and the other yellow.

João stepped to them. "Good day, travelers."

The tall man looked down at him. His eyes were colorless, the pupils defined only by a glassy ridge in the shape of a pupil. Even the iris was clear. "Superb day, sir. What is this place?"

"A fine city of decent-mannered people," João said. The clearness of the man's eyes was like looking at someone whose insides were made of water. "I am Commander Alejo. Allow me to escort you to the Mayor. She meets with all visitors."

"Does she? I don't believe I am a visitor. I like the feeling of this place. There's energy here like I've never felt before. I think we've found it, boys." The man glanced at the one in yellow. "This is the energy we saw on the Global Glamour Atlas."

"Nevertheless, the Mayor wishes to speak with you," João insisted.

"That is a strange custom. Perhaps one day you and I should discuss it over a beer."

Running footsteps sounded from behind, and João turned to see Eristol trotting toward him. "A word, Commander," Eristol said between huffs.

He stepped away from the croppers and bent so Eristol could speak. "Yes?"

"Do not bring this cropper to the palace. The Mayor insists. She's not ready to meet with him yet."

"That is unlike her."

"Yes, well, that's her message."

"Understood."

Eristol returned to the palace, and João turned again to the tall cropper. "You are free to explore the city."

"Yes, I am."

"The Mayor will wish to speak with you at some point."

The cropper said nothing, but he sauntered away toward the market, his fellow travelers in tow.

"The Scale and Tentacle will offer you a free meal and free bed for your first night," João called after them. "And ask for the Salon. Croppers find comfort there."

"I can find my own comfort, Commander."

The cropper's confident and ecstatic attitude was a contrast to most.

What was the Mayor up to? João strode to the palace and found the Mayor in her office. She had just finished with another cropper, a man well into his seventies who looked confused and sad as he passed João. The Mayor stood behind her desk, looking older than the gentleman. She leaned heavily on her cane.

"I want that man followed night and day," the Mayor said.

"That man?" he asked, pointing to the doorway.

"No, the one you spoke with, the cropper with two followers."

"How—"

"He carries something with him that is very dangerous. He must not enter this building while he carries it." Her form wavered and she became a child. It was always difficult to take orders from the child version of her, but her eyes and the three streaks of gray hair reminded him this was still the Mayor.

"If he's such a threat, why not escort him out as usual when you deem it necessary?"

"I do not believe you can, and there's no deeming about it. The magic informs. I simply observe and sense. This man brings his own magic power, potentially a great disturbance. No one before has entered the city with that kind of energy. Few are aware of their own power, but he is very aware. An attempt to remove him forcibly might lead to a disaster. Just follow, observe, and report until I can figure out what to do."

"What if he does something overtly threatening to the public?"

"Then you will have to protect them as best you can. Make it known to your most trusted Brigade leaders that they are to be ready. Put them on alert, but do not tell them why. I need to know what this man is capable of and what he is planning before I can figure out how to thwart him."

João noticed the Mayor did not say *if* she needed to thwart the man. It was a fact. He saluted and left the palace to find Padrok, the Brigade's captain.

CROYDON SAT in his favorite upholstered chair in the Salon. He came once a week, hoping there would be a new cropper his age. There had been a few, and he'd made two friends. John was from Alaska during the Gold Rush, and Thato was from an African tribe on the Vaal river. He had seen white people for the first time only a month before, when he'd walked into the city while hunting. The only problems with Croydon's new friends were that John had already left the city and Thato was difficult to engage with, a loner.

This week there was no one his age, but there was a new cropper named Zosimos. He said he was a magician.

The magic of the city, like Nico and Shaday's, Croydon had accepted as interesting and useful. João's ability to know who arrived and who left was important. It had taken a while to adjust to the various magic people could perform, to accept that it was real. But unless his entire existence at the city was a dream, magic was very real. Still, none of that magic was entertaining, and Zosimos promised entertainment.

The Salon was full. Croydon sipped the last of his special root beer, which Asami had brewed. She had made kegs of it, but now it was gone. He wished she still cooked. Why had she stopped? Did she lose her magic? Kana had never provided an answer other than that she no longer worked in their kitchen and would not leave their house. João had reported no wrongdoing by van Neck, and Croydon had even followed the man around the city a few times but didn't learn anything useful. Van Neck met with Kana regularly, but the rest of the time he was at the harbor or the market. Sometimes he went with another man, who was heavily muscled and bald, into the Fated Gale. Croydon couldn't bring himself to ask Kana about him. Prying seemed like something she'd told him once, about tramping in someone's garden.

Harmony Vental stepped onto the small platform that served as a stage. A bright lantern radiated around her. She wore a form-fitting sparkling red gown, and her bright golden hair was piled in waves on her head. She smiled with perfectly white teeth. If she had been in his time, she would have been a movie or TV star. He had no idea what she had been in her own time.

"Good people," she said. She threw her arms open in a broad gesture. "Tonight, we have a new entertainment like you've never seen before. Welcome, Zosimos the Akhmim!"

The audience applauded, and Croydon joined them fervently. A tall man wearing a red plastic helmet and tight red unitard took the stage.

"Thank you. I will not bore you with preamble but get right to the point. You sir, may I have your hat?"

A man near the stage tossed Zosimos his hat. Zosimos caught it and placed it gently on the floor, then he hovered his hand over the hat and said, "Rise." The hat lifted from the floor and floated around the stage. When Zosimos waved his hand at the audience, the hat flew over them like a bird. Then he pointed to the hat's owner and the hat returned to his head.

The audience burst into applause. Before they stopped, Zosimos pulled a metal plate from a table behind him. He placed it, floating, in the air, then set an ordinary-looking pine cone on the plate. He looked at the audience, smiled, winked, and said, "Fire." The pine cone burst into flame. The audience applauded loudly again.

Zosimos kept the magic coming. He made a mug of ale erupt and spray everyone close to the stage by speaking only the word, "Flood." He played at the air with his hands like he was making a snowball, and when he had finished, he held something between his forefinger and thumb about the size of a golf ball, but clear and wavy. He let it float and said, "Burst." It exploded like a large firework and made Croydon's ears ring.

After demonstrating his abilities for nearly an hour, he stood at the front of the stage and said, "Good evening." Then he vanished. The audience roared. The lamps flickered and came to full bright, and Harmony took the stage.

"Well, wasn't that amazing? Zosimos the Akhmim!" The audience shouted and clapped for more, but Zosimos did not return. Eventually, everyone filed out of the Salon and Croydon dashed home. He couldn't wait to tell Nico and Shaday what he'd seen.

THE COTTAGE HAD EXPANDED to now house five rooms: three bedrooms, a kitchen, and the sitting room with the fireplace. Nico and Shaday sat at the table in the kitchen under the soft glow of two lamps. Shaday wove a tiny basket while Nico read a small Portuguese book João had given him, which was described as a pocket guide to the duties of a soldier. Nico had also taken down the map that usually hung on the wall. It was a circular map of the city that Nico said had led him to the End of the World. He was looking at the back of it, which was covered in tiny Japanese or Chinese characters. He and Nico had gazed at the map several times and puzzled over the writing. Nico remarked each time that he should take the map to Kana, but he kept it on the wall. Croydon never asked why. Right now, Zosimos's magic consumed his attention.

He described the performance. Shaday was wide-eyed, but Nico just nodded. "He was fantastic, like the magicians on TV," Croydon said.

"TV?" Nico asked.

"Um—like a stage performance, but in little pictures on devices in our homes. Everyone can see it at the same time."

"I don't really—"

"Never mind. This guy, though, he made things float and catch fire, and then at the end, he vanished."

"Sounds impressive."

"The ladies and I will have to see his next performance," Shaday said. "Did Harmony say when that would be?"

"Tomorrow."

"Did he charge?" asked Nico.

"The Ventals never charge," Shaday said.

"I know, but did this Zosimos seek tips or anything after the performance?"

"No. We never saw him after he vanished." Croydon helped himself to a slice of bread and some cheese. He missed Asami's light, herb-flavored bread.

"I don't like it," Nico said.

"What are you thinking?" Shaday set her work on the table. "He's just an entertainer. No different from musicians and actors. Nice to have something new for a change. The tumblers were fun a few years back, but they left after a week." She studied the basket she was working on. It was simple, like those used to collect fresh berries. "There, that one's done. How many did you want?" she asked Nico.

"A dozen."

"Do you think I'll be able to do magic?" Croydon asked.

"Likely so," Shaday said. She stood and placed her hands on his shoulders. "Once you get through puberty."

"I think he's through it," Nico said.

"Why would that make any difference?" Croydon asked. Nico's pronouncement was welcome news, but what he really wanted was magic of his own.

"Who knows? Maybe it doesn't, but I don't recall the younger children ever reporting magic."

"I bet the Mayor knows. Doesn't she know everything about this place?"

"I suppose," Nico said. "But you'll find your magic soon enough."

"Kana said she thought it was my trustworthiness, but that's not magic."

"It might be," Shaday said. "You are an earnest boy, and João is an outstanding man to learn from." Nico cleared his throat. "And Nico's been your best influence."

"Being trusted doesn't feel like magic." He looked at Nico, who stared at the map again, drawing a finger along the Goresetch road to the edge of the circle where it ended. Other roads existed outside the map but did not connect to it. "How do you know I'm done with puberty? I don't feel normal yet."

"It takes as long as it takes. But your old normal won't return. You're becoming an adult. What interested you as a child won't seem so interesting."

"I want magic, and I still want a sword."

"Endless fates," Shaday sighed. "Why do men obsess over weapons?" She left them for her bedroom.

"Are we obsessed with weapons?"

"Not obsessed with weapons," Nico said, turning from the map to his reading. "But we are obsessed by the trouble they bring and the trouble they protect against. And it's not just men. Look at Lieutenant Tabray."

"What do you mean the trouble they bring? João and the Defense don't bring trouble, they defend against it."

"Where there are people with weapons, other people with weapons are sure to find and challenge them. And that's not to say the weaponless are safe. Some with weapons give no heed to innocents in war, or invasion."

Croydon cut another slice of bread.

"Have you finished your numbers? I don't want to see another note from Headmaster Ardens that you've shirked your lessons."

Croydon shoved the slice into his mouth, rewrapped the bread, and headed for his room. School wasn't any different at the End of the World. He hated math just as much. "Did you ask Kana about the writing on that map?" he asked over his shoulder.

"No. But I will."

STINA ONLY HAD two free nights a week. She spent one, based on the Defense's rotations, with João. If there was music or a play, they went to the Salon. She spent Monday nights at the Salon as well, but with Almariss and Shaday. This Monday it was all about the entertainment. The great Zosimos the Akhmim was to perform right, proper magic. The city buzzed over his performances. She hadn't seen a magician since her father had taken her to the London Theater when she was twelve. She couldn't recall that magician's name, but he'd been funny.

She met Almariss walking up the street from the harbor. The entrance to the Salon was lit with many lanterns in shades of red, yellow, blue, and green. There was a line waiting outside for the Ventals to open the doors.

"Zosimos has made quite a name for himself already," she said to Almariss.

"Yes, but the Mayor hasn't requested him for a visit yet."

"João mentioned it at dinner last night. She doesn't seem to trust him."

"Neither do I."

"Why is that?"

"I can't put my finger on it. I can see he has some terrible memories, the kind that change a person and sometimes not positive changes. He's more than he seems."

"Has he told anyone where or when he came from?" They reached the end of the line.

"Nico chatted with him in the market this morning. He didn't reveal much, but apparently he says he came out of the year 2304."

"Three hundred years into my future? Wow." What was the world like that many years after hers? What science did they have? Had they colonized Mars? Cured cancer? She would chat up Zosimos herself if she could meet him.

Shaday arrived. "Such a crowd," she said. "Croydon did say he was a wonder."

They filed in with the rest and found spots on temporary

benches the Ventals had set up for Zosimos's performances. They were jammed elbow to elbow and five rows deep. The cacophony of hearts beating inside Stina's chest threatened to crush her own.

The central lamp lit Harmony Vental as she took the stage wearing a long, flowing, diaphanous blue dress. "Dear friends, tonight I present, for your entertainment, Zosimos the Akhmim!"

The audience applauded, and the lamp focused on three deep red chips floating over the stage.

Stina heard Almariss groan and then fall away from her side onto the floor. "Almariss!" She leaned over but couldn't see Almariss's face in the dark. The aisle was full of legs and feet.

Shaday leaped up. "Is she all right?" Those seated nearby sat frozen, caught in the surprise of seeing the dockmaster fall. The lamps brightened.

"Move or help, Davious!" Stina shouted at the man closest to Almariss's head. Almariss still hadn't moved. "Help me get her outside." Davious was a sturdy man, not as tall as Almariss but strong enough to lift her shoulders off the floor.

"She needs fresh air," said Shaday.

Stina grabbed Almariss's feet. Others came to help now and placed their arms under her body. They jostled and stumbled their way out of the Salon to the back patio, where Harmony and Wilcott had laid out a blanket and pillow. The helpers laid Almariss down on the blanket.

"I'll send for Physiker Korbath," Wilcott said.

Stina kneeled on one side of Almariss's head and Shaday on the other. Shaday held her hand.

"Is she breathing?" asked Harmony.

Stina listened at Almariss's mouth and nose and watched her chest. "Yes, she's breathing." She felt the beat of Almariss's heart, hard and rapid, as if she were running and not lying on the patio floor.

"Everyone back inside," Harmony said. "Give her room. The physiker will be here soon. She'll be fine."

All but the Ventals and one woman returned inside. The woman wore a heavy sweater and tight but threadbare Urbletics. Stina had never seen her before. She would have remembered the athletic clothing; she had several pairs just like them back in her time.

"Interesting," the woman said, then she went inside.

Almariss groaned again. Her eyes opened, and she blinked as if waking from a long sleep.

"Oh, thank the fates," Shaday said. "Are you all right?"

"I . . . I don't know. I think so, now."

"You passed out," Stina said. "Out cold. You sick?"

"Maybe. I've got to get to the Mayor."

"Just sit. Physiker Korbath will be here shortly."

Almariss pushed herself up and started for the steps. Wilcott and Harmony reached for her, but she batted their hands away. "I'm fine. I must see the Mayor."

Stina pulled Shaday up and they both followed. "We're coming with you."

Almariss whirled on them. "No. This isn't for you." Then she turned and strode into the dim streets. "Stina," she called without turning. "Fetch my hat and pipe. I'll pick them up tomorrow."

"What the bloody hell was that all about?" Stina asked.

"I've never seen her like this." Shaday gripped Stina's arm.

Inside, the audience clapped. The show had resumed. Wilcott folded the blanket and Harmony opened the door for them. "Ladies."

Stina looked at Shaday, who was looking at her, likely with the same thought. "Not tonight, Harmony. Thank you."

Harmony nodded kindly. "I understand."

.   .   .

"You've got to meet with him," Almariss said. She had found the Mayor sitting in her office, in the dark except for a single lit candle on her desk. "If he's trouble, have João escort him away." The Mayor stared at the Affinity Globe. It spun, but slowly and not at a steady pace. Each rotation was faster or slower than the previous. That was enough evidence to confirm Almariss's suspicions. A disturbance.

"I do not know if he is a danger or a boon."

"Isn't that enough reason to meet with him?"

"The danger he may pose flows in a single direction. If I open that path and he is dangerous, there is no recovery. It will be too late instantly."

"You mean if he steps foot in the palace and means to do harm—"

"I will not be able to remove him. Nor will João, not with the Defense nor the Brigade."

Almariss paced. She wished she had her pipe, but then again that might make her feel worse if she drew closer to the magic.

"Tell me what you felt again," the Mayor said.

She didn't want to relive it. It hadn't been a physical pain, but an emotional one. Like those first days when the Mayor had stepped away from their romance.

"You've come much closer to the power than I imagined," the Mayor said. "It was a mistake for me to allow it. Not the first mistake my heart has led me to in relation to you."

Almariss sighed. "The room spun. I was nauseous. Then I felt something breaking—no, tearing. Like layers of my soul peeling away. His magic burned against me, and his memories. He's walled them off but he draws on them to amplify his power. I couldn't see him, but where I imagined him to be there was a bright aura, and he laughed. He was deliriously happy. He is strong."

"The strongest ever, and he might also be drawing upon the

191

energy of the city. That is why he cannot come here. If he were to control the Fount, I would never regain control. The city would be his."

"Does he know?"

"I don't think he knows entirely yet, which is our only advantage. If he knew, he would have come here at once. His dallying with entertainment fills some vanity of his. João and the Defense have been following him. He's courting the citizens, trying to win them over and using magic to do it. He's passing glamours over them. Recruiting them, but to what purpose beyond simply liking him, I can't tell."

"All the more reason to have João escort him and his assistants out of the city."

"Like I said, I don't believe they could."

JoÃo LED ALL twelve members of the Defense and the four members of the Brigade—Padrok, Nico, Abeo, and Datu—to the Salon. "Surround the building. Keep your weapons covered. Blend in with the crowd as they leave, but do not let him or his assistants slip by."

"But if they're invisible?" Private Sai asked. Others snickered. João ignored him and waved everyone to take positions.

They waited. Applause erupted several times, then people filed out. The patrons excitedly recounted the magic they had witnessed, especially the magician's levitation and final disappearance. Mostly they ignored the Defense and Brigade spread among them or only waved and offered simple greetings or nods.

Once the crowd had dispersed into the night, Zosimos's two assistants emerged from the Salon. The darkness between them rippled as they walked, then formed into a shadow which solidified into Zosimos.

"Outstanding evening, Commander."

"Zosimos. Another entertaining show?"

"Very, yes. The people of this fair city seem to love good magic."

"We do, but I am afraid your magic does not fit. You and your assistants must leave the city."

"That sounds like discrimination based on magic. Your city's magic is good, therefore my magic is bad? I suppose I'm not surprised a backward city would hold such views. Like all the racial, sexual, economic, and you-name-it discrimination prior to the twenty-third century, different is judged as dangerous. But you have no proof I'm a threat. I'm only an entertainer. I sought and found your city to provide magic like no one has ever seen."

"Your magic is real, not entertainment." The Defense and Brigade stepped toward them and surrounded Zosimos and his assistants.

Zosimos laughed. "Of course it's real. I studied the magic sciences for ten years. I understand it deeply."

"Magic science?"

"People learned long ago, in the twenty-second century, that magic was not some mystical, never-to-be-understood, or superstitious thing. The scientific unknown is just magic we don't understand. Once we understood magic, we undid the mysteries of science. And this place has made my magic strong. We have no intention of leaving."

"We'll force you."

Zosimos laughed. "Swords against magic? You don't even have gunpowder. Why haven't you? I find it odd you've never picked up any guns or gunpowder in all the places this city in its timeless vortex has bumped against."

"I have such a cache, but I prefer not to inflict horrible collateral damage on my citizens."

The man's eyes might have tinted a pale green color, like a stain in their perfectly clear glass pupils. Something vibrated in

João's feet, or under them. Not the comfortable hum of the city, but something sharp. The man was using magic against him.

Zosimos's face was now devoid of a smile. "Well, if you will force us to leave, you'd better get your guns."

"Defense!"

The Defense and Brigade drew their swords and rushed the magician, but he and his assistants vanished. Padrok fell heavily against João and his sword sliced against João's ankle.

Someone grabbed João's head and lifted him off the ground. It felt like his head would separate from his neck. Something inside drained away, leaving him with a numb exhaustion like after a long, intense battle. Whatever held him let go, and he crumpled to the street.

Nico was first to his side, then the others. João could not speak.

"He's alive," he heard Nico say. "Someone get Korbath."

HE WOKE to the smell of sage, pine, and candle smoke. The air was icy. He opened his eyes to bright candlelight and found the Mayor standing over him. The cut in his ankle stung, but not badly. He could feel that it was wrapped tightly and that he was seated. He tried to stand, but he was still weak—exhausted—and only fell back.

"I knew you would try," the Mayor said. She was gray and old. She looked as weary as he felt. They were in her office.

"What is he?"

"A magician."

"But he drained my strength."

"More. He took your magic."

At her words, he felt the truth of them. There was a quiet where there was once a comforting hum. An emptiness. Once he'd realized he had magic, he couldn't imagine not having it.

It was like it had always been there. King Sebastião would have called it the Devil's work, but it was as natural as breathing. And it was gone.

"Why am I here?"

"Physiker Korbath bandaged your ankle but thought you needed a different kind of healing."

"You can restore my magic?"

"No. I didn't give it to you, and I can't return it to you."

Too great to hope. If she could just help him regain his strength, it would have to be enough.

"Who knows," she said. "If the power once favored you with magic, it may again." She lifted a few pine nuts from a bowl on her desk and placed them into her mouth. When she had eaten a couple, she continued. "We need to remove Zosimos as soon as possible, but not with swords. It needs to be with cunning and quickness. His presence and his ability to tap into the magic could be disastrous for the city. If he knew the source, he would take it for his own use."

"Could he use it all?"

"No. It would use him first. But if the disturbance was great enough to land the city in a time and place permanently, the magic could dissipate. The magic would consume first, and he would dissipate with it, but we would lose it. The city would be just another place."

"What would happen to you?"

"I would die. I've lived well beyond my years, but the power sustains me. Others—many others—would die too."

The confirmation that those who remained in the city gained immortality made him dizzy. He chose not to think about it just yet. "What do you wish me to do?"

"For the moment, go back to the barracks and rest."

"Does Stina know?"

"Know what? That you were fool enough to try saving the world with just a sword? She knows. She's waiting outside."

What was he supposed to have done? He was commander of the Defense. It was his duty. "How do we defend against Zosimos?"

"I'm still working on that. Cunning, misdirection, and quickness are what any magician relies on. We must divert, be more cunning, and become far quicker. Go rest."

He limped out of the office and into the ministerial offices. Stina was there with her arms crossed and head cocked to one side. "Once a warrior, always a warrior, I suppose," she said.

"Always a fool."

She slipped her slender arm under his and he leaned toward her, though his limp wasn't bad. The strength of her arm was reassuring, and he leaned just a little more.

CHOICES AT THE END OF THE WORLD

Not all paths lead to the golden city.
The road makes a single promise:
To lead you to, or away.
The choice belongs to you.
- Notes of a Traveller

The Mayor paced, leaning on her cane though she was the vibrant twenty-year-old version of herself. Almariss sat in front of the game table, but there was no game laid out tonight. There was plenty of tea, and she helped herself to a third cup.

"I heard about João."

"He will recover." The Mayor stopped pacing and pointed her cane at the Affinity Globe. "We've escaped a minor crisis. Look."

Its spinning was more regular, but still not normal. "It's growing stable?"

"It is, though I've had difficulty detaching. But the more we remain disconnected, the quicker the power should stabilize."

"Then Zosimos is not a threat?"

"He is most certainly a threat. He just isn't using his magic now. He hasn't scheduled another performance, has he?"

"Not that I know."

"He's had a taste of what it means to draw strength from the magic here. He'll want more."

"I don't understand. How?"

"He brought his own magic here. His own power. In his time, they learned to find their interior sources of personal power and use it. But here, he's found a source greater than his own."

"If we try to force him to leave, he'll just draw on the magic of the city and grow stronger."

"Exactly. And maybe tip us into a permanency that dissipates the magic altogether. He won't be a threat then, but it will be too late for us and the city."

What the Mayor was saying hit her. They and others connected to the power beyond their normal life spans would die without it. Long life wasn't for everyone; some sought a more natural death and eventually left the city. But she did not want to die. Not as long as the Mayor lived. "How do we prevent this? All he has to do is wander through the city and eventually find the source, if he hasn't already. He's found the Finger Light. He and his assistants are staying there."

"João said Zosimos's people mastered the science of magic. They studied and learned it, which means they have to remember how to use it."

"He isn't likely to forget."

"Actually, he might. You mentioned the wall inside him hiding his memories." The Mayor thumped her cane on the floor twice. "That's it."

"What is?"

"I have a task for Shaday and Nico. Tonight. Now."

∼

I⊤ WAS PAST MIDDLE-NIGHT, and the streets were vacant except for the Defense sentries. Could something so simple work? Almariss left the palace for Shaday and Nico's cottage by the sea. The Mayor's plan was to use a simple distraction. Zosimos had shown himself drawn to signs of the city's magic, so they needed a powerful distraction.

Shaday opened the cottage door and let her in. Nico made tea.

"Zosimos is a danger—a significant danger," she told them.

"I knew it," Nico said.

"But the Defense cannot attack him or force him out of town. We need your help."

"What can we do?" Shaday asked.

"The Mayor wants a basket of your special weave in the shape of an inverted bowl."

"No problem, but how will that help?" Shaday immediately pulled out her reeds.

"Part of a distraction. Nico, we'll need a glass, large and in the same shape as the infinity knot of the palace banner."

"She wants a Memory Glass?"

"Yes." Then she explained the rest of the Mayor's plan.

Shaday constructed a glimmering, inverted basket shaped like a mound the size of half a melon. Nico, with Croydon's help, took the Mayor's infinity knot design to Pearcy, the glass-blower. While Shaday and Pearcy worked, Almariss ran through the streets, past Lookout Road and Lookout Hill, to Elana and Mando's farm. Despite the deep hour of night, they welcomed her and she explained the Mayor's request. Then she went to Laraine, the dressmaker, and last she stopped at Kana's. She would have brought Asami, too, but Kana said she was ill. They assembled at Shaday and Nico's cottage just before sunrise.

Nico and Croydon returned with a beautiful glass infinity knot and attached it to the top of Shaday's wicker mound. But it was not yet complete. They needed something powerful inside the knot.

She, Elana, Mando, Laraine, and Kana were some of the longest-lived citizens of the city. Each of them added memories to the knot, and even Shaday, Nico, and Croydon added their own. While memories captured in glass still belonged to the owner, they were much more difficult to retrieve, especially if the glass wasn't close to the memory's owner. No one would own this glass, so no one put memories of great value in it. Some were dreadful things they didn't want to recall, but they were still powerful memories. Others donated simple but significant recollections of the city. Decades and decades built into centuries of memory. When they were finished, the knot pulsed a rainbow of colors, swirling clouds that entwined with an inky purple and gray. The magic inside was palpable.

"That's a lot of memory," Nico said.

"Let's hope it's enough to draw Zosimos's attention." Almariss thanked everyone for their effort, and they returned to their homes.

After sunrise, João arrived. He limped slightly but seemed healthy. "Is it ready?" he asked.

"It is," Nico replied.

"Good. Tonight you, Almariss, and I will take it to the church."

"Nico," Shaday said. "Be careful."

"I will. I'm just there to activate the magic."

"Yes, but who knows what will happen then."

Almariss agreed. Zosimos might already be strong enough to drain the energy of the knot along with her and Nico's magic, just as he had done with João.

～

LATE THAT NIGHT SHE, Nico, and João arrived at the tiny church of St. Christopher's. Private Sai was stationed at the front doors, and João and the others slipped in through the rear door. Nico carried the basket and glass knot.

"Put it in the nave," João said. "No one will notice. This place doesn't get visited much since Father Al left. Few Catholics remain in the city."

"Don't you still come here?" Almariss asked.

"I do, but there is no service. I come to pray and ponder. I ponder more than I pray."

Nico placed the basket and knot in the nave. "How long do you think it will take him to find this?"

"I don't know," Almariss said. "Hopefully it will be a brighter, flashier energy to him than anything else in the city."

"The guards will watch night and day," said João. "That should help make this place look more important."

"But if he wants in badly enough, he might do to them what he did to you."

João shrugged. "That is the duty."

All they could do was wait and watch. The plan was for Nico to stay hidden inside the church at all times. Almariss would stay the nights with him but she couldn't leave the harbor untended, and João would come several times during the day. Hopefully Zosimos wouldn't approach during the day. If he did, she would have to run from the harbor to the church.

João left them for the barracks just across the street. Almariss slept lightly and not for long. The hard pews were meant to keep you awake.

In the predawn, she left Nico and the church via the rear door and walked to the harbor. She scanned the gray horizon above the sea. The waves were tall and white-tipped. Something seemed off, but she couldn't identify it. No ships approached.

~

DURING THE LATE AFTERNOON, Zosimos and his assistants walked past her house and into the city. Lieutenant Tabray, in civilian clothes, trailed them. Almariss finished her tallying while the sun set, then she stopped at home for some bread and sausage. While she ate, she looked out the window toward the end of the quay and the Finger Light. The red glowing light warning sailors away from the quay's finger was out. Zosimos had drained the light's power. She packed a pouch of pine and sage for her pipe and some bread and sausage for Nico.

When she walked past the Commons, she saw Anne and her wolfhound. A week ago, she would have wondered what the woman was up to, but tonight she didn't care. Zosimos was a bigger, more urgent threat.

~

NICO PACED. Almariss tried to sleep huddled against the end of a pew. She never understood the pull of complicated religions. João was Catholic. There were others who were Buddhists, Zoroastrians, and Taoists. Many with complex rituals and rites. Those things vexed the time she had left behind. Neighboring villages had warred with each other over which god or goddess was true, but Almariss's family and much of her small town were not religious, and they were spared most of the violence. They had poetry, sung and spoken, and believed not in the stars or heavens or hells. They believed in each other. If you didn't, nature ended you swiftly. Through her time as dockmaster in the city, she had learned so much about the world and all the times and places in it, but few knew as much about people as her own.

The glass knot cast a spinning rainbow light against the church walls, and the symbolic wooden cross on the wall appeared to warp and bend. Even João's god wavered in the reflected power of shared memory, or was it energized by it?

The rear door clicked open, and a wooden step creaked. Nico bolted behind the nave.

There was probably no hiding from Zosimos, and that wasn't the plan. Confrontation was the plan. She stood up and waited for him to appear. He slowly melted into view under the colored light. He held out a hand and looked at it, apparently surprised his hand was visible. Then he reached for and took the color-pulsing glass knot.

"I knew you would be drawn to this," Almariss said. "And yes, I can see you."

If she surprised him, he didn't show it. "Can't fool one immersed in the magic," he said. "I knew you were connected to it, the way you reacted to me. Many of you connect to the city's magic, which is useful to me."

"Useful?"

"Hiding the magic inside a church was not terribly clever. It's easy to spot the difference between spiritual power and magic. And you know you cannot prevent me from taking it, so why watch me do it? Your mayor isn't here. She will not watch me take her magic."

Almariss swallowed. "Like you, I'm a student of magic. I'm curious. For me, magic comes naturally, but you learned yours."

"You spoke with the commander. Yes, I mentioned it before I took his magic."

"When you did that, did you feel nothing? Were you oblivious to what he felt and what the magic was doing to you?"

"I was aware—"

"Aware that magic flows in all directions at once? They did teach you that in your magic university, didn't they?" She had to press now, to get him to dredge up memories and the specific memory of how he did things. If not, he would drain the knot, and her and Nico, and he'd eventually tap into the magic of the city.

"We call it the Chronos Property, although that's a poor name for it since Chronos flows only one way."

"How will you defend yourself from the magic? It will see you as a powerful source and seek to use you. I know you don't use charms or spells, so how will you conjure a defense?"

"It's simple," Zosimos said. "I think of what I need and arrange the molecules and atoms of the world in my favor."

It had to be now. All or nothing. If the Mayor had miscalculated, Almariss was going to be dead. Fitting. Perhaps it was time after all. Perhaps it was best to die before the Mayor, because how awful would it be to survive her? She sought and found the magician's colorless eyes while her own beckoned with azure. She felt the light of magic that was not light beam from her and connect to his eyes. It was hot on her end and cold on his. "Defend this."

Zosimos took a step back, clutching the knot. "With ease."

She could see him working, or at least his emotions working. She laid them bare. Clawed a hole in his wall of feelings. She looked into his memories through her own, caught in the glass he held. She knew all his efforts and failures. Others had belittled him because of his intelligence, bullied him, and he became the bully once he mastered magic. He floundered at love. Two relationships. One with a woman had ended with her draining him, in a sense; she took every material thing from him, but mostly she took his pride, and worse—his confidence. The other, a male, had used him and his magic almost as slave labor. He did the work while his partner enjoyed the benefits. Working magic in his time was an easily exploitable resource. Magic had become so common no one noticed it. It awed no one, and no one paid what the effort was worth.

Something happened to the partner. She probed deeper. Zosimos struggled to protect himself from her and the memories in the glass which clouded his own. As long as he remained defensive she was safe, but if he chose instead to draw upon the magic, she was finished.

She found it.

Zosimos had attacked his partner's power. He had soaked up whatever power his partner had, and his partner literally faded away—too thin and weak to keep breathing. Zosimos was a killer. She delved into his deepest emotion, tied to his strongest memory.

"That was a neat trick," he said. He was fully visible now, and his smile was wide and out of place, as if he couldn't control it. He squeezed his eyes shut, then took one hand from the knot and raised it toward her.

Almariss braced herself, but she felt nothing. Had it worked?

"I will rip the magic from you and this city, and you'll feel every inch of the flaying."

Still, nothing happened. "Can't quite recall how to do it?" she asked.

"I know how. Just a second ago—it was there, it will come back."

As he struggled to remember, Nico jumped from behind the nave and tore the knot from Zosimos's hand, then he fled as João and Private Sai rushed in.

"What—"

"Memory is a funny thing," Almariss said. "It can be fleeting."

"I know how to—"

"You once knew, but you've forgotten. Perhaps you'd like to meet with the Mayor now? I'm sure she's willing to meet with you." Whatever Zosimos might recall of his power would not be clear or complete—a dangerous predicament for a wielder of magic.

"How did you—"

"I did nothing but look into your emotions. A small gift from the city. Apparently the city took a great deal from you. Just like I said it would."

JOÃO SAW Zosimos clearly for the first time in the bright light of the Mayor's office. Zosimos's eyes were still transparent, but there was a stain of weary red in them. He had the look of a cropper now. The Mayor, middle-aged, held her attention on the spinning globe. She warped in the light and then appeared to be a twelve-year-old girl.

"You face the same choice as any cropper," she said. "You can leave or you may stay, but earning a living here will be difficult. What you will find outside the city today or tomorrow, I can't tell you. But you do have a choice."

He shook his head. "Not really. Without my magic, I have no skills. It will be difficult for me to get by anywhere. Why would it be more so here?"

"Your emotional past is more of a burden here. Out there, no one will know, but this city knows. It knows you more clearly than you know yourself. It remembers what you did and knows what you might do."

"Just as it knows you. You've been too close to this magic for far too long. Look what it's done to you. You can't maintain your authentic form for more than a few moments. How long before you cannot hold it at all?"

"There is always a cost. I've been willing to pay that price for the safety and preservation of this city and its people. A day will come when I am unable to pay it and someone else will have to."

"Steep price for helping others."

"You need not decide today or tomorrow. When to stay or go is also a choice."

"I've already decided. This is no longer a place I can trust."

He rose to leave.

"What about your assistants?"

"They can make their own choices. Good day."

After he left, the Mayor turned to João. "He's wrong. The End of the World is the one place he can trust."

ANNE WATCHED the magician leave the palace. He was not in a particular hurry, but he walked directly down Main Street and toward the Goresetch road. It was the first time she had seen him without his two assistants, but she knew where they were. They were fond of gambling, and she had sent Frank to keep them busy while she monitored Zosimos. She hadn't been sure what to expect. An explosion had not been out of the question. He also might not have left if he suffered whatever fate had befallen John and Juli.

His presence outside, and his lone departure, confirmed much of what she guessed from the bits of information Kana had provided. The phenomena he'd brought into city had definitely caused issues with the city's own. Issues big enough to prevent the Mayor from seeing him right away. The Mayor was vulnerable to outside power, and that was worth knowing, but Anne suspected the real nature of the issue was with the phenomena itself. Zosimos had somehow been defanged and was no longer a threat, and the Mayor had not wanted him inside the palace while he was a threat. Kana had provided enough information to know that something inside the palace —probably under it, as Jacob noted—was very special and off limits to everyone.

She couldn't step into that fucking building without suffering John and Juli's fate. It had been clear for a while and was now confirmed: the key was getting the Mayor away from the building. She strolled to the Horn of Plenty with Noble at her feet and waited outside for Frank. Noble explored the surrounding buildings and bushes. She didn't have to wait long. Frank and Zosimos's assistants walked out of the tavern within a few minutes.

"Thank you, boys, for an entertaining afternoon," Frank said.

"I'm afraid it was more profitable for you than entertaining for us," said the one in yellow.

"I really can't feel my fingers and toes," the other said.

"Be careful what you wager here." Frank donned his green beret.

"What did you wager?" Anne asked the assistant in blue.

"My sense of touch . . . but that isn't possible."

"Don't you believe in magic?" Then she looked at Frank and frowned. "That means you're twice as sensitive. Do you think that's smart?"

He winked. "I lost most of the feeling in my hands in the war. Doctors said bombs damaged my nerves. I have a normal amount of sensitivity now."

"Where do you suppose Zosimos is?" the man in yellow asked.

"He's left the city," Anne replied.

"Not without us."

"He has. I watched him go myself. He walked directly from the Mayor's Palace to the Goresetch road."

"Why wouldn't he tell us?"

"It was his choice. He's abandoned you to your own miserable choices."

"What choices?"

"Did he explain what this place really is?"

"A city of magic caught in a time vortex."

"Yes, that's what it is, but do you understand what it means?"

They gave her blank looks.

"Come with us, and I'll explain."

PART III

LOVE AT THE END OF THE WORLD

To some this place is rich; to others a place of desperate poverty.
For many, this place lacks love.
For some, love grows like trees in a forest.
- Notes of a Traveller

K ana and Jacob arrived on time, just as they had for the past two years. Kana never missed the chance to see her sister for a few minutes. Anne had expected them to grow out of their need for each other, just as she had her own sister. As adults, such a bond was unnecessary, perhaps even unhealthy. But not these two.

She met Kana in the boardroom after her allotted fifteen minutes with Asami. Frank sat by the door, and Jacob joined them at the table. Erk and Onit, abandoned by Zosimos, now took some of Frank's duties and were in the city, scouting and observing. It had been a small boon to have fresh eyes, especially eyes familiar with phenomena similar to the city's.

The boardroom needed refreshing. The table was fine, but

the chairs were in sad repair. Marta had converted two of them into three-legged chairs, but further refinements would have to wait. It was hard enough feeding all of them now. You could swap only so many Red Chips to croppers for their valuables, and those valuables would only be valuable once they controlled the phenomena. Trading a few trinkets or coins for real chips—and spending them quickly—was barely a means to get by. The most profitable way to slip Red Chips into circulation was through gambling, but that held its own risks. Frank, at least, was good at that. Or a good cheat.

Kana sat opposite her at the table, Jacob beside her.

"What news this week?" she asked Kana.

"I have noticed little. The Mayor meets only with new croppers. Almariss hasn't even been in."

"You've said the same for the last three months. Are you sure you're looking? Have you become complacent? Do you think just showing up each week will get you your fucking fifteen minutes with your sister? You need a sister more than I need a fucking cook."

Worry took over Kana's face. "It is the truth. Nothing has happened since the magician left."

"Well, something is about to fucking happen. Asami, bring the pie."

Asami entered the boardroom a moment later bearing a wrapped meat pie. She kept her head down and did not look at her sister as she placed it on the table and then left. Kana looked at the pie and then at Anne, then the pie and back.

"A gift for the Mayor. Tell her my fate has granted me a small retention in chip-value and that it was no doubt because of her kindness in not forcing me out of the city like a murderer that has led to this. A gift of thanks. Go, while the pie is still warm."

Kana and Jacob rose. Kana hesitated to pick up the pie, but she did and they left.

"A gift for the Mayor," Frank said. "Shit, that's rich. How much chip-value will that gain you?" He laughed and left the room.

There was nothing funny about this plan. It was a risk. She took her pale, faded chip from her sports bra and worried over it with her fingers. It was true the Mayor had left her alone and had not forced her out of the city—and it had gained her nothing. There was barely a discernible line between her situation and that of the worst criminals. And that was a line the fucking Mayor now forced her to cross.

Almariss walked through the ministerial offices. She snuffed out her pipe and held her thumb on the bowl. She was nervous and excited. This would be the first tea they shared in weeks. As she neared the Mayor's office, she noticed the scent of meat pie spices mingling with the palace's sage and pine. The scent came from her left, from the desk of the young Minister of Commerce. Kana looked up, surprised and nervous. The pie was wrapped like a large onion.

"I thought your sister retired from cooking."

"She did. This is not to be eaten."

The Mayor, sharply elegant and spry in her forty-year-old self, stepped out of her office to greet Almariss. She noticed the pie.

"That is a large lunch for one, especially you," the Mayor said.

"I'm not eating it. No one is eating it."

Almariss shook her head. "Shame to waste—"

"Hold a minute," the Mayor said.

"What?"

The Mayor took Almariss's pipe, placed it in her mouth, and inhaled—puffing it back to life.

"What are—"

"A disturbance, but from inside, not without." She stared at the pie.

Almariss looked at the pie and recalled what Kana had said about no one eating it. "Kana, poison?"

Kana cried and covered her face with her hands. "I didn't want to. I warned you so you wouldn't. I—"

"Who made you do this? Not Asami?"

"No! Never—I can't say."

"Why not? Has someone threatened you?"

Kana slumped in her chair and wiped her tears, but they kept coming. Her breathing came in irregular heaves. Almariss went to her and stroked her hair. "Easy, Kana. No one will hurt you. You aren't the poisoner."

"But she knows who is," the Mayor said.

"Don't." Almariss held up a hand. "She needn't tell us anything. I can guess who's behind this. Anne Fields and the Connectionists."

The Mayor closed her eyes, then opened them and nodded in agreement. "Kana. Say nothing of this to anyone, especially not Anne. You delivered the pie, you have done what she asked. You are clear."

"But Anne will expect you to be poisoned," Almariss said. "When she learns you weren't, she'll make good on whatever threat she made to Kana."

Kana shook and sobbed more.

"I have an idea," the Mayor said. "Almariss, bring the pie into my office. Kana, just report that I received the pie. That was all she asked of you, right?"

"Yes, Your Honor."

"Good. Almariss."

~

THE MAYOR UNDERSTOOD MORE than she said, and now she paced.

"Anne has become a bigger problem than I realized. I thought her ploy through reasoning last year ended it and she would eventually leave."

"I don't think she can. I think she's stuck here, too afraid to leave."

"Meaning her only alternative to a miserable life without chip-value is to break the magic."

"Do you think she knows?"

"Knows what? How the magic works? She's been using Kana to learn about me. She likely learned through Zosimos that the power can be disrupted. This disruption—from within—is off balance, like a spinning toy wobbling. I can't shake the feeling the world has suddenly begun spinning in the wrong direction."

They both looked at the Affinity Globe. It did appear to spin in a different direction, and it wobbled. Almariss felt the vibration beneath her feet syncopate. "João should escort Kana home."

"She needs protection and help, but if the commander of the Defense suddenly starts escorting her, Anne will know we know. I suppose they've threatened her somehow through her sister. Those tears weren't for herself."

"So what do we do? Do you think Asami's in actual danger?"

"If Anne is willing to kill me? I'll have João secretly alert the Brigade."

"What about you and the pie?"

"I think I'll gift you the pie. Make certain you're seen with it on the way home. The more people who see one of Asami's pies, the better. People will talk and maybe put some pressure on Anne, then you'll disappear for a few days. Let her think you ate the pie."

"To keep her from escalating right away."

"Exactly. For a few days. You must get to the docks if any ships arrive, but I'll try to steer the town toward pre-ship-building times. I can't promise anything."

"If they've done something with Asami, she's probably at the Connectionists' house. Will you send the Defense there?"

"We need to draw Anne and her enforcers out. It's too dangerous otherwise."

Almariss lifted the pie and tried to ignore the scent. Even knowing it was poison, the call to take a delicious spoonful was hard to resist. She left the palace and took the most public route home. People did indeed notice and point at the pie. She imagined the line forming at Asami's door.

AFTER THE NIGHT at the moonlit pool, dinner with João had become the highlight of Stina's days. That and walks through the city after. The shared-heartbeat thing was a hell of a drug. Sometimes she thought it too intense, yet still she longed for it. When he wasn't close, she felt empty despite the beat of dozens of others beside her own.

Tonight they started with dinner, as usual, but João seemed distracted. She suggested they visit the Salon; there was music tonight. But João preferred a walk along the quay. The night was cloudless and cool, the sea calm, and the sound of gentle waves spending themselves against the shore was lulling. She wrapped her shawl tighter and João pulled her close with his arm around her waist. They strolled, though she sensed he was anxious. His heartbeat was rapid. "You seem far away."

"I do not want to worry you, and I can't tell you much, but there is genuine danger. I am helping the Mayor manage it."

She stopped and looked at him. "What kind of danger? Like Zosimos?"

"I cannot say. But there are things I will need to do. Things

I will need you to do. This might be the last chance we have to ourselves for a few days."

"Commander of the Defense. Always on duty."

"There are causes greater than our happiness."

"Are there?"

"Your safety and the safety of everyone in this town is the greatest cause."

"The danger is that great? Should I worry?" Too late, anyway.

"I do not know, but the Mayor seems at least as concerned as with Zosimos. But she's been through this before, even before Zosimos, so don't worry."

"Well, let's make the most of tonight. It's not too late for the Salon. The music won't have started yet."

"If you like, though I desire a few moments with just you."

"As you wish." A memory flashed through her mind and she added, "Dear Wesley."

"Wesley?"

"A private joke from the future. One day I'll tell you a tale about true love."

He pulled away slightly and looked up at the stars. "I make a steady income, though it isn't much. It only really increases when people are in trouble."

"Like your reckless attack on Zosimos, and when you ran that thief down the Goresetch last month? Or now?"

"Right. I am thankful the End of the World is a peaceful place, but it will not make me wealthy."

"Why do you want to be wealthy?"

"I do not. I . . . I just want enough."

Where was he going with this? His heart was not so much beating as fluttering.

"I grew up raising swine and fowl. I'd like enough room for that."

"Will a farmer sell and leave?" Stina asked.

"I don't know. Maybe. I've heard Jabu and his wife are discussing it. They have the wheat and barley fields at the farthest end of Tower Road."

"Nearly in the forest."

"At the edge, yes."

"You want to be a gentleman farmer and the commander?"

"It will take a very long time."

Everything with João took a long time. He was always thinking and planning, but that was his job. Still, left to his own wandering, off-target conversation, he might never get to the point. "What else do you want?" she asked.

"Nothing." Then he looked into her eyes and added, "Well . . . you. I mean, I want to be with you."

"You are with me. I'm not going anywhere. Fate placed us both here. I waited a year for you to ask me—to court me. And we've been together another two. This has been the slowest courtship I've ever had. In my time, if I felt this way about a man who was as careful as you, I would've taken the lead."

"I am sorry."

"Don't be. You're true to your time, and that's important to me. My world's way is probably why I had no courtships that worked out. Never had many actual courtships at all. Maybe one when I was a teen."

"'Take the lead' means what?"

"Women ask men on dates, make the first move—I mean initiate something, like a kiss."

"Oh. I had not imagined that."

"Which is why I . . . why I wait for you to do what is natural for you."

"You are a strange and fascinating woman. I do not know what my mother would have thought."

"You would have introduced me to your mother?"

"Yes, naturally. You are my—you would—she would have to meet you."

She lowered her head, recalling her own mother. She'd been eighteen the last time they were together. "I would love to have met your mother."

João squeezed her hand, but he stared at the sea and remained silent. Was he thinking about marriage? She couldn't assume anything. The episode with his letter had taught her that. The centuries between them were tricky to negotiate, but damn, this was painfully slow. Time to be direct. "João, are you asking to marry me?"

"What? I—well, I should ask your father, or your mother. I don't even know if you are Catholic, or if that even matters. I've learned faith and religion are two distinct things."

"You didn't answer the question. Are you asking to marry? Do you want to marry me?"

He looked at her. The light of the stars was enough to see his smile and dimpled chin. "I think you just asked me."

Her stomach threatened to heave her dinner and her head felt light. She was sweating. Not what a marriage proposal should feel like, yet the anxiety made absolute sense. It felt just the right sort of panic, danger, and life-altering loss of time. Bloody terrifying. *Go with it.* "Like I said, not unheard of in my time. What's your answer?"

His brow furrowed, but still he smiled. "I do not know what power you have, but you always make the discomforting things easy. Yes, I want to marry you. In any place and any time, I want to be with you always. I want to save enough for a home large enough for the children."

She really would heave. Now they were getting to it. "How many?"

"It is not for me to ask. God or fate determines. One is blessing enough."

His Catholicism required no birth control. If his views on religion were changing, he needed to start with that. Her body was no baby factory, especially in a town with medieval technology and a single physiker. "Perhaps God or fate will inform me."

"Do not joke."

"No joke. Didn't God send a messenger to Mary? He might have already told me that two blessings will fill our lives. And that we should know each carefully at other times."

"That sounds like strange doctrine."

"It is my doctrine." She wrapped her arms around his shoulders and lifted herself up to kiss him.

A SHORT WHILE LATER, they strolled close to Almariss's small home on the quay. There was no light inside. She must have been out. João let go of her hand and placed his hand on her arm. "I have to do something now and I need you to let people know that Almariss is ill, but you need to know it is not true."

"What?"

"The Mayor needs people to think Almariss is ill. My soldiers will guard her place and the physiker will come and go, but truthfully she is fine."

"Why?"

"It is complicated."

It was Commander Alejo looking at her, not the vulnerable João who'd just been proposed to by a woman from his future. There was a threat, which meant he was in danger too. "Be safe," she said.

He drew her close and kissed her lips, then her neck. The pleasant nausea returned, and shivers climbed her spine. "As careful as I can," he said. "Always, for you."

Reluctantly, she left him while he spoke with Private Sai at Almariss's door. As she walked through the city, she pulled the glass turtle from her pocket. Twisting clouds, one of green and one of blue, folded around each other. "Did you hear that,

Mum? I'm to be married." The blue cloud crystalized and shone an image of her mother dressed in hiking clothes walking beside her. The green light also crystalized, and Angi appeared on her other side. *Real damage.*

So many feelings. It was never like this before, never hope and sadness simultaneously. She returned the turtle to her pocket. By the time she reached the Scale and Tentacle, pale predawn light filtered through the streets.

"THE PHYSIKER WILL BE by after sunrise. Let no one else inside," João said to Private Sai.

"Aye, sir."

He turned to look at the sea across the harbor. The water was flat and still. The glow of the coming sun spread into the horizon. Something hit him in the chest like a cannon fired at him from across the water. He buckled to one knee and struggled to catch his breath.

"Commander? Are you all right?"

He choked on air but managed to stand. "I am—I am fine. No one but Korbath."

"Aye, sir."

He ran for Nico and Shaday's cottage. His magic had returned, and the croppers heading into the harbor were unlike any before. The signal of their arrival was strong enough to raise a battlefield of dead soldiers. He knocked on the door. Croydon answered and told him everyone was in the back. He followed the boy around the cottage to the marshy shore. Shaday, Nico, and Almariss stared at the glassy orange sea. Almariss turned to him.

"How many?"

"Thirty plus the captain, a dog, and another I can't see as human or animal, but very alive."

"What does that mean?" Nico asked. "Who are they?"

"Pirates," he said.

"Oh, dear fates," Shaday said. "I still can't see any ship."

"They'll be in the harbor in a few hours," Almariss said. "I have to get there."

"So much for the ruse."

"It doesn't matter now, João. This is bigger. Tell the Mayor."

"On my way. Nico, alert the Brigade. Tell them to be ready to come at my whistle." He left them and ran for the Mayor's Palace.

"FINALLY," Croydon said.

"Finally what?" Nico asked.

"My first action in the Brigade."

"No," Shaday said. "You're not a full member yet."

She never let him do what he wanted. Nico had to beg her to allow João to teach him with his steel sword. She'd practically shook when he revealed the shiny weapon he'd purchased, and she had fought him on joining the Brigade as a junior member. Well, he was almost sixteen and he would do what he wanted. "I'm getting my sword."

"Croydon, you're not a full member until you're seventeen."

"You're not my full mother either." He stomped to the cottage.

SHADAY BREATHED SHORT, and tears welled at the corner of her eyes. Nico placed a hand on her shoulder. "Actually, I think you are quite fully his mother," he said.

"Don't let anything happen to him. You know I couldn't bear it."

"I know. I'm sure once the Mayor explains how the city

works, the pirates will leave like all ships do. João's just being cautious."

"I hope so, but Almariss seemed worried."

"Yes, well, she had quite a scare with the magician. I've got to wake up Padrok, Toby, and Scott."

She grabbed his hand and held it. "Nico, I couldn't bear it if anything happened to you either."

He squeezed her hand, then bent and kissed it. "I know. But keeping you safe within the magic is why I go."

PIRATES SAIL TO THE END OF THE WORLD

Some suns are best
Silver stream leads to glistening sea
like memories at the end of distant tracks
sisters, mothers; roaming brothers, and fathers
the world was full; memory was full.

Some suns are cold
exposing bones in the shade;
the world empty but for those
walking solo under a cold dead moon.
- Notes of a Traveller

*A*nne stood on her veranda drinking a cold herbal brew Asami had blended. It really was far better than any of Maggie's concoctions. It was a wonder that Asami had not tried to poison her yet, but then people like Asami—people who earned and maintained chip-value—were too confused by conscience to do something selfish. They were trustworthy. Was that how the Mayor did it? A kind of personality test when meeting the croppers? Well, why should she be the fucking arbiter?

Once Anne controlled the phenomena, she would decide who stayed and who had to leave. She'd already made a list. People like Asami, useful people, would stay. Foolish, unhelpful people like the fucking Ventals had to go.

Jacob stepped onto the veranda. "The pie failed," he said. "I mean, it is working, but on the wrong person. Almariss. She is in her shack with the doctor and a guard outside."

"I'm not surprised. I thought something like that might happen. I had hoped maybe the commander and a few of the Defense might receive it from the Mayor. Still, if Almariss dies the Mayor gets a little more vulnerable. We know they work together. If she loses Almariss she's a little weaker."

She watched a ship bearing no flag and no colors sail out of the harbor. She drank more of the tea and had a perilous thought. What if making a poisonous meal had tainted Asami's chip-value abilities? She'd definitely compromised her conscience to make the pie. "Jacob, take my glass to the kitchen."

"Madam."

ALMARISS SAT at the game table staring at the stacks of tile. There would be no game tonight. The Mayor leaned on her cane. She was, for the moment, older than she'd ever seen her. Frail.

"If what's on that ship is so powerful, why let them return?"

The Mayor allowed herself to fall into her chair opposite Almariss. "What the ship carries cannot return to the world. It does not belong there. When they sailed into harbor today, I felt a disturbance like no other. We all did, and I was glad to know they left. I did not want that disturbance here. But a deeper look revealed I'd made a mistake. They had to return."

"What does it carry?"

The Mayor sat silent for several breaths, as if gathering the courage to speak. "According to some, it's called the Orphic Egg. To others, it's the World Egg. It came from primordial time—from the making of the world. The thing inside made, and is destined to unmake, the world."

"There's a demon in the egg?"

"No. There's a god in the egg. The eldest god and progenitor of all other gods. It's called Phanes. The ship's captain holds the key to releasing and re-capturing that god." She melted into a younger woman of ninety. "We face a terrible choice. If I hold the ship here, the captain may unleash the god. If so, it will use the city's power to grow and break its bonds—to break out of time's control. It will start by destroying the city, and then it could appear at any place and any time— the End Time. At the End Time, Phanes is to unmake the world and return all matter to the chaos of the void."

"Our other option?"

"Let the captain take it back to the world and allow him to wreak endless smaller havocs for eternity. It really isn't a choice, because eventually he will end up here again. Phanes is the maker and un-maker of worlds. That's its job. As long as it remains in the egg the world remains made. Outside of it, the world unravels."

"How do we know it isn't the appointed end time?"

"We try to stop it. If we succeed, it wasn't."

"Then what do we do?"

"For now, we must hope the captain is reasonable and will make a trade for freedom."

"That doesn't sound like something a pirate would do." Almariss's tea was cold, but she didn't feel like having any more.

. . .

THE ENTIRE BRIGADE, twenty strong, sat or stood facing João in a semi-circle behind Nico's cottage. A dim gray glow spread up from the sea's eastern horizon into the starry sky. Nico wondered, were they ready for this? Were any of them?

Shaday stood near. Croydon sat on the trampled grass at the front of the Brigade, his steel sword at his waist. He'd earned it. He'd worked odd jobs and studied his lessons—and endured long hours of practice with João. Nico understood Shaday's fear for what might happen, but Croydon was a young man now. They had to let go. Besides, Croydon was better with a sword than Nico was with a pole ax.

"Again," João addressed the Brigade, "this may turn into nothing. The Mayor is working on how to deal with the pirates. When they return, our job is to ensure no group of pirates—no two or more—leave the docks at any time. I will allow the Captain and one of his officers, if he chooses."

Toby interrupted. "If, say, four of five should try to leave and they don't listen to us, do we fight?"

"You call for the Defense first. There will be members of the Defense on the docks at all times. Let them confront the pirates."

"But if the pirates fight the Defense?" Croydon asked.

"Then by all means, help them." João waited for other questions, but none came. "Watches start now. Who's on first watch?"

"Toby, Scott, and Croydon," Padrok replied. He wore his Brigade captain coat and held a pike. They left and the rest of the Brigade drifted toward their homes. João returned to the city.

"You know I don't like this," Shaday said as she and Nico stepped inside the cottage.

"The early watches should be uneventful. Croydon will be fine."

She gave him a look he knew well. She didn't believe him. Nothing he could say would put her at ease. "What makes this lot so different?" she asked. "We've had pirates here before."

"They probably aren't different. Everyone is just a little more careful after Zosimos."

"I hope that's all it is. I wasn't able to get the shimmer into my weave yesterday when that ship was in harbor." He tried to hide the surprise on his face, but she saw it. "Did you try putting a memory into glass?"

"No." If the pirates' presence affected the magic, these pirates were different. Perhaps he shouldn't have been so supportive of Croydon. "I'm going to check on the first watch."

"Excellent idea, but you've got second watch so get back for some rest."

"I will."

Outside, the arc of the sun stained the sky a dull orange. He looked up at the fading stars. They never stood in the arrangement of his home, never the same as the ones that shone on Lura. This dawn, though they had dimmed, it felt as if the distance to them had somehow shortened. They felt oppressively close.

THE SUN BURNED hazy over the harbor. Anne stood on her veranda sipping her own terrible herbal brew. She considered the news that Almariss had survived. Was it Asami's fault? Had she failed to poison the pie sufficiently? The girl needed reminding of her sister's fate if she did not do as told.

The bigger concern was what to do now. Nothing changed. All her plans had failed, and Red Chips barely kept them fed and housed. The Connectionists needed an alternative plan. They had to destroy the phenomena, or they needed to use the threat of destruction to get the Mayor away from the palace. There were weapons in the city, but not much to make a bomb with and not enough to do the kind of damage that would force the Mayor to step outside. The building was stone and brick, difficult to burn without lots of accelerants.

She watched as the same sailing ship, the one flying no flags that left the harbor the day before, returned.

Ships never returned. What the hell?

A fortune-shaking event. Was the town stable? Was it fixed to a place and time? Was the fucking phenomena changed, broken, or weakening? She called to Jacob, and he appeared at once.

"Jacob, what do you make of that ship?"

He studied it for only a few seconds. "A pirate vessel, madam."

"Why would it make a return trip to the harbor a day after it left?"

"I do not know. I've never seen a ship return, unless it never truly left the harbor."

"Meet that ship. I want to meet the captain."

"Pirate."

"Fine, pirate."

"Yes, madam."

Alone once again, she took a sip of her tea and gagged. "Frank! Bring Asami here now." Not only did Asami need reminding of her place, but she needed to make something special for the captain. Meetings always went better with food.

CAPTAIN LONG BEN strode from the stifling docks in full boots, a long coat, and a hat. He was used to the steamy heat of the Caribbean, but this harbor wasn't on any Caribbean map. He marched toward the Mayor's palace. The Mayor knew who he was—what he was—so there was no pretense to be anything other. She had stationed guards on the docks, watching over the ship and over him as he left. They might inform her of his movements but she could not know what lay hidden in his cabin, and that was his advantage.

The sun cast long, dim shadows along the road, and for a city, even a small one, there were few people along the way. He had evaded the Dutch East India man at the docks. The few people in the streets quickly averted their eyes as if they had not seen him. No doubt they were worried about his sword. No one in this sleepy port besides the guards carried a weapon. It was as if they didn't know privateers existed.

That would change.

Meeting the Mayor—or a governor, or any authority—was fraught with politics and agendas. Sometimes officials got full of themselves and made examples of sea rogues. The Mayor knew about privateers and pirates. He just hoped the Mayor hadn't yet learned of the gold he and his crew had acquired the day before—or how. Heavy taxation was not a positive start to a new relationship.

And a relationship they would have. The secret of this city and its habit of appearing and disappearing could be quite profitable. It had already proven so. The British, French, and Spanish navies couldn't follow. He could plunder and hide. The good life. This sleepy little port was about to wake up as a privateer haven, and the Mayor needed to understand that. He jingled a bag of gold coins at his belt. Small, private taxes paid to such authorities were a reasonable cost of doing business.

He jogged up the steps of the Mayor's palace and stood between two identically dressed men. Not really guards, as they were unarmed, but some official door minders.

"Hello, gentlemen. I believe I have an appointment with the Mayor, or so the dockmaster tells me."

The door minders looked at each other, apparently uncertain about letting him in. They came to some silent agreement and swung the doors open.

"Thank you." The town fairly crackled with magic, and any magic that could work in his favor was good magic.

There were offices on the left and right sides, and one large one at the back. Clerks and ministers worked under various-colored lights. There were no windows, and the place smelled of fresh-cut wood and sage—more magic. He walked to the rear, where a woman watched him. She was probably fifty, tall, had gray-streaked brown hair, and was dressed in a white dress with a fur stole. She leaned on a cane decorated in jewels and gold scrollwork.

"Captain Long Ben," she said, followed by a broad smile. "Fair sailing yesterday?"

"Fair enough."

She welcomed him into her office and pointed to a chair in front of a long white table. At the table's center was a rotating globe of white, gold, and lavender. It was spellbinding, but experience told him not to stare at such things for too long. Lit candles on the walls, on tables, and on shelves filled the rest of the room. The sage definitely emanated from this room. The Mayor pounded her cane against the floor once. A short bald man in striped pants arrived immediately.

"Eristol, some port please."

Eristol nodded and left the room. This was off to a better start than he'd imagined.

"How far did you sail yesterday?" she asked.

"Forty nautical miles, roughly. Why?"

"You arrived early yesterday, then put out immediately. Why?"

"Well, most people call us pirates. It's what we do."

"But normally you stay a few days and let your crew carouse."

"When it's time for shore leave, yes."

Eristol returned with a clay jug and two clay cups. He poured the port and handed one cup to him and one to the Mayor. The port was excellent.

"Eristol, please pick up this month's supply of candles this morning."

"Your Honor." Eristol nodded again and left.

The Mayor took a thoughtful sip. "So you just landed, talked with someone—likely the dockmaster—and then set sail immediately."

"That's about right."

"She told you that you needed to see me within a day, but you don't care for authority so you left."

"Sure."

"But if that were true, you wouldn't have found your way back. I note your ship lies a good five feet lower in draught. You're full. As you said, you're a pirate, so I'm certain you did some pirating. But you returned."

"Closest port in a storm, as they say."

The Mayor turned to fiddle with a candle on a shelf, then faced him again. She was now a much younger woman; full black hair with white streaks. Definitely a witch.

"You and I are more intelligent than that, Captain Long Ben. After you spoke with the dockmaster you figured it—you figured out what it meant to be at the End of the World. This city isn't on your charts. Perhaps you're just mad, or maybe a gambler. Maybe you're cunning enough with magic to believe this place would provide a literal safe harbor. It would disappear from your enemies' eyes and they could not follow if you outran them."

"You guessed it. The dockmaster warned me we might not locate the harbor if we tried to return. But we were quick, and I made sure we returned quicker than those following. What's the problem?"

"There won't be a next time. I intentionally kept the city

connected to your seas. You represent a significant disruption to the functioning of this city, but worse, you represent a threat to the wider world. I cannot allow you to repeat your journey. It's best if you do not leave at all until you relinquish what's aboard your ship."

"Best for whom? What does it matter to you if I do some pirating? You don't answer to any authority." No need to admit there was anything on his ship but treasure. She was reaching, trying to trick him into revealing his hand.

"I answer to an authority you can't understand. It is my responsibility to preserve the city. Your ship's entrance to the harbor with that thing threatens this city—and the world."

Definitely fishing to know more about the thing. No clue would escape his lips. "Why let me back? Why not just let me go—disappear before I returned, leave me to my fate?"

"I'm bound not only to this city but to the world itself."

"Sounds like an unfortunate career choice."

The Mayor ignored that. "A question, and mind you if you speak a false answer you can never step inside this building again."

"Why would that be, should I wish to?"

She tossed him a wooden coin, gray as the sea. "Answer while holding that. How many people did you kill on your little venture yesterday?"

"None that I'm aware of. Privateers steal when they can and kill only when they must." It wasn't a lie. His crew had killed no one. What Phanes did—well, that was out of his control. And she hadn't asked about Phanes.

"Is that a code?"

"It's practical. Killing people causes . . . entanglements and difficulties."

"Show me the chip."

He held it up. It might have been a shade darker, like an angry sea.

"Good," the Mayor said. "But I wouldn't step into this building again until that chip looks pink."

"Why?"

"Your fate, reflected by your choices and actions, may prevent you from entering my official space and send you to a place from where and when you cannot return."

"And if I ignore your ban and sail again?"

"That is no longer a choice. Your ship will not leave unless I allow it."

He played the chip across the fingers of his left hand. What was she getting at? Could she really hold his ship? Was she stronger than Phanes? Unlikely.

"What will you do with your gold?" she asked.

He shrugged.

"People here value gold only for its appearance. You can buy little with coin. That wooden chip is the only currency here, and if it isn't at least a little pink, you'll starve."

He took a moment to let that sink in. He tried to avoid the spinning globe, but it seemed to push him deeper into his chair. Magic was thick here. If she held the ship, he couldn't do much with the gold. "Well, no one will be tempted to steal it."

"No, not many. Though to a few I'm sure your ship looks tempting."

"They would have to have a small army to take the *Fancy*. But you have a bigger problem. A security problem. My crew, without money, will take what they need, if you understand me."

"Which is what I was getting at. I suggest you keep them aboard until I can meet with each one. If they can earn chip-value, they can become valued citizens of the city."

"That will take a few days. Can't we reach agreement?" He needed time. He wasn't about to lose his crew to this witch.

"Agreement?"

He placed the purse on the desk with a metallic thud. "This gold won't change your mind about letting me leave harbor?"

The Mayor smiled. "That is correct. What's in that purse might get you some meals once traded to the changers for pink chips, or it could be traded as a decorative metal. Everyone likes gold jewelry and features such as this." She held up her cane and pointed to the fine gold inlay. "But we might find an alternative agreement. If you agree to leave behind that prize aboard your ship—the egg—I can let you sail back to the world."

He pulled the purse back, rose, and fastened it to his belt. How did she know about Phanes? She was more than a witch, and he should have seen it. "You cannot withstand what I could unleash." She said nothing. It was only a hunch, but he'd struck right with that. "Good day," he said.

THE DOORS CLOSED behind him with a definitive thud. The door minders kept their attention forward. The pale gray coin in his hand looked paler in the sunlight. With no place to spend and trade treasure, the city was useless except as a temporary place to hide. Yet the Mayor wouldn't allow them to leave—something that needed testing.

Perhaps she just needed prompting. He tossed the chip and caught it. She'd said it herself. She was bound to the power and the people of the city. If she failed to protect the city, she would become unbound to it. That was her weakness.

The Dutch East India man slipped from between two buildings in front of him. Damnation, he'd been waiting. There weren't any East India ships in the harbor; no ships of any size besides his own. But once a pirate hunter, always a pirate hunter.

"Good day, Captain," the man said.

"I'm not in the mood. Take your good day——"

"I'm not what you think. I've become a bit of a rogue myself. I think there might be a bargain beneficial to us both, if you will hear me."

Long Ben did not slow. "I'm listening, but you have until I reach my ship to convince me. Then you can decide how good a day it is."

"A meeting, on your ship and on your terms, to discuss something of mutual benefit between my party and yours."

"Your party?"

"People with no love for the Mayor."

"She claims my ship cannot sail. Can you get her to release my ship—if it is indeed impounded?"

"I'm certain that can be arranged."

"Hmm. I'm disinclined to believe that, since you didn't know the situation until just now. But I'm listening. How many in your party?"

"Four."

"All right, I'll hear your proposal. But I have no time for anything that doesn't profit me, and those who waste my time find themselves chum for the sharks." They had arrived at the ship. "Bring your party aboard at once."

"Thank you, Captain." The Dutch East India man tipped his hat and left.

Long Ben walked up the gangway and called to his first mate. Master Robinson appeared on deck immediately.

"Sir?"

"Set sail at once."

"Aye."

If he could sail out of the harbor, he didn't need the Dutch East India man's proposal. He gave the orders to lift the mooring lines and lower sails. Then he watched the docks. A few curious onlookers and the Mayor's guard stared back.

"Captain, the sails are tied in knots the crew cannot undo,

and the hawsers won't loose. It's as if the ship's a mind of its own, or under a strange spell."

"Indeed." He needed to get the Mayor away from her magic or he'd have to unleash Phanes, and then they would see who held more power. The only problem with that was the possibility of Phanes destroying his own ship in the process. "Master Robinson, we need a little leverage. Let's see how the Mayor fares when she must rescue one of her precious citizens."

SLAYERS AT THE END OF THE WORLD

Bones, yellow-brown and weather-worn,
thrust through green moss,
flesh and form long gnawed away;
tears, mourning for failed return.
- Notes of a Traveller

The small one has returned. Her lavender blouse is torn and muddied. She has hurried to the resting bones. She sings her mantra. Sounds of care; sounds of loss. She has no flowers today. She trembles, but not with fear or sadness. She trembles with a feeling the large one understands well—rage.

The large one steps heavily but with care from the deep forest. The slayers know she can sense fear. Do they not understand she can sense all emotions? Slowly, she approaches the little one. Something has broken inside the small body. Anger and rage roil like a storm.

They are close now. Embracing trunk within arms and

around the small body. The small one speaks and the larger one listens. She does not know how she understands the words, but she does. She knows them and feels what drives them. She has lived them. She still lives them.

They are sisters who have lost sisters.

They must deny the slayers.

THE DISTURBANCE from within careens city, forest, and shore against the jagged edges of places and the undertow of time.

Aberration and oasis.

Time's arrows have been flung, but time's origin burns brightly and draws closer like a crushing furnace.

DESPAIRING AND FEARFUL, the maple, oak, larch, and pine clutch each other and watch the pair—large and small, furred and lavender—march toward the city.

The city whirls with certainty toward the weighted flame of the beginning.

LONG BEN STOOD in his cabin behind his chart-cluttered desk, staring at the egg in the clutter's midst. An egg like no other. It was the size of an ostrich egg, its surface swirled with blue, green, aqua, and fire-orange. A slim silver serpent wrapped itself around the egg, as if holding it together, and when he looked closely he saw that a series of dark, thin lines had appeared under the egg's undulating colors. Hairline cracks. The magic of the city was calling to Phanes, and Phanes would answer that call. Sure, if that happened he could read the incantation and release the serpent to return Phanes to the egg—maybe. But if the city's magic helped Phanes, would the serpent be strong enough? Watching it struggle with the cracks in the egg did not give him confidence. The Mayor would have a real problem on her hands if she didn't let him leave. Did she understand that as well as she knew everything else? Possibly. But if so, why dally?

"Captain," said the bosun, knocking at his door. "Your visitors."

"Let them in." He really didn't have time for this nonsense. There was little chance the Dutch East India man's party had anything to offer. He tossed a small gold satin cloth over the egg.

Five people entered. One was a small woman from the Orient, carrying food. She placed it on his table and arranged it artfully. Wheels of white rice and seaweed wrapped around centers of rich colors: orange, red, pink, and green. Another woman, light skinned with brown hair, entered; then the Dutch East India man, who was followed by another, larger, Mediterranean-dark man—a bodyguard. Last came a pale, petite, light-haired woman who carried herself as though she were in charge.

"What's all this?" he said to the East India man. "I thought there were four of you?"

"There are," said the petite woman. She wore a light but threadbare sweater and revealingly tight hose. "Asami is my caterer. A welcoming gift of fine sushi."

"And you are?" He helped himself to one wheel of orange —fish and rice. Delicious.

"My name is Anne."

Asami fell to the floor with a thud. The Dutch East India man and the brown-haired woman rushed to her and helped her upright. Asami regained consciousness, but she pointed at his desk. "It does not belong," she gasped. Then she slumped again.

Wary of a diversion, he kept his eye on the egg and on Anne. She was clearly trying not to look at the silk-covered egg.

"Jacob," she said. "Take Asami home, then meet us at the chip-less camp."

"Madam," he said, and then he helped Asami out.

The silk moved. He needed to get rid of these people. It had been stupid to agree to this meeting.

JOÃO WATCHED Eristol barter with the chandler. The little man was a cunning haggler. During his four years at the End of the World, João had learned that even though the value of chips was determined by one's favor in God's eye, there was still room for deal making, of which Eristol was a master.

"The more you contribute to the Mayor's duties—your candle tithe, as you call it—the more the Mayor benefits," Eristol said to the chandler. "Therefore, the city benefits, which enriches you."

The chandler shook her head. "When I give them away, I gain a little chip-value, but when the beekeeper charges me more for his wax, that chip-value doesn't cover the cost of materials. If everyone agreed just to do in kind for each other we wouldn't need chips, but that's not how it works."

"That was the Wandering Master's vision. He meant the chips only as a transition."

"Well, the Master wandered away from the End of the World right after he handed out chips, so what does that tell you?"

"That you should take the four chips it costs you to cover the wax and donate your time making the candles to the Mayor."

She sighed and held out her hand.

As they walked away from the market, João asked, "Why do you do that?"

"Do what?"

"Haggle people to the bone. Doesn't that decrease the value of your chips?"

"It probably would, but I don't have any."

João stopped. They had reached the foot of the steps to the Mayor's Palace. "Are you a Connectionist?" His hand rested on the pommel of his sword. There had been one spy in the palace, why not more?

Eristol laughed. "No. Though I cannot earn much chip-value."

"Does the Mayor know?"

"Yes. The Mayor knows everything about everyone. You should understand that by now. I get by through the generosity of others. In return, I do my job. I don't lose chip-value as quickly as some. So, while I'll never be wealthy in chips, I never want for anything."

"What about love?"

"What about it?"

"You don't have it. If you can't gain chip-value, you probably can't give or receive love. Unless it is Christ's love, which comes to everyone."

"That's lovely, but I don't believe I'm missing anything. Good day, João."

"Good day, sir."

Eristol climbed the palace steps and João headed across the street to the barracks. Four years. The small stack of chips he kept beside his pallet grew slowly. It might never be enough to give Stina the house and life she deserved, but at least his chips held their value.

Shouts came from behind him—from the palace and the door ministers.

"They've got Eristol!" shouted Taffet.

"They're taking him toward the harbor," added Tiffet.

. . .

243

ANNE RECOGNIZED ASAMI'S FAINT. Almariss had done the same when she was near Zosimos. Asami had pointed to something on the captain's desk. Something under a gold silk. The silk moved.

"What is your proposal?" the captain asked.

"You have broken the city's phenomena by returning. You carry something of power."

"Not exactly. The Mayor . . . arranged things. What of it?"

"I take it things did not go well with the Mayor. She wants you to leave and never return."

"It did not go well, but not as you imagine. She will not allow us to leave."

Anne refused to let surprise show on her face or in her stance. "Hmm. She wants you to stay? That can only mean she thinks you're a greater danger to the world than the city. She also told you not to step foot in the palace again."

"Bright lady, but what is it you offer me?"

"Control."

"All I want to do is leave the city. I'll not be returning. So again I ask, what can you do for me?"

She had to think quick. She had been confident she could find something to bargain with, though she did not know what. It was like those investor pitch meetings. You came prepared with numbers, a prototype, a slide deck, and the ability to wing it. She always thought best on her feet in front of a client. Whatever moved under the silk sheet on his desk was the key. It was power, and it had brought him back to the harbor when return should have been impossible. That was the power she needed, the kind that could destroy or master the phenomena. She was close to the answer now. "Will you kill the Mayor, if it comes to it?"

"I do not intend to kill the Mayor, but maybe a citizen or two if that's what it takes to get her to grant my freedom."

"But as long as she refuses, you're at a stalemate."

"She won't refuse for long. Now, for the last time, what can you do for me?"

She had it. Really, it was simple. She lowered her voice as low as it would go. "What if I brought you the power of the city? What if your ship could come and go through time and place?" She gave him her best intense gaze and allowed a moment for her offer to sink in, then pushed to close the deal. "Wouldn't a ship that could travel to any time and any place be better than just a safe harbor in an untrustworthy city?"

The captain scratched his bearded chin. "Indeed, it would, but how do you propose to achieve this, and what does it profit you?"

"Without the power, the city will become a normal place. Fixed—connected. There will be no need for the Mayor. I can become mayor then, if I wish."

"So you don't care for the city's magic."

"I loathe what this city has done to me," Anne said. She'd had to scrape, lie, cheat, and steal just to keep herself fed.

"And how will you acquire the city's magic?"

"I have a spy in the palace. I know where it is and what it is. Just get me and my crew inside and we'll rip it out and hand it to you."

"Simple as that?"

"Often the best answers are simple."

A pirate officer arrived at the captain's door with another pirate and the Mayor's valet under pointed sword.

"Captain, we have the valet," the officer said.

"Take him to the brig."

"Aye."

Anne continued to stare at the captain, again not allowing a trace of surprise. That he had the Mayor's valet was interesting, but it changed nothing. He was trying to get the Mayor away from the palace and her source of power, but she knew the Mayor would never do that. She'd find another way to meet her obligation to protect the valet, while also not leaving the palace. The captain cocked his head and considered her, then stepped over to his desk.

"You can truly deliver the city's power to me? You haven't taken it for yourself because you can't get in?"

"Correct. I just need something powerful to get me inside the palace. Just as for you, she has a trap waiting for me."

"And if you gain possession of the power, why not use it yourself rather than give it to me?"

"I could, but I will be satisfied if you use it to do me one favor."

"Which is?"

"Land the city in my own time. Allow me to get on with my life."

He considered for another half-minute. "You have a deal." He pulled the silk off the object. It was an egg with swirling colors and a writhing serpent crawling about the outside. "All you need to do is crack this egg open in front of the palace doors. Destruction will ensue. I'll be watching through my spyglass. Once the creature in the egg has broken open the doors, I'll call it back to the shell. It will return to me, but you'll have your entry."

Anne took the egg in her hand. It moved—undulated. The serpent struggled and twisted, as if trying to break the egg. She recognized it as soon as the captain had pulled away the silk. The Dogon egg; the essence of all things. Powerful phenomena, and hers to control. The true culmination of Project E266. The essence of all things would rip through the palace. It was fate. The pirate was a fool. Her cheeks warmed with joy.

The officer returned, and she raced off the ship with the egg wrapped in its silk. Frank and Marta followed. From the dock, they headed for the chip-less camp.

. . .

MASTER ROBINSON STARED at him with a look of accusation: an accusation of betrayal. But Long Ben knew he couldn't use Phanes to retrieve the power. Phanes would use and consume it and then be beyond control.

"Phanes will hatch soon. The egg is cracking," Long Ben explained. "It's drawn to the city's magic. If that woman succeeds, we'll have an unbeatable ship and the Mayor will be powerless to stop us. If she fails, we're no worse off. Even if she tries to double-cross us, Phanes will kill her and her crew, and likely many in the city. That should demonstrate to the Mayor what she faces. She'll have no choice but to let us go."

"If Phanes taps into the city's magic—"

"We must make sure that doesn't happen." He picked up his spyglass from his desk and drew from his pocket the yellowed bone tablet containing the serpent's unbinding spell.

JOÃO UNSHEATHED his sword and gave chase after the pirates who'd taken Eristol. He blew the whistle around his neck. It sounded everywhere at the End of the World; the off-duty Defense and the rest of the Brigade would hear it. Four years of peace. Four years, except for the magician, but this was different. His warrior's sense told him peace was over.

He bolted through the market and met Lieutenant Tabray running toward him. "Did you see them?" he asked.

"Who?"

"Pirates. They've taken Eristol."

"I just left Private Sai at the ship, but they could have taken Braken Street."

They ran down the small hillside to the harbor. As they ran, Lieutenant Tabray caught him up on events. "The Connectionists are on the pirate ship. Private Sai blew my whistle, and when I reached him I saw one of the Connectionists, Jacob, take Asami off the ship and head toward the Connectionist cottage on the hill."

"The Connectionists are with the pirates?" For a second, the weight of failed responsibility descended on him. Once he had learned they held Asami, he'd wanted to launch a rescue attempt, but the pirates' arrival had taken his attention. He should have listened to Croydon's concerns months ago.

A commotion erupted around the *Fancy*. It held thirty crew, Eristol, a dog, and something else; not human or animal. Whatever that was, it had to stay on the ship, except—it was not there. It was moving somewhere in the city. What had happened? Had the Brigade allowed too many pirates off the ship, or had they been overrun? It was his responsibility to keep the Mayor, Eristol—everyone—safe. He'd failed Eristol. He'd failed Asami too. He leaped over barrels and ducked under fish nets, then stopped at the ship's gangway. Two dozen pirates bearing swords faced his day watch made up of Brigade members Scott, Toby, and Bohai and Privates Anatoly and Cristobal of the Defense.

The *Fancy's* captain stood at the railing. "Ho, leader of this small, brave military. I think you'll find the danger is no longer me or my ship. It approaches your mayor's palace."

The remaining half dozen members of the Defense arrived behind him with swords drawn, ready to fight. "Lieutenant Tabray, he's right. Everyone to the Commons, now!"

"Commander," she said. "Should we open the gun armory?"

He stopped and considered for a moment. "No. Not yet." She nodded. He knew she second guessed him. But there were no isolated battlefields in the city. He would not bring gunfire into the streets.

They ran back to the Commons. A crowd filled the steps of the palace and the street below. The thing was at the landing in front of the palace doors. He couldn't see it, but he felt it reaching out, sucking magic toward it like a cloth soaking up spilled water. It tugged on him. "Lieutenant, gather the Brigade and Defense. Surround the front of the palace. Let none of the Connectionists leave."

"Yes, Commander. What are you going to do?"

"I have to get that thing away from them."

"What is it?"

"I do not know. It is not human or animal, yet it lives. It is reaching for the city's magic like Zosimos, but this is much more powerful. If it enters the palace, it will destroy it and everyone in it."

"The Mayor!"

"And others. And likely the magic of this city. Go!" He pushed his way through, up the steps to the landing. "Make way! Mayor's Defense, get away! Take safety, get away!"

The crowd parted but did not leave. The Connectionists stood on the landing with the door ministers. Anne was at the door with the thing in her hands. He had to get close. He bolted to her side, and the Connectionists pressed in on him immediately, blocking his escape. But escape was not on his mind. Frank, Jacob, and Marta surrounded him with swords and knives. The wolfhound watched, and Anne had a look of mild surprise which quickly turned to annoyance. Zosimos's two assistants, Erk and Onit, each held knives to the door ministers' throats.

Frank pressed a dagger blade to João's neck and took his sword. Only then did he pull his blade away from João's throat, but he kept the sword pointed at him. Anne stepped closer to the doors. He was close, but not close enough. "What are you doing here?" he asked. "If you enter, you'll be sent—"

"To whatever time and place sucks me in, I know," Anne said. "I have no intention of going inside until it is safe. If you wish to save the Mayor's life, call her out. The pirates expect her to try to save the valet's life. You should know I'm not here to kill, that was never my intention. But I will take the city's phenomena, which will probably kill her. Choose quickly. I'm not very patient."

He looked at her hands. A gold silk cloth covered the thing writhing beneath. He felt its power. It pulled on his own magic, stronger than that from Zosimos.

"Come on. It's not really such a quandary," she said. "Call the Mayor out, or die with her." She pulled his uniform lapel and guided him to stand in front of the door. She raised the object and prepared to throw it at him and the doors. "Once this blasts through the doors, the phenomena will be mine. I will control the city. The people—your girlfriend—will have to live by my rules. Last chance."

She didn't know the power of what she held, nor what the Mayor was protecting. The pirate had fooled her and given her the means of her own destruction, and the destruction of the Mayor, the palace, and the magic. If she unleashed that thing, it would destroy everything, not just the phenomena. The pirates would be free to leave, but the city and everyone in it would be lost. The thing had to leave the city. He had to get it out.

Erk and Onit's attention was fixed on João and Anne, and Frank threatened with the sword. He looked at Tiffet, who held his key out just enough to reveal it to João. Taffet winked.

UNMAKING THE END OF THE WORLD

Silence, so longed for, comes rarely,
yet often the price paid
for silence is sorrow.
- Notes of a Traveller

*N*ews of Eristol's abduction by the pirates reached the Scale and Tentacle like a yell of fire. The tavern emptied as everyone left to see what was happening. Padrok, leader of the Brigade, was already out, so only Hallea remained with Stina. Neither was about to stay behind. They threw off their aprons and ran outside. Hallea headed for the harbor, but Stina considered where João would be. The harbor with the pirates? No. The pirates held Eristol—he wouldn't assault the ship with just the Defense and Brigade. Not the barracks. No, João would try to protect the Mayor.

She ran to the palace but stopped short when she neared. A crowd had gathered, filling the landing at the doorway between the columns with people from the city. Harmony stood among the onlookers at the edge of the Commons. João's heartbeat was near, but slow and calm, not racing like everyone else's.

"What's happening?" she asked Harmony.

"The Connectionists have captured the door ministers and —" Harmony looked at who she was speaking to and covered her mouth with her hand. Then she breathed, "—and João."

"Oh, bloody hell—where's the rest of the Defense?" Stina looked around the sea of faces. Nico and Croydon and some Brigade members assembled on the far side of the Commons. The rest of the Defense surrounded the palace steps.

She crossed the Commons to Nico. "What's happening?"

"They've got João and the door ministers," he said. "The Connectionists have a weapon."

"What kind of weapon?"

"I don't know, but something powerful. You should get back, we have to get everyone back."

She turned to the crowd. A weapon? A bomb? She heard Lieutenant Tabray give orders to the Defense. She held a gun —an ancient rifle, maybe a musket. Bloody hell. Stina began pulling people—Hallea, Harmony, Wilcott, and others—away from the palace and deeper into the Commons, where Croydon and some of the younger Brigade members stood in reserve.

CROYDON'S HAND was sweating around his sword's grip. He wiped his palm on his jeans. He ran through João's lessons again and again. Despite knowing how to wield the sword— how to parry and step and thrust, he realized he didn't actually know how to fight. What would it be like to cut another person, or to kill them? What was it like to be cut, and to die?

Did he have the courage to risk his own life to take someone else's?

He watched Padrok step onto the lowest palace step. He

shouted, "Madam Fields! Let everyone go. We have you surrounded."

There was a light, brief laugh. "Are you ready to take on Connectionists *and* pirates? We'll pinch you in the middle."

"Hold steady," João called.

A loud crash sounded behind the barracks. Something bellowed, filling the air like an enormous trumpet. The ground shook.

LONG BEN STOOD at the helm with his spyglass to his eye. He saw up the hill to the palace and could just make out a crowd in front of the doors. It wouldn't be long now. The serpent couldn't contain Phanes. He lifted the bone tablet. The first passage, the one to unleash Phanes, he ignored; the second, which gave the serpent wings to fight and kill Phanes, was the only one that mattered. He'd have to utter that phrase the moment Phanes burst free. Even that might not work.

He recalled the terrifying feeling he'd felt when he held the egg and tablet while standing on the deck of his ship in the harbor at the End of the World. It connected him to streams of magic as old as the world. He was a buffer between them, but if he became the conduit, he would die. Everyone would die. The world would be unmade. The Mayor had suggested he might be a gambler. Neither of them had understood just how much of a gambler he was.

JOÃO PICTURED his stack of chips—too small, too pale. Anne said it was a simple choice, and it was. He gave a slight, hopefully imperceptible nod to each door minister and stepped closer to Anne, who raised the object threateningly. A breeze blew the silk from the object, revealing a multicolored egg the size of a small melon. It cracked. A small, winged serpent seemed barely to hold the egg together. The egg had to go. The entire city was about to be destroyed in an explosion of magic. He could not let that happen.

"Time's up. You've made your choice." She pulled her arm back to throw the egg.

João glanced at the door ministers. Each manipulated their keys in the air. He lunged forward and grabbed Anne around the waist, then yanked her toward the doors. She lost her grip on the egg.

"What are—"

The doors swung open, and a blast of frozen mountain air slapped against them. A sea of blue sky and the edge of a mountain summit fell away before them. He pulled her through the doors and onto the windy mountain top. Wintry wind stung his eyes.

Or perhaps it was the memory of a future he no longer shared.

SOMETHING EXPLODED LIKE A FIRECRACKER—BIGGER than an M80. Croydon couldn't see what was happening on the landing. More bellowing and crashing took his attention. A roar rushed toward him, and he turned to see a wooly beast bulleting down Tower Road and toward the palace. It bellowed and snapped its trunk like a whip, swung its tusks like a winnowing rake. A tiny figure in lavender sat on the creature's back, clutching its fur.

"Kana?"

A shout ripped from the palace. Then more shouting, and the chime of sword against sword. The Brigade swarmed up the steps. A woman tried to flee down the steps, shouting, "I give up!" She tripped and tumbled to the street. Croydon, at first frozen by the sight of Kana and the mammoth, ran to the woman and pointed his sword at her as she lay moaning.

"I give up," she said. "I'm not a thief, I don't want to be one of them. She made me do it." Then she cried. Croydon lifted her to her feet and pulled her away from the steps and into the Commons beneath an oak, where they both collapsed to the ground.

He glanced back at Kana and the mammoth. Kana was looking into the sky, and he followed her gaze. The sky was black—filled with roiling clouds that looked like smoke descending rather than rising. They were all going to know what dying felt like. The panicked certainty of death came to him again.

A being with wings and flaming horns streaming from its skull descended onto the edge of the Commons facing the palace. Twice as tall as a human, yet human-shaped and naked and bronze. It crackled with power. The eyes weren't visible at this angle, which was just as well for his sanity. It raised its long right arm and gestured in a circle. A finger of swirling cloud descended—a small tornado—and twisted into the small knot of people at the bottom of the palace steps. Croydon caught Nico among them. It lifted and spun their bodies in a wide circle like litter.

The panic was full on him, but he was a few days shy of sixteen. João had trained him. Panic was not allowed for a soldier, and João wouldn't let panic stop him. There was a clear path between Croydon and the demon. He rushed forward, his sword poised for a low but deadly jab at the beast's back.

The two feathered, golden wings struck him and swatted him away as if he were an annoying fly. He crumpled to the turf. The woman crawled toward him and grabbed his shoulder. He felt his strength draining, as if he were bleeding energy. He should have gone to Kana, but it was too late. He couldn't move. He had no energy to move. He had to concentrate on breathing.

"What—is—that?" the woman asked.

Stina fell to her knees beside Croydon and the woman. "Croydon, are you okay? What's happening? Where's João? What the hell is that thing?"

"I don't know."

The winged demon stepped closer to the palace. The ground shook beneath him with each step, as if he weighed as much as a mountain. Croydon had never felt an earthquake, but he imagined this was what several at once was like. A deep, rippling vibration turned the ground into waves. A steady, deep hum. A glowing light, white-blue like lightning, became a growing tendril like a vine. It spread out of the vents at the base of the palace, pulsing and surging toward the demon. The demon made beckoning gestures with its arms, drawing the light to it.

The light jumped forward, struck the demon, and pushed it into the air. The demon beat its wings furiously and floated away from the palace steps. It made a swipe at the columns with its arm. A fiery wind scorched between them and scoured the landing, forcing those caught on the landing to jump away. One of the door ministers was aflame, as was the Dutchman, van Neck.

LONG BEN SAW the egg erupt and began the binding chant immediately. When he finished, he felt nothing. He was no longer connected to any magic. Through the spyglass, he watched in horror as Phanes reached to absorb the city's magic —drinking it in. The unmaking had begun. Only the serpent could save them now—and only if it acted before Phanes gained the city's power.

CROYDON'S STRENGTH RETURNED. He pushed himself to his knees. The mammoth, still bearing Kana, rushed at the demon.

Its tremendous bulk stepped into the light streaming from the palace, breaking the connection with the demon. The snap of disconnection sent the demon reeling onto the turf. It turned its attention to the mammoth, which charged again, glowing with the white power of the light. It rammed the demon. The collision was like two trains slamming engine to engine. The impact sent Kana flying over the demon. Its flaming horns scorched her clothes.

Croydon jumped to his feet and ran for Kana, but Stina pulled him down and held him. "Look!" she cried. She pointed to the sky. A winged serpent descended from the black sky in a long, sinuous arc. A demon and now a dragon. Croydon crouched low, clutching Stina and the Connectionist woman.

The demon, still concerned with the mammoth, flung an arm sideways. The mammoth flew away from the Commons and into the Horn of Plenty. The front of the building collapsed. The dragon dove at the demon and tore one of the demon's wings from its body. The demon howled and threw flames at the serpent, but the serpent dove close again and ripped away the other wing before retreating into the sky and disappearing into the swirling clouds.

The demon roared. Its rage was the anger of thousands of centuries held captive. It stepped toward the palace again. The tendrils of light and power surged again as the demon beckoned for it.

A small running figure caught the corner of Croydon's view. Kana ran to the light; then she stepped into it. The tendrils wrapped around her until she was no longer visible under the brilliant blue-white pulsing beam.

"Kana, no!"

The demon, bereft of power, sank to one knee, and then the other. It wailed. Croydon had never heard such a cry. It was, he imagined, the sound of thousands of people dying at once. The thing twisted and shriveled and sucked into itself like a raisin. A writhing cloud touched a finger to the demon and sucked it up into the black sky with an ear-splitting roar.

∾

THE CONNECTIONIST WOMAN FLED. Croydon ran to Kana. The light receded and slipped back through the palace vents. She lay unmoving on the ground. He grabbed her wrist but couldn't tell if the pulsing was hers or his.

"Kana? Kana!"

She groaned and opened her eyes. They were wide, full of terror—and blue. Her nearly black irises were blue like the edges of lightning. The terror drained as she recognized him.

"Trust," she said.

He helped her to her feet and she ran for the mammoth. He followed. The mammoth appeared unharmed. He stayed back, but Kana went directly to its side and began petting and caressing it. Finally, the enormous animal pushed itself up like a tired dog.

Someone put a hand on his shoulder. Nico. Blood streaked his cheek from a cut above his eye.

"Glad Shaday didn't see this," Croydon said.

"She will know," Nico groaned as he arched his back. "Then we'll hear it." He grinned.

None of Croydon's friends back home would believe this. He barely believed it.

He looked back at the palace. Lieutenant Tabray tugged a Connectionist, Frank, away. Padrok had van Neck, his flames extinguished. Anne's dog paced back and forth at the door, sniffing. The door ministers, even the one who'd caught fire and had burned tatters for a uniform, returned to their posts and shooed the dog away. The doors, which had been full of bright blue sky moments ago, were closed tight.

Stina walked up the steps and reached the landing. "No!"

she screamed and fell against Hallea. They slumped against a column. Stina sobbed and clutched Hallea. Harmony joined them and wrapped her arms around Stina from the other side.

"What happened to João?" Croydon asked.

"He's gone," Nico said. "He dragged Anne into the unknown, took that demon away from her. I imagine he saved us all by preventing her from achieving whatever she was doing."

"Gone—forever?"

"Forever. The same as walking out of the city. Gone to some other place and time."

João gone? He couldn't imagine it. No João? That's not fair. He felt the welling of tears. Some soldier he was, but damn . . . João?

"Croydon," Kana said. He turned. She had remounted the mammoth. "Help me free my sister."

"Free her? Where is she?"

"The Connectionists."

"Right," said Nico. "I'll get the Brigade."

THE PALACE STOPPED SHAKING and the strange film that had fallen between Almariss and the Mayor dissolved into the normal dim light of the Mayor's sitting room. She reached for her pipe but didn't light it. "Is it over?"

"Phanes is back in the egg, but it's not over."

"That was close, wasn't it? Close to destroying the palace and the city."

The Mayor faded and re-emerged as the version of herself that was fifty. Stately, wise, assured, and deadly beautiful. "It was close to destroying the world, not just the city. Phanes seeks ever to destroy and remake. It does not belong in the world until the appointed time of unmaking. The egg must leave the world."

"How do we get something out of the world? Destroy it?"

"We cannot destroy the egg. It must be removed, and I have an idea."

"I knew you would."

"I won't always." The Mayor shot her a look. A mother reprimanding a child, except the Mayor wasn't her mother. They'd shared a different love. Tears built, but she didn't know why. The magic of the city had been so disrupted, everyone connected to it would suffer something.

The Mayor grew slightly younger. "Almariss, I need something from you."

Was there anything left to give? Without hesitation she said, "Anything."

The Mayor leaned close. Her hair was darkening and her eyes glinted brown like the flash of a stream. She placed her hands on Almariss's head, thumbs caressing ears, and pulled her to her lips. The fires that had long ago dampened, though never extinguished, roared to life. Two centuries of unrequited love was a burden no one should bear. They released it.

Everyone knows love is magical, but do they know passion is the incantation to summon it? The thrum of the city became the rhythm of their hearts. They fell into the sway, the ebb and flow and the swirl of the city striking the edges of places. A sinking ship dragged—rushing toward some distant point of darkness. It was glorious and terrifying. This moment might not come for another two hundred years, so Almariss opened up to it and sank endlessly.

IT WAS OVER ALL TOO SOON, as she knew it would be. The Mayor pulled away, realigned her gown, and used her cane to pull herself from the sedan. She was even younger, her hair fully black with just the ever-present shock of white strands. How could anyone not love a woman such as that?

The Mayor lifted two closed wooden boxes from the gaming table. They were black with ornate carvings of endless knots decorating their surfaces, their intricate clockwork mechanisms hidden beneath their lids. "These are the palace locks. They are locked now. The door ministers have the keys. When I leave, retrieve the keys and let no one in today."

"You're going out—to the pirates?"

"Yes. Mind me. No one, not even a new cropper, enters today."

"Except you, when you return."

"Yes . . . right."

Together, they descended the stairs and approached the doors.

Almariss gazed at the Mayor. The scorch of the past moments lowered to a simmering warmth, a wholeness shared between two. "I love you, Mereneith."

The Mayor stopped and turned to her. She appeared young, almost innocent, but she leaned over and kissed her gently. "And I you. Always."

Mereneith stepped away and flung open the doors. Her hair caught the afternoon sun like dark and silver fire. She strode out and surveyed the scene. Almariss followed. The landing and Commons were empty. Only the door ministers remained. Mereneith sighed and placed a hand on the shoulder of Door Minister Tiffet. "My dear and loyal João," she said and sighed again. "If he left any chips, Stina will be quite wealthy, though she will not find much solace in that."

"Let me go with you," Almariss said.

"No, you must keep the palace. Gentlemen, give Almariss the keys and come with me." They did as instructed and escorted Mereneith down the steps and across the Commons.

When they disappeared from view, Almariss closed the doors and retreated to Mereneith's sitting room.

THE MAMMOTH LUMBERED up the hill to the house overlooking the harbor where the Connectionists had lived. Croydon, Nico, and Scott of the Brigade followed. Croydon thought, if there were any Connectionists left, they were about to get quite a surprise. Kana wasn't riding the mammoth but walking beside it, and Croydon next to her.

"Why didn't you tell me?" Croydon asked. They could have rescued Asami long ago, especially with João.

"I could not. I could not risk losing her. If they took her out of the city, I would never have seen her again. She would be worse than dead, because I would know she lived."

Two years was a long time. Only love made someone keep such a secret. He suddenly felt the empty weight of his own sister, lost to him yet still alive. They arrived at the cottage, and the mammoth huffed at the door.

Before Croydon could knock, the woman he had pulled from the palace steps shouted out of the window. "You can have the cook if you let me walk out of here safe. Keep that beast under control or the cook won't see sunset." She flashed a knife.

"You can walk out," Nico replied. "And keep walking. In fact, Scott here will see that you are unmolested all the way down the Goresetch road."

"Suits me fine."

"Are there any others?"

"No. I swear."

There was a rustling inside, then the door opened. The Connectionist walked out behind Asami. Asami looked unharmed for having been held hostage for so long. Kana ran and embraced her sister. The mammoth embraced them both.

"Incredible," Nico said.

Croydon agreed. "Unbelievable. Never thought I'd see a mammoth, or a demon, or a dragon."

"Oh yes, those too. But I was thinking about love's ability to hold us through anything, even when we don't see each other."

Croydon had thought he understood that kind of love—Nico's endless love for his wife, Lura, a love he equated with romance. But there were other kinds of love, and they weren't equal. Romance was a fiery thing—passion, adults called it—and maybe it ignited love, but it didn't keep it; didn't make it grow or bind it. Love after romance, or even without it, was stronger. That was the love that grew and bound. Asami, Kana—he would always love them. Not as in a romance, or even like sisters, but a bond.

But another binding had come undone—cut as if carved out of his chest. Without João, a hole grew inside of him; a hard, cold pit that had been full of warmth and surety just an hour ago. It wasn't fair. He wiped a wet sting from his eyes.

Long Ben stood between the Mayor and her valet, who was held by the bosun. He felt the urge to pace across the deck, but the Mayor blocked his path and his crew surrounded them. She had come unarmed, leaving her door minders on the dock. She appeared as a frail old woman, bent and leaning heavily on her cane.

"You have me," she said. "I trust Phanes is safe aboard this fine vessel." She emphasized vessel with a bang of her cane against the deck.

"True, you are here, I suppose fulfilling your obligation to protect your valet. And yes, my little pet is safe." He pulled the egg from his pocket, whole and encircled by the serpent. For the moment no cracks splintered its surface, but he felt Phanes moving inside. It wouldn't be long before the cracks appeared again. The city's magic still drew Phanes. They had to leave.

"What is your plan?" she asked.

"We leave. You accused me of being a gambling man, so I'll wager you can't control the magic from here. I'll keep you aboard and sail out of this port."

"Not exactly. The ship will not return to the world." The Mayor banged the cane again, emphasizing *world*. She scowled. "That egg can never return." Then she smiled. "Fate acts upon the individual, but no one's fate exists by itself. Ours are all intertwined. What I choose as my fate also affects you." She struck the cane a third time.

Three strikes of the cane. Long Ben looked up at the sky, which had become gray and was growing black. "What have you done?" He grabbed the Mayor's shoulders and shook her. She smiled infuriatingly and her age melted away. She was young, a maiden. Her black hair flowed in the wind with white streaks not unlike Phanes's flaming horns.

"I have sealed our fates and preserved those of the End of the World, and of the world that contains us."

"Captain!" cried his first mate. "The mooring lines have slipped, we're adrift."

"Drop anchor. We're not going anywhere until I give you a heading." He pulled his dagger from his belt and thrust it against the Mayor's throat. "Are we, Your Honor?"

"I'm afraid the bottom of the harbor is rather sandy and deep. I don't believe your anchor is as firmly entrenched as you hope."

"Densen!" But he didn't need confirmation. He saw the ship drifting away from the dock at an unnatural speed. The gangway fell. He pressed the knife tighter against her skin. "What are you up to? Where are you taking us?"

"Where that egg belongs."

"You may guide the city, but no place can contain the egg."

"No place, but one time. Primordial time, where and when the egg was created and where it belongs."

"You—what about the city? With no one to guide it, haven't you left the citizens to the mercy of whatever random and dangerous times and places it runs into?"

"No. I've left the town in better hands than mine."

The sound of the *Fancy's* sails unfurling at once rolled like thunder. The ship gained speed and hurled itself at the growing storm outside the harbor.

"Damn you, Mayor."

"Damned us all, I'd say."

LEAVING THE END OF THE WORLD

This place is magic
This place is phenomena
A place always rising and always falling
This place, the once-blue oasis, is all those things.
- Notes of a Traveller

Almariss led Stina and Shaday up the stairs to Mereneith's sitting room. No one spoke, and the silence was uncomfortable, but Almariss was loath to break it. She gestured for them to sit, and she poured each a cup of tea. Then she sat in a chair she had brought and set near Mereneith's. She couldn't sit in that chair. Not yet; not ever. Shaday and Stina shared the sedan.

"I can't believe it," Shaday breathed.

"Which part?" Almariss replied.

"All of it. Well, I *can* believe Croydon would attack a demon."

"It was a god, actually. Phanes, the first and last god."

Stina's eyes were as red and puffy as she imagined her own to be. She considered lighting her pipe, but that would just bring the magic of the city deeper within her, and she wasn't ready for that again.

"There's no way for you to return to the place and time where João . . ." Stina practically whispered his name. Her voice was hoarse.

"I don't know what I'm doing, so no, unfortunately. Even Mereneith, the Mayor—even she said she could rarely get close to a specific place or time. The trick is to see what's coming and take the least dangerous option."

"The Mayor—you're the Mayor!" Shaday gasped.

"I suppose . . . in name, perhaps." She had only read part of the letter she found inside one of the locked boxes. But that letter said she was now in control of the city's destiny. She was the Mayor.

Stina sobbed. "There," shushed Shaday, holding her.

Almariss's own eyes grew wet and blurry. She concentrated on the tea, which helped, though like the pipe it brought the surging, swirling energies of the city into her. "I suppose the important thing is that the city is whole and the magic is intact. João, Mereneith, even Eristol did what they did to preserve it and us."

"Damned greater cause," Stina sniffed.

"I feel awful for you two," Shaday said. "I still have Croydon and Nico. It's foolish, but I wish there were someone I could give each of you."

Almariss gave up her chair for a spot beside Shaday and wrapped her arms around both women. "We have you."

Shaday held something glinting—a small glass—against the back of Stina's hand. She winked at Almariss. "I think you might need one of these too."

~

It was nearly dawn when Shaday and Stina left. Almariss hadn't wanted them to leave. Alone in the palace, she felt as empty as the building. But when the sun rose, she would have to unlock the doors, hand the door ministers the keys, and let the clerks and ministers in. Then she would have to sit in Mereneith's office—her office—and begin the duties of navigating the city. Already, she was working hard to steer it away from the worst, most dangerous times and places—if she could identify them quickly enough. That was an art, one she doubted she would master quickly. The city was in for a rough ride for a while.

The letter was lengthy, but it was direct and full of explanations and instructions. Only one part was personal and written most recently. That was the part she wanted to read again and again and also dreaded reading.

Almariss,

I leave everything to you, my student, my love. You will loathe me for what I've done to you. For all the things I've done to you, especially for ever loving you. What I told you was the truth. When I could no longer maintain my age close to yours, I could not bear our love. As you know now, passion, when one is deeply connected to the magic, is too intense for a human to bear, but because I loved you I bore it longer than I should have. I was selfish.

You will despise me for training you as my replacement without telling you. You never asked to be mayor, only to understand the magic—the power you felt. But I knew you had to be next. I should have left the city in your hands long ago.

You are wondering why I asked for that last moment between us. Yes, I planned it. I needed a memory, one I could relive again and again. Shaday and Nico made for me a small eagle in a basket. My eagle-eyed love. I held it as we loved each other a final time. If you feel like it, you may ask them for your own. We may share that moment across time. Though we are not together, I will never be apart from you.

She felt herself smiling and crying. The letter continued with explanations.

~

IF YOU ARE READING THIS, then I was successful. I had to get the egg and Phanes out of the city. But I could not allow it to return to any place in time save for one—primordial time—the time of the making of the world. As you now see, all times and places swirl about the city constantly. Only when something disturbs the city does it slow down and edge toward a particular place. By moving the ship and the egg, I hope to create another disruption and use all of my energy (and a good deal from everyone in the city) to slip toward the instant of creation. What Long Ben doesn't understand is that Phanes's power is available to me.

If I've succeeded, the egg and Phanes will be safe in primordial time. Eristol, myself, Long Ben, and his crew will live in that time and place—a place of endless creation full of power, a great magic. We shall live there until the appointed time for the world to be unmade.

Now, there are some things you must do immediately. The rest can come as you learn and grow comfortable living in the city's magic.

This world—our world—and the city built within an oasis, must be preserved. It is as natural as anything else on Earth. It is remarkably strong and efficient at repairing its bumps and tears, its jagged edges that catch on time's rippling shores. What takes longer and costs us more is bringing wholeness to the fractures caused by its inhabitants—by ourselves and those who come to it.

Maintain a defense against those who seek, intentionally or not, to alter the city's nature, lest you find yourself repairing a hole from the inside.

First, you understand the source of the power is the Fount, which is located beneath the palace. It is what Phanes tried to gain and what I never wanted Zosimos to find. Let no one near. I repeat—let no one near the Fount of Energy.

Second. Constant disruptions buffer the city. Outside forces (magnetic flares from the sun, earthquakes, etc.) catch the city. But you must be most careful of those who cause disruption from within. I repeat—internal disruption is the most difficult to recover from. The job of navigating the city—your job—is to keep the city disconnected from any place and time for as long as possible. When it connects, the power decreases, and it is difficult to get it going again. If it stays in one place too long, I'm afraid it will lose its magic and become just like any other place—stuck wherever it landed. If this happens, those who have lived beyond a normal lifespan will die. Keep it moving and keep out the disruptors. Those who cannot earn and maintain chip-value are the easiest to spot, but that's not one hundred percent accurate, nor are they the only disruptors. People change. They may enter with no ill intent but develop it as the city affects them. Protect the city and its magic for those who choose to live within it.

∾

SQUEEZED in the spaces between paragraphs was a recent addition to the letter:

∾

THIRD. Your ability to see all times and places at once in your mind will be much to bear. You need tea, cool air, darkness, and lots of rest. You'll need a valet. I suggest Asami, but the choice is yours.

Fourth. You will grow very much older than you already are. You will be lonely. Spend time with Shaday and others. They will distract you from the barrage you will experience.

Fifth. You need to identify and train your replacement. I strongly suggest Kana. Her encounter with Phanes and her ability to communicate with all beings and to survive direct contact with the Fount suggests to me she is strong, perhaps the strongest of us all.

∾

THE LETTER WENT on for pages about the minutiae of the navigation, how to maintain her physical energy, and so forth. Already she sensed the city falter; its whirling tumble through time—there was a wobble. She had to focus on how to disconnect the city at once.

STINA STARED at the small satchel containing João's things. It sat unopened on her pallet in the Scale and Tentacle's attic. His sword and bearskin scabbard lay beside the satchel. The memories of their four years together were less painful to replay now, three weeks later, but they still brought an emptiness, a bottomless hole. The place where his heart should be was forever empty.

She clung to flickers of memory, even those of the first years when he fumbled at learning how to get close to her. He got so tangled in his religion sometimes she couldn't help but laugh. They were each lost, having left loved ones and a life behind through no choice of their own. Then they found each other. As improbable a couple as anyone could imagine. Now he was lost to her, and he left her behind. He chose a greater cause than themselves. He saved them all. Saved the entire world, according to Almariss. Could she really expect anything else from him? He'd sacrificed his future—their future—to be stuck somewhere with the woman who had tried to kill him. He would always choose the greater cause. *Is that fate? The culmination of our choices? The choice we always make because it's who we are?*

She undid the drawstring of a purse and pulled out a handful of chips, each as red as her grandmother's roses. It was wealth beyond counting and had come at a sacrifice beyond reckoning. You could reason fate and a noble cause, but you could not reason what your heart wants. *Why, João?* Tears came easily again.

When Angi left, Stina had cried herself to sleep for days—a

combination of recent loss and homesickness. In the weeks since João fell into the unknown, tears kept her awake. It wasn't like they had been part of some magical fairy tale—and yet, it was. It was exactly that. A fairy tale full of love and magic. Like the Mayor said, love is unlikely, but we find it everywhere. João had loved her. He had saved for a house and wanted children. It wasn't the life she had planned, but it would have been a wonderful life—and she had wanted it. She couldn't share it with her family and friends back home, but she and João would make their own family. She had wanted that more than anything.

João was gone. The door ministers' magic didn't allow them to know where or when they had opened the doors to, they had just opened the doors to a place that wasn't the End of the World.

Stina added her own things to João's satchel. Her cell phone —maybe it would work again—the glass and wicker turtle with green and blue memory clouds swirling around each other; her minidress; a blanket; keys to the VW; and the dress she'd had made to impress João. She gathered her toothbrush, hair pick, and watch. The watch still worked. It was three in the after-noon in Downderry, 30 November, 2018. It was also ten in the morning at the End of the World in an uncounted year.

She slung the satchel over her shoulder and João's sword across her back, then went downstairs. She gave Padrok one of João's chips. "That should cover my room and leaving you shorthanded for three weeks. I'm leaving."

Padrok took the coin in his fat fingers. "That will cover your room for years."

"I won't need it," she said, and she started for the door. "Give it to croppers."

"Nevertheless, it's yours if you return," Padrok said, and he gave her a great bear hug.

~

THE SUN WAS STRONG. Gulls squawked, soared, and dipped over the harbor. Stina walked past the sign. The End of the World—sure as hell was—an end of many worlds. The Goresetch road led through a wide meadow, as it often seemed to, then rose slightly over a taller, grassy green rise. If there was anything that looked like the twentieth century, or the twenty-first, she was in.

Over the summit was an expanse of wind-rippled wheat fields. The ocean was still at her left, but distant. The road narrowed to a track between the fields. She heard heartbeats; distant, but many. At the next rise, a house was visible on the horizon. A few olive trees provided shade. The house was stone and looked a little like those she once saw in Greece, but no poles or wires. No cars. Still, it could be the early twentieth century. Not every place was wired before the Second World War. She could live with even that if it were early enough—maybe. Living through the world wars wasn't appealing. Perhaps the late twenty-first century had devolved away from cities and tech.

The house was a small manor. Grape vines grew in the clearing behind the building. People in simple gray linen draped over their shoulders harvested the grapes. Old men and women and children. They saw her but said nothing.

After a few moments, as she drew closer, a woman approached. The lady of the house? Her garment was blue. She lifted the skirt as she stepped along a stone path. She spoke a question, but in what language? Latin? Greek? The accent was heavy, but then Stina realized what the woman had said. The city's magic still at work. "Are you free?"

"Yes."

The woman crossed her arms and frowned. "Report to the magistrate."

Stina shook her head. Life outside her own time, racist as it was, would never be easy. She shrugged her shoulders and held her palms upward, hoping to appear unthreatening. She suddenly thought of João's sword on her back. Not a great impression.

The woman pointed down the road.

The pull of the End of the World tugged at her as insistently as her father pulling her from a puddle when she was small.

"Thank you," she said to the woman, and then she turned back to the End of the World. She could try again tomorrow.

No TEARS KEPT STINA AWAKE, and she slept like someone on vacation: no cares, no worries, no lover to occupy her mind, no job. Padrok had given Angi's pallet to a new cropper. A girl, Black like her, and fierce. Only seventeen, but angry and refusing to speak.

Stina woke before the sun. The girl was somewhere else. She placed one of João's coins on the girl's pillow, then left the inn with her satchel and João's sword strapped to her back. She took to the Goresetch road again. She could have gone to the Lookout, but the problem was often that the place you viewed from there vanished by the time you climbed down the hill and took off for it. People who spent time at the Lookout only had a notion to leave. She meant to leave, and that meant actually leaving.

It was cold, and windy. Snow fluttered softly around her as she stepped over a rise. The ocean was no longer visible and there were snow-covered fields and forests as far as she could see.

She shivered and threw the small blanket over her head and

shoulders. The road became just a trail of footprints in the snow. Large footprints.

~

THERE WAS A HEARTBEAT AHEAD. A single one, strong. A break in the snow revealed the mammoth covered in white. It turned to face her, its eyes large and black. She wasn't afraid. Kana had ridden it. It had protected them against the demon—no, a god—Phanes.

Heartbeats ahead, maybe a dozen, and smoke rose over the horizon. The heartbeats grew stronger. She skirted ahead of the mammoth to the edge of a rise. Below was a group of fur-covered domes dotting a snowy field. People dressed in fur pelts chanted around a fire. Men with spears walked up the slope toward her.

She ran back to the mammoth. "You don't want to be here." She wished Kana was there to communicate with the animal. The mammoth just looked at her. It had that confused and sad look of a cropper. The heartbeats drew closer. She reached out and touched the mammoth's trunk, and it gripped her hand. "This way. You have to get out of here," she said. She tugged on the trunk, and the animal followed her up another slope. "Run! Either back to the forest or out there, but you have to run!"

It slipped its trunk around her waist, then slid it up to her face. It ran the cold, wet tip against her skin and she felt its breath. It smelled of pine and sage. Then it let go and ran into the snow. It galloped and shed the snow covering it.

The heartbeats were closer. It wasn't any safer for her than it was for the mammoth. She trotted back through the snow, following her footprints to the End of the World. In a while, other footprints mixed with her own and then divided. Which ones were hers? If the world still held to the arrangement she remembered, the tracks leading to the right should lead her back. But the journey was taking longer than the walk out. Her watch showed two hours. Bloody rot—*come on, Almariss, don't pull away yet.*

She hurried her steps and saw the ocean. She reached the shore and a long sweep of frozen beach. But no city, no ships, just miles of ice jammed against the shore. She'd taken the wrong tracks, or Almariss had navigated the city away. A hole opened in her stomach, gaping with the fear of being alone—the most alone she'd ever been.

Bloody hell.

And she'd lost her way. A sinking weight like a stone down a well. It threatened to pull her to her knees. Death in the freezing wind might come before she ever found her way back to the hunters' camp, which wasn't any kind of actual destination. Tears came again, followed by the absence of João's sure arms around her and his heart pulsing inside. She reached into the satchel for the dress to wrap around herself, but her hand landed on the glass turtle. She pulled it out.

WARM WAVES POUNDED against pure white sands. Towers of mirrored glass and painted steel loomed behind her—a great, gleaming city. Palm trees ran in a line along the interior of the beach. She held something in her hands—small, pale hands. What she held was alive. A turtle. Small enough to fit inside her child-sized hand. A gecko scurried across her bare pink feet. She carried the turtle gently across the beach and stood in the surf. The water was warm and clear. She smelled salty waves and felt the slow simmer of sand under the sun's glare. She lowered the turtle into the water and it swam away, knowing the vast sea full of predators and storms was a richer life than hiding on an island under the shadows of glass and steel towers.

◠

Her knees were deep in the snow. The glass turtle in her hand was warm. She pressed it to her cheek. Her own memory floated around Angi's. The memory of a summer holiday in the gullies and valleys of Snowdon with her mum. They hiked for days and spent nights drinking wine and laughing. So much laughing. But the chill of snow returned. Her feet were numb; her fingers too. The glass was freezing. It lacked other, more recent memories. Tears warmed her cheeks then grew cold and froze to her skin. "Nico!" she shouted to the wind.

She struggled to stand, then forced her feet and legs to move. The snow was knee-deep and she could barely recognize any tracks leading to the fork in the path. She almost missed the fork. The glare of snow and the gray sky fused into a vision of nothing, like walking through clouds. She tripped and fell. Sleep pulled her into a chill embrace.

◠

Another heartbeat. No—two.

She called out. At least she thought she called, but maybe her jaw had frozen; maybe no sound emerged.

◠

Hands grabbed her elbows and pulled her up. The heartbeat was strong inside her. A shocking intimacy—and familiar. She'd steeled herself against any such intrusion after João. The second heart beat rapidly. She forced open her frozen eyes. Croydon. "What are you doing here?" She hadn't seen him since that awful day, and the sight of him as a grown man struck her. Still a teenager, but not the twelve-year-old boy hiding and crying behind the sign. Sixteen. And he'd attacked Phanes with a sword. Every bit the protective fool João was.

He wrapped his thicker, larger blanket around both of them. "I watched you leave today, and yesterday." The wolfhound that had followed the woman, Anne, sniffed at her legs. A flash of the memory of that day tried to break into the forefront of her mind, but she pushed it away.

"You watched me?"

"Yes. I was curious."

"Enough to get up before dawn and follow a woman around? Creep much?" Feeling returned to her face and fingers. Her feet were still numb as stone.

"Sorry. I just figured if you found someplace else to go it might be good for me too."

"You want to leave?" She saw he carried a satchel—a creel like Nico's. His sword slung at his hip. He'd been planning this for a while.

"I do. I don't feel I belong now that I'm older. I never really felt I belonged."

"I get you." She jabbed her thumb into the air at the wintry landscape behind them. "But that ain't the way."

"Nico and Shaday are great. They've always looked out for me. Sometimes I wish I had treated Shaday better. I've disappointed her again and again, and now I'm sure I've made her sad in a big way. But as she said, I know she will always love me and I'll always be alive to her."

"Yes, she'll come around eventually. Nico will explain you did what you had to. And yes, she will always be connected to you. Memories are not like photographs. Memories connect us. They exist in the minds of everyone who has the memory. A shared connection. But . . ."

"But?"

"It's not my business. You made your choice."

"It's just us now. My business is yours."

279

"You were close with the sisters, Kana and Asami. It can't be easy leaving them behind."

He looked away. "It's not."

~

THEY WALKED HUDDLED TOGETHER with the hound scouting ahead until the thick snow gave way to an icy, packed and rutted path that became a road. Croydon checked his watch. "This should be where the sign sits."

She thought, where the VW once sat stuck in the mud. Where she had found Croydon hiding behind the sign. Now just snow and ice, no city. "Almariss may have disconnected it, Croydon."

"Disconnected. Gone, like home. We've really made our choice, haven't we?"

They had. There was no return, not home, not to the homes they made at the End of the World. They intended to leave, and in following that intention, they made their choices final. She noticed a change in the terrain ahead. "Look, there's mud and grass sticking out of the road. Let's get out of this snow." She left the shared blanket and took the lead. She still gripped the Memory Glass turtle in her hand. A last plea. *Not yet, Almariss. I need Nico's magic.* But she knew it was too late.

The snow and ice melted away after a few miles and the air warmed to something comfortable. As they traveled farther, it became hot and humid. Insects flew and buzzed around them. One kept trying to land on her nose. "So bloody irritating." She swatted the space vacated by the fly.

"Horsefly," Croydon said. "Like summer back home."

The dirt road led to a bridge, and they heard a river. Croydon ran to the bridge. "This might lead us home—well, to my home."

Hope and disappointment fluttered in her stomach. "Was it nice? Was it a friendly place?"

"Yeah. Small town and icy winters, but it was nice. Not much happened. Nothing happens in New England towns."

"New England?"

"Yeah, New Hampshire, right in the middle of the north."

"That's close to Canada. My mum's in Canada." She realized she didn't know when Croydon came to the End of the World. He was definitely twentieth or twenty-first century, but she'd never asked him. "In the 2010s," she added.

"2010s?"

"Twenty-fourteen, or maybe you Americans say two-thousand-fourteen."

Croydon's mouth dropped open. "You're from the future."

"Well—your future, I guess. What year did you come to the End of the World?"

"1975."

Stina stared for a moment, "Oh my."

"What?"

"I'm twenty-four and you're sixteen, but you're older than I am. Some thirty-odd years older."

Croydon considered that. "I guess you're right." Then he laughed. "Imagine that."

They crossed the bridge. "This isn't—" He looked around. "It's not my road."

Stina said, "The End of the World actually is beyond us." Tears built again. Nico could not help her now. "We're stuck wherever we are." And stuck without the magic memories of João. She and Croydon had abandoned the city and been abandoned. Placeless, homeless. Nomads through time.

"What do we do?" he asked.

João had done what he had to do to protect her and the city. The city was safe and gone to wherever and whenever was next. She and Croydon were just two—three, the hound's cold nose reminded her—and all they could do was keep each other safe. Nomads made home wherever they were; they carried home with them. She looked at him and said, "We survive."

~

THEY WALKED until the road passed through fields of grain. Many heartbeats filled her senses, and she warned Croydon of people ahead. Men, women, and children of all ages and varying shades of skin worked the fields. Some stopped to watch them pass. Beside the road, a small manor stood on a hillside overlooking the fields. Similar to the one she saw before, but larger and wealthier. There were no cars, no power lines, no planes. A banner flew over the manor.

"That's the flag of of Septimius Severus, Roman emperor in the second century," Croydon said. "I read about it for summer homework the year I got lost."

Stina took his hand and pulled him back. "Rome won't be terribly welcoming for either of us. And we can't speak the language."

Croydon pulled a large leather purse from his satchel and shook it. It jingled richly. "Everyone speaks the language of gold and silver."

"You've thought this through better than I have." She sniffed back her tears. "Maybe we can buy passage north, where they speak Old German or Old French or whatever came before. I might get by with that. I had years of French and some German." She still squeezed the turtle, and it cramped her left hand.

Croydon noticed. "That reminds me," he said, pointing at the turtle. He fished through his creel and produced a glass bear poking its nose from a wicker cave. "Shaday and Nico taught me how to do this. I guess my magic was the same as theirs. I put some of my memories of João in it when we finished our practices, and I think Shaday put some of yours in."

"How did she do that?" Croydon shrugged, but then she recalled the night she, Shaday, and Almariss had mourned together. Shaday had held something, but Stina had never looked at it. She took the bear, and it filled with a golden cloud. The certainty of João's arms hugged her tight. His face appeared in front of her. The smell of his body filled her breath, and the boyish hope in his brown eyes sent a rush of emotions and physical responses flooding through her. The pulse of his heart thrummed inside her. Her cheeks heated. She turned from Croydon, and tears came freely. She placed the bear in her satchel and caught her breath. The memory was too intense for anything but a private moment.

"I'm sorry," Croydon said. "I didn't mean to—"

"Thank you, Croydon." She turned and smiled at him, then hugged him. "Whatever we find will be easier now."

"The magic worked? I wasn't sure if it would outside the city."

"It does." Her smile came unbidden; the first since she'd lost João. It felt broad and warm across her cheeks.

He drew a glass elephant from his pocket. It wore a woven saddle, and a lavender light appeared before his face. He wasn't leaving Kana and Asami entirely, after all.

She undid João's sword from her back and handed it to Croydon. "You should have this. You earned it." His eyes widened and the unrestrained smile on his face was like the Christmas day João had agreed to teach him sword skills. "He'll expect you not to dishonor the Urso de Batalha. Practice."

"Practice at all things makes anything possible. I'll do my best."

Do their best was all they could do now. That was part of fate—doing your best—over and over wherever you are and with whomever is at your side. *Not such a deep and mysterious thing, really. Fate is not pre-ordained; it's molded by what we do, the choices we make again and again.* Stina decided fate resulted from free will and not its limitation. *It's not thrust upon us or some guiding light over a path to follow; it is the path we make from our cumulative choosing.*

Croydon pulled a parchment covered in Asahi's or Kana's writing from his creel. He unfolded it, revealing a map. The center was a faded circle with a faded image Stina couldn't make out. But the four corners were filled with roads, forests, rivers, and mountains; even an ocean in the west. He pointed to the top left edge. "We're between Ostia and Antium. This road bypasses Rome." The map still held whatever magic Kana and Asami had embedded in it, revealing their surroundings as they traveled, even noting places in English. Despite the strangeness and fear of walking a road in the second century, she held to shreds of comfort: the glass bear, the magic of the map, Croydon's presence, even the hound.

With the map as their guide, they walked forward under the warm sun of the Roman Empire. Two people, pulled from separate points in a future that has not yet passed, and a wolfhound that was neither wolf nor hound. They entered a strange world with only what they carried, but what they carried was magic.

ACKNOWLEDGMENTS

Without these dear people, this novel wouldn't exist.

Thanks to my daughters, Seanna, Serena, and Sam who give me the space and encouragement I need. And to the rest of my family and friends who have listened to me talk about writing for so many years. Your unwavering support keeps me afloat.

My first and trusted reader, John, keeps me on track. John's been subjected to my stories since we were in high school, and the fact that he still accepts them with any eagerness says more about him and his charity of time and energy than it does about my writing. Thanks to all my early readers for their gracious expenditure of time on my behalf.

Author and editor, Kat Howard took on editing a collection of six related short stories and encouraged me to turn them into a novel. Her wisdom and feedback was invaluable. Rachel Oestreich from Wallflower Editing made the prose better, so much better. Ana Grigoriu-Voicu produced the magical cover.

The encouragement I received for my work in the Writing the Other Novella Writing Workshop from K. Tempest Bradford and Nisi Shawl was what I needed when I needed it. And the ongoing support from my workshop mates Shiv, Leonie, and Danielle are boosts I continue to rely on.

ABOUT KEVIN J. FELLOWS

Kevin J. Fellows is a poet and writer of fantasy and speculative fiction. He's a member of the Science Fiction & Fantasy Poetry Association. *At the End of the World*, is his debut novel. He lives in the desert southwest, has lived in upstate New York, but was born in the wilds of New Hampshire. He fumbles with his guitar, runs, and bikes, all less than he should. For more about his upcoming books and poetry, visit his website:

kevinjfellows.com.

For regular news and updates, sign up for the Infectious Magic Digest. Readers of the Digest also receive cover reveals, occasional free poems and stories, and opportunities to become ARC readers.

You can also receive original stories and poems, as well as behind-the-scene updates, private chats, and more from Kevin's Patreon.

Author photo by Seanna Fellows

COMING IN 2021

The first book in the new series by Kevin J. Fellows, *The Arcane Depository*.

Sophia and her team scour the world for dangerous magic during the early years of the 1900s. They must acquire that magic and put it away, safe from those who would use it and tip the world toward a global magical war.

ABOUT THE TYPE

This book was set in Baskerville, a typeface designed by John Baskerville (1706-75). He was an amateur printer and type founder. The typeface was cut for him by John Handy in 1750. The typeface found a resurgence of popularity in 1923 when the Lanston Monotype Corporation of London used it for many titles. The Mergenthaler Linotype Company in England and the United States cut a version of Baskerville in 1931. It remains a popular typeface today.